EVE *of* DARKNESS

EVE *of* DARKNESS

Sylvia Day writing as S. J. Day

TOR®

A TOM DOHERTY ASSOCIATES BOOK
NEW YORK

EVE OF DARKNESS

Copyright © 2009 by Sylvia Day

A Tor Book
Published by Tom Doherty Associates, LLC
175 Fifth Avenue
New York, NY 10010

www.tor-forge.com

Tor® is a registered trademark of Tom Doherty Associates, LLC.

ISBN 978-0-7653-3748-1

First Trade Paperback Edition: January 2013

Printed in the United States of America

0 9 8 7 6 5 4 3 2 1

A story doesn't blossom into a published book until it is loved by an editor. A published book doesn't reach enough readers if it isn't championed by its editor. An author doesn't spread her wings fearlessly without the security of a supportive (and patient) editor.

I am grateful to Heather Osborn for her enthusiasm for the Marked series. There is nothing in the world like having an editor whose hopes and dreams for your stories are as limitless as your own.

Thank you, Heather.

ACKNOWLEDGMENTS

The art department at Tor, especially Seth Lerner. Months of work went into the packaging of the Marked series—design tweaks, background changes, multiple cover models. . . . The amount of time and effort that was invested in the covers means a great deal to me.

Melissa Frain at Tor, Nikki Duncan, and Joy Harris for loving this book and prodding me often to hurry up and finish the other two, which kept me motivated while doing so.

Denise McClain for the extremely thoughtful and helpful feedback.

Jordan Summers, Shayla Black, Karin Tabke, and Sasha White for being there for me whenever I needed a caring ear at the other end of the phone line. How blessed I am to have friends like you!

Gary Tabke for answering my questions regarding police procedures. Any errors are entirely mine.

Frauke Spanuth for her brilliant marketing branding and help with German translation.

Tina Trevaskis for her honesty and friendship.

And Nikola Tesla for the radio, remote controls, and AC power, none of which I could have lived without while writing this book.

Sin is crouching at your door; it desires to have you, but you shall master it.

—The Lord to Cain, Genesis 4:7

EVE *of* DARKNESS

CHAPTER 1

The Devil is in the details.

Evangeline Hollis understood the true gist of that saying now, surrounded as she was by thousands of Satan's minions. Some wore Seattle Seahawks baseball caps, others wore San Diego Chargers jerseys. All bore detailed designs similar to tribal tattoos on their skin that betrayed both what species of cursed being they were and what their rank in Hell's hierarchy was. To her enhanced eyes, it looked like a damn festival for sinners. They were drinking beer, devouring nachos, and waving giant foam fingers.

In reality, the event was a football game in Qualcomm Stadium. The day was classic Southern California perfection—sunny and warm, the eighty-degree temperature balanced by a delightfully cool breeze. Mortals mingled with Infernal beings in blissful ignorance, simply enjoying a bit of afternoon spectator sport. To Eve, the scene was macabre; like watching hungry wolves sunning themselves alongside lambs. Gore, violence, and death were the inevitable result of any interaction between the two.

"Stop thinking about them."

Alec Cain's deep, sensual voice made her shiver inside, but outwardly she shot him a rueful glance over the top of her sunglasses. He was always telling her to ignore their prey when they weren't on the hunt. As if rogue fae, demons, mages, werewolves, dragons, and thousands of variants of the same were easily disregarded.

"There's a woman breastfeeding her child next to an incubus," she muttered.

"Angel." His nickname for her moved over her skin like a tangible caress. Alec's voice could turn driving directions into foreplay. "We're taking the day off, remember?"

She blew out her breath and looked away. At a few inches over six feet, Alec was blessed with a powerful chest and tautly ridged abdomen that were noticeable even through his fitted white tank. He had long, muscular legs presently showcased in knee-length Dickies shorts and biceps so beautifully defined they were coveted by both men and women.

He was her lover . . . occasionally. Like all sweets, Alec was delicious and satisfying, but too much of him caused a sugar crash that left her dazed and reeling. He'd also ruined life as she had known it. Her career aspiration had been interior design, not Infernal bounty hunting.

"If only it was that simple," Eve groused. "How can I go on vacation when I'm surrounded by work? Besides, they stink even when I'm ignoring them."

"All I smell is you," he purred, leaning over to nuzzle his nose against her cheek. "Yum."

"It creeps me out that they're everywhere. I went to McDonald's yesterday and the person serving me at the window was a faery. I couldn't even eat my Big Mac."

"Betcha ate the fries." Pulling down his shades, Alec looked at her with somber eyes. "There's a difference between staying on your toes and paranoia."

"I'm cautious, not a basket case. Until I find a way out of this mark business, I'm making the best of it."

"I'm proud of you."

Eve sighed. Having Alec for a mentor was such a bad idea, and not just because it was the equivalent of a Hollywood casting couch in most Marks' eyes. Never mind that the true "casting couch" was the exchange of sexual favors in return for a position you *wanted*. No one ever wanted the Mark of Cain.

The Marks' hierarchy started at the bottom with the newbies and topped off with Alec, the original and most badass Mark of them all. There was no way to surpass him. There was also no way to work with him. He was the quintessential loner, the very definition of the word. Yet here was Eve, a six-week newbie in the field, perched solidly at the top because he didn't trust anyone else to watch her back. She was important to him.

The other Marks thought working with God's primary enforcer had to be a vacation. While it was true that Infernals didn't mess with Alec unless they had a death wish, it didn't make things any easier. Demons now targeted *her* as a way to get to him. To make things worse, Alec had been marked so long that he'd forgotten what it was like to be new and confused. There were things he expected her to simply "know," and he became frustrated when he realized she didn't.

He squeezed her hand. "What happened to the girl who just wanted to forget about everything for a couple of hours?"

"That was before she was kidnapped and nearly blown to smithereens." Eve stood. "I'll be back. I need to use the little girls' room."

As she stood, Alec caught her wrist. Her brows rose in silent inquiry.

"Angel." He kissed the back of her hand. "When I tell you to stop thinking about them, it's not because I want you to live in a fantasy world. I just want you to see the good stuff around you. You saw a mother nursing her baby, but you didn't see the miracle of it. You were too busy looking at the demon next to her. Don't give them the power to ruin your day."

Frowning, Eve absorbed his words, then nodded her acceptance. Alec had lived with the mark since the dawn of time and could still see miracles; she could try.

"I'll be right back," she said.

He released her. After inching her way past the other spectators in their aisle, Eve sprinted up the wide cement steps. She still marveled over the speed, strength, and agility that came with the mark burned into her upper arm. She'd always been athletic, but now she was Supergirl. Well . . . she couldn't fly. But she could jump really damn high. She could also see in the dark and bust through dead-bolted doors, talents she'd never anticipated needing or appreciating.

Eve reached the concourse and followed the signs to the nearest restroom. The line protruded just outside the entrance. Luckily, she wasn't desperate. More than anything, she'd just needed to get out of her seat.

So she waited patiently, rocking in her flip-flops with her hands in her pockets. An occasional breeze passed by, ruffling through her ponytail. It carried the mingled scent of evil and rotting souls, a pungent stench that made her stomach roil. It fell somewhere between decomposition and fresh shit, and it amazed her that the Unmarked couldn't smell it.

How had she lived twenty-eight years of her life in complete ignorance? How had Alec lived centuries in complete awareness?

"Mom!" The young boy in front of her was crossing his legs and wiggling madly. "I have to *go*!"

Although the woman looked as if she could be the child's sister, Eve wasn't unduly surprised. Many women in Southern California didn't age. They just became plasticized caricatures of their youthful selves. This one was bleached blonde with a perfect tan, breasts a size too large for her slender frame, and plumped, glossy lips.

The mother looked around.

"Let me go in the boys' bathroom," he begged.

"I can't go in there with you."

"I'll be done in a minute!"

Eve guessed the boy was around six years old. Old enough to pee by himself, but she understood the mother's concern. A child had been killed in a public restroom in nearby Oceanside while his aunt waited outside. The demon who orchestrated that horror had used the oldest trick in the book—pretending to be God.

The harried mother hesitated for a long moment,

then gave a jerky nod. "Hurry. You can wash your hands here in the girls' bathroom."

The boy ran past the drinking fountains and ducked into the men's room. Eve offered a commiserating smile to his mom. The line moved incrementally forward. Two teenagers joined in behind her. They were dressed in the predominant fashion of layered tank tops paired with low-rise jeans. Expensive perfume saturated the air around them, which created a welcome relief from the odor of decay. In the stadium, the crowd roared. One of the Chargers' outside linebackers was a werewolf. From the high-frequency praise of the Infernals in the crowd, he'd done something worth cheering about.

"Why is the line so long?" the girl behind her asked.

Eve shrugged, but the woman in front of her replied, "The bathrooms down there—" she pointed to the left with a French manicured nail "—are closed for repairs."

As if on cue, the mark seared into Eve's deltoid began to tingle, then burn. She sighed and abandoned her place. "You can take my spot. I don't have to go that bad."

"Thanks," the teenager replied.

Eve headed to the left, muttering to herself, "Some vacation."

"You were bored anyway, babe," purred a familiar voice.

Glancing to the side, Eve watched as Reed Abel fell into step with her, his mouth curved in a devilish smile that belied the wings and halo he occasionally sported for shock value. He was a *mal'akh*, but there wasn't much angelic about Alec's brother.

"That doesn't mean I wanted to be put to work."

Reed was the handler in charge of her assignments, which was just a nasty trick in her opinion. Why God allowed and encouraged dissension between the two brothers was beyond her comprehension.

"We could blow this taco stand," he suggested. "Go have some hot, sweaty fun."

She wasn't touching that invitation with a ten-foot pole. Like his brother, Reed scorched a girl in both good and bad ways. "Are you kidding about the assignment? Do you need me for something more substantial or what?"

"You thought it was substantial enough before." He winked mischievously.

Eve smacked him. "Don't be crude. I refuse to be the latest toy you and your brother fight over. Go find something else to play with."

"I'm not playing with you."

There was something sincere in his tone. She ignored it by necessity, although less circumspect parts of her perked up.

"The bathroom?" she asked instead, when the yellow Out of Service sign came into view.

"Yeah." He caught her arm and tugged her closer. "Raguel suggested it was time for an extension of your classroom training. I'll go get Cain."

Raguel was the archangel whose jurisdiction she fell under. He was the bail bondsman, Reed was the dispatcher, and she was the bounty hunter. It was a well-oiled system for most, but her road had been bumpy from the very beginning.

She sniffed the air. The acrid stench of Infernal wrinkled her nose. "You know . . . this is like sending a medical student into brain surgery the day she first reads about it."

"You don't know your own strengths, babe."

She glared. "I know when I'm getting my ass kicked."

"You're batting a thousand so far. This one's a wolf and you're good with them. But be careful anyway."

"Easy for you to say. You're not the one risking your hide."

His lips pressed to her temple in a quick, hard kiss. "Risking yours is enough, trust me."

Skirting the Out-of-Service sign, Eve entered the men's restroom, lamenting the fact that she was wearing her favorite flip-flops. Due to the rigors of her "job," she'd taken to wearing combat boots whenever she left home, but Alec had coaxed her into going casual today. She should have known better.

The harsh ammonia smell of stale urine assaulted her nostrils. Finding her target was easy. He stood in the center of the room, alone. A teenage werewolf who was eerily familiar.

"Remember me?" he asked, smiling.

The boy was tall and thin, his face long and unremarkable. He wore a dirty gray hooded sweatshirt and jeans so low his ass was hanging out. A dark spot moved across his cheek and came to rest on his left cheekbone. His detail—swirls around a diamond shape. Like the mark on her arm, it served a similar purpose to military insignia.

Recognition hit her hard, followed by an immediate chill down her spine. "Shouldn't you be in Northern California with your pack?"

"The Alpha sent me down here to even the score. He

thinks Cain needs to learn what it's like to lose someone he loves."

"There was no way to save the Alpha's son," she argued. "Cain doesn't pick and choose his hunts. He follows orders."

"He made a deal. For you. And he broke his promise."

Eve frowned. Alec had never mentioned a deal to her. But that was something she would explore later. There was a more immediate question. "You think you can take me by yourself?"

His smirk turned into a grin. "I brought a friend."

"Great." That was never good.

The large handicapped stall in the back slammed open and something absolutely horrific thundered out. *Holy shit.* An Infernal that large should have reeked for yards. Instead, the only thing Eve smelled was wolf.

The dragon hadn't fully shifted. He still wore his pants and shoes, and dark hair still covered his head. But his mouth was a protruding muzzle of razor-sharp teeth, his eyes were those of a lizard, and all of his visible flesh was covered in gorgeous multihued scales.

"You smell tasty," he rumbled.

She'd heard that Marks smelled sickly sweet to Infernals, which made her laugh inwardly. There was no such thing as a sweet Mark. They were all bitter. "You don't smell like anything."

We failed, she realized with a sinking feeling in her gut. Infernals still had the means to hide themselves in crowds.

"Brilliant, isn't it?" the wolf asked. "Obviously, you didn't wipe out our operation completely."

The dragon roared and it was a fearsome, deafening

sound that echoed in the confined space of the bath-room. The mortals couldn't hear it, though, and Eve's eardrums were invincible despite their celestial sensitivity. Another boon granted by the mark. The dragon shoved the wolf aside and stomped closer.

"Guess that's my cue to leave," the kid said. "I'll give the Alpha your regards."

Eve's gaze remained riveted on her opponent. "Yeah, tell him he screwed with the wrong chick."

The wolf laughed and departed. Eve wanted to do the same.

For all her bravado, she was out of her league. If she had been capable of physical reactions to stress, her heart would be hammering and she'd be short of breath. No doubt about it, she was going to be suffering when this confrontation was over, *if* she was still alive. A religious person might pray for Alec to get here soon, but that wasn't an option for Eve. The Almighty did exactly what he wanted and nothing more. The purpose of prayer was to make the supplicant feel like he was doing something. It made Eve feel like she was wasting her breath.

"Where's Cain?" the dragon growled, approaching her with his hulking, lumbering stride. "I smell his stench on you."

"He's watching the game, which is what you should be doing." Eve couldn't risk telling him that Alec was coming. He might just kill her quickly and bail. In his mortal guise, with no odor to betray him, he could slip right past Alec. But if the dragon thought he had time, he might toy with her. Infernals liked to play.

"I need a snack." His voice was so guttural she could hardly understand him. "You'll do."

"Have you tried the nachos?" she suggested, her hands fisting. Deep inside her, power coiled. Hunger and aggression, too. It was base and animalistic, not at all the elegant sort of violence she might have expected God to employ in the destruction of his enemies. The surge was brutal . . . and addicting. "The chips are kind of stale and the cheese is from a can, but it's a lot less dangerous to your health."

He snorted, which shot a burst of fire out of his muzzle. "I've heard about you. You're no threat to me."

"Really?" She tilted her head, frowning in mock confusion. Demons used sarcasm, evasion, and lies to their advantage. Eve did, too. "When's the last time you got an update on me? Does Hell have a newsletter? A chat room? Otherwise, you're probably behind the times."

"You're cocky. And stupid. You think that sting in Upland made you a hero? Hell's branches are like the Hydra, bitch. Cut off one head, we grow back two."

An icy lump settled in Eve's gut. "More to sever," she managed, albeit with a slight tremor.

The dragon held up his hands. As thick, sharp claws grew out of the tips of his fingers, he leered and drool ran from his gaping maw. "You're a baby. Should make you juicy and tender."

"A *baby*?" she scoffed, fighting the urge to step back. "Do you have any idea what I've been through these last six weeks? I have some serious workplace rage."

Eve widened her stance, raised her fists, and took a deep breath. This was going to hurt. "Ready to see for yourself?"

The dragon's chest expanded on an inhale and he altered, his body assuming its natural reptilian appearance. He loomed above her, his head bent on a long graceful neck to accommodate the ceiling. He was a beautiful creature, with iridescent scales and lithe lines. Problem was, that stunning hide was like cement. Any attempt to kick or hit it would only lead to pain. For her, not him.

Their hide has very little vulnerability, Raguel had taught in Dragon 101. *Points of weakness are the webbing between their toes, the joint connecting the forelimbs to the torso, their eyes, and their rectum. The first will not cause mortal wounds, the second and third require proximity that can get you killed, and the fourth . . . well, as the kids say, you do* not *want to go there.*

Holding out her hand, Eve requested a blade. A sword appeared, hovering in midair, ablaze but for the hilt. Fire. Fire in Hell, fire in Heaven, fire blasting from the dragon's nostrils forcing her to leap backward to avoid being singed.

Pyromaniacs, the lot of 'em.

If she had a choice, she'd prefer her revolver. But she couldn't carry all the time and the Almighty preferred the flame-covered sword. Never let it be said that God didn't have a flair for the dramatic. He knew his strengths, and a bit of flashy intimidation was one of them.

The dragon laughed or chortled or choked . . . whatever. He wasn't impressed. The sound of his amusement gave Eve the willies and she rolled her wrist, using the substantial weight of the blade to limber up. She'd started out being the sorriest swordsman in her class. Now she was passably proficient, getting better every day.

"You missed me," she taunted grimly, wincing when

her flip-flops clung to the sticky floor. Stupid footwear choice.

One of the many things she'd learned since getting saddled with this job was that presenting a formidable appearance went a long way toward hiding her deficiencies. Her enemies could smell her fear and they thrived on it. Throwing them for a loop with a little cockiness was sometimes the only way to gain any sort of advantage.

The dragon took a step toward her, his talons gouging into the tile, his weight vibrating the ground beneath them. The barrage of flames had made the room hot, but she didn't sweat. She couldn't; her body was a temple now.

Swinging at her with one short forelimb, the beast roared with terrible intent. He countered her evasive leap with a lash of his tail, which boasted a hard weighty scale on the tip that was used like a mace. It sank deep into the spot she'd occupied before she stumbled out of the way with a yelp. He yanked the appendage free in a shower of ceramic dust.

As she ran past him, he pivoted, his swinging tail ripping several sinks out of the wall. Eve darted around his side and managed to dislodge one of his scales with a hurried thrust of her blade.

He'd demolished the bathroom, she gave him a paper cut.

"Stupid cunt!" the beast bellowed, seemingly oblivious to the water spraying madly from the broken pipes. The depth of hatred and malevolence in the reptilian eyes added to the growing layer of hardness on her soul that was slowly changing her. Permanently.

Eve's fury rose to mask her terror. Infernals such as this guy were for much more advanced Marks. If he hadn't masked his scent and details, she wouldn't be fighting him.

She was in deep shit. And damn it, she was sick of being soaked all the time. Every Infernal she came across doused her with water.

"Reed." Her voice was not her own. Lower and deeper, it was the language of Marks. Known as a "herald," the tone was instinctive and indecipherable to Infernals. "Hurry up. I'm in trouble."

The sensation of a hot summer breeze moved over her—Reed's reply.

Lifting her free arm for balance, Eve began to feint and parry, her torso canted to the side to present a smaller target. She ducked behind her sword when another burst of flame spewed from his nostrils. The back of her hand was charred by the heat and she screamed. The damage would heal in moments, but that didn't prevent the initial agony.

Eve fell back, tripping over broken tiles and sobbing as a sharp piece penetrated the sole of her sandal and dug deep into her heel. Viscous warmth and the resulting slipperiness of her sole betrayed her blood loss. The dragon roared with triumph at the smell of her wounds and snapped at her with his razor-sharp teeth.

She wasn't going to die in a men's bathroom. No way.

"How the mighty have fallen," Alec drawled.

Eve gasped with relief at the sound of his voice. She ducked the beast's lashing tail, then rushed to peer around his body.

Alec lounged against the tiled threshold of the bathroom with both arms crossed. He looked relaxed and slightly bored, but there was a terrible darkness in his eyes when he hazarded a glance at her. She was his only weakness, a vulnerability he struggled to hide.

"Cain," the dragon rumbled, his posture wary.

"Damon? You used to be The Man. A courtier in the court of Asmodeus." Alec made a chastising noise with his tongue. "Now the best you can do is terrorize rookie Marks?"

"Hey," Eve protested. "Compared to the bathroom, I'm doing all right."

The fact that her opponent had his back to her and didn't seem to think that was a danger chafed. What the hell did she have to do to get some respect?

Frustration wiped out her fear and left only angry determination behind. Eve moved to the dragon's left side and leaped the full height of the room, putting the weight of her body behind the downward slash of her blade. She attacked the slender fold where his tiny forelimb attached to his torso and it severed cleanly, the limb splashing onto the floor with a thud. Crimson blood spurted from the newly made hole and mixed with the water spewing from the distorted pipes.

The dragon howled and spun around, knocking Eve to her back. She skidded several feet in the gore-stained lake that covered the decimated tile. He retaliated with a burst of flame. The inferno engulfed her, melting hair and skin from the top of her head down to her feet, boiling her in the flood that washed over and around her. The agony was such that she couldn't voice a sound and when the flames ceased abruptly, she hoped for the relief of death.

But she wasn't going alone.

Fueled by adrenaline and the animosity of a woman completely fed up with her life, Eve vaulted to her feet. She slammed into the beast's neck and belly where she clung to the tips of his scales with one-handed desperation. The impact to her raw, burnt flesh was devastating and she cried out, nearly dropping her sword.

Alec was there before her, one arm banded around the dragon's neck while the other hand gouged at the eyes. The beast flayed and screeched, whipping its neck to and fro in a vain effort to free himself of his attackers.

As Eve plunged the length of her blade through the vulnerable flesh created by the missing forelimb, she felt massive talons tearing into her spine. Her body arched, forcing her weapon the final inch needed to penetrate the dragon's heart.

The beast howled, then exploded in a burst of white-hot embers.

Eve crashed to the ground, paralyzed by her wounds. She lay blinking, gasping, surrounded by the requiem created by the shower from the pipes.

The vibration of footsteps pounding through water assailed her, then Alec was pulling her gingerly into his lap.

"Angel . . ." His hands shook as he tentatively touched her ruined skin. "Don't you dare die on me. You hear me? I just got you back, damn you—"

"Alec." She tried to open her eyes, but the effort required more energy than she possessed. Shivers wracked her abused frame and rattled her teeth. The faint chemical tang of tap water filled her nostrils, as did the scent of ashes, demon, and blood. *Her* blood.

She could finally smell and taste the sweetness of it.

"I'm here." His voice broke. "I-I'm here."

"The Alpha did this."

"What?"

"The Alpha. He wanted . . . his son . . . he tried . . ."

"Shh. Don't talk, angel." A hot tear splashed onto her raw skin. Then another. "Save your strength."

"We missed something in Upland," she whispered, sinking into an encroaching blanket of darkness. The pain was fading, the fear receding. "Go back . . . We missed something . . ."

CHAPTER 2

Six weeks earlier . . .

E ve knew, the moment her eyes met his, that they were going to have a torrid, extremely brief affair.

His shoulder brushed hers as he walked by. The scent of his skin lingered in her nostrils for a delicious moment and she shivered, her blood thrumming with anticipation. She didn't know his name, she didn't know *him,* but the compulsion to take the handsome stranger home with her was powerful and irresistible.

A tiny voice in her mind urged her to use caution, told her to slow down. Think twice. She wasn't a "casual sex" woman, never had been. But one look, and lust had hit her like a freight train.

His face . . . God, his face looked so much like Alec Cain's they could have been brothers. Smooth olive skin, night-black hair, and espresso-brown eyes. Sex incarnate. Though a decade had passed since the night Alec had ruined her for other men, Eve doubted he'd changed much. Men like Alec just got better with age.

The man who'd just passed her carried that same air of dangerous, tightly restrained power. That sense of being barely leashed. The urbane Armani suit that draped his tall, leanly muscled frame only emphasized that primitive quality she hungered for. The animal attraction was intense, quickening her pulse and knotting her stomach.

Her heels tapped a rhythmic staccato upon the golden-veined marble floor. Somewhere deep inside her, alarm bells were ringing. She felt almost as if she were fleeing, as if the sight and smell of a dominant male were something to fear. But parts of her were far from afraid.

The vast lobby of Gadara Tower was congested by business-minded pedestrians. The steady hum of numerous conversations and the industrious whirring of the glass tube elevator motors failed to hide her rapid breathing. Fifty floors above her, a massive skylight allowed natural illumination to flood the atrium. It was that drenching sunlight gleaming on thick, inky strands of hair that first drew her attention to her mystery man. The gentle heat from above combined with the lush vegetation in planters created a slight, sensual humidity.

All together, she was feeling turned on. Hot under the collar. One look at a seductive stranger had incited a dark, unfamiliar sexual urgency. It was riding her hard. Cracking the whip. From the moment she entered Gadara Tower she had felt odd, jittery, as if she drank too much coffee. Never prone to nerves, she didn't feel like herself. She longed to go home and take a hot bath.

Eve's hand flexed, adjusting her perspiration-slick

grip on the handle of her leather portfolio. Within the zippered confines rested a dozen of her best drawings; the reason she was here. Raguel Gadara was expanding his real estate empire and she was one of a select few interior designers under consideration. She had poured her heart and soul into her presentation. She'd been certain she would leave the building with the job in the bag. Instead, she cooled her heels in his waiting room for twenty minutes before being informed that Mr. Gadara would have to reschedule. Eve understood the message—*I have the power to select you or not.*

Gadara was about to learn a hard lesson about Eve Hollis: *she* had the power to *accept* and she wouldn't work with a man who played power games. He'd just power-played himself out of the best damn interior designer in the country.

To say that she was horribly disappointed would be an understatement. She had latched on to the opportunity to pitch to Gadara with uncustomary fervor. For weeks now she'd felt excited. Expectant. Like a roller coaster poised on the downward slope, ready to race. Now she felt like she'd rolled back into the station without going anywhere.

The elevators to the parking garage were ahead of her and she quickened her pace. Then she spotted a gray-painted door that bore a Stairs sign.

Compelled to move in that direction, she veered off course, almost as if she were a passenger in her own body, just tagging along for the ride.

The moment her hand wrapped around the door handle, the mystery man was with her, his chest to her back as he propelled her into the airless stairwell. She was spun around with barely tempered brute strength and pinned to the closing door, sealing them in. Her precious portfolio fell to the cement floor and was promptly forgotten.

"Oh!" Her heartbeat stuttered, shifting gears from trepidation to sexual hunger. Her neck arched as the man licked and sucked at her tender throat, his much taller body hunched over hers. The rich, spicy scent of his skin inundated her senses, rushing through her blood like a potent aphrodisiac. Her hands slipped between his jacket and shirt, caressing the straining length of his tautly muscled back. He was hot, his skin burning. Pressed up against her as he was, he was making her sweat.

His left hand engulfed her breast through silk and lace, squeezing and kneading the achingly swollen flesh. His right hand caught the edge of her pinstriped pencil skirt and yanked it upward roughly. A loud tear echoed through the space as the slit in the back gave way under the pressure.

"Slow down," she begged, even as she grew more aroused. "I-I don't normally do things like . . . this."

He ignored her, cupping her thigh and hauling her tighter against him. Eve felt his erection thick and hard against her belly, and she shivered. It had been a long time since her last sexual encounter. Too long. She was primed, and when he reached between her legs, he knew just how ready she was.

"Temptress," he rumbled, his voice deep and aggressive. With a clench of his fist, he tore her thong and dropped the remnants on the floor. He released her long enough to shrug out of his suit jacket. "Unzip me."

The command was undeniable.

Eve fumbled as she worked to unfasten his belt. His strong fingers were rubbing between her legs, sliding through the slickness there. The hand at her breast gentled, his thumb stroking back and forth across her puckered nipple. She whimpered and spread her legs wider, helpless against the hunger.

A monotonous droning noise caught her attention. A quick glance up confirmed her suspicions—a security camera was pointed in their direction, the flashing red light beneath the circular lens confirming that it was fully operational.

Flushing with embarrassment, Eve wondered what she must look like with her knee-length skirt bunched around her waist. A wanton. A slut.

What the hell had gotten into her? She'd never done anything like this before.

But she felt delicious, despite her consternation. The man who reminded her of Alec Cain was pushing all the right buttons. The ones that turned off her inner morality police.

"Hurry," he growled.

Jolting at the sound of his rough voice, Eve resumed her task, somehow managing to tug the belt free and open his trousers. The waistband clung to his lean hips for a moment, then collapsed into a puddle around his ankles. When she lifted the wrinkled tails of his shirt, she discovered he was going commando. He was thick, long, and ready.

"Oh God," she breathed, her body clenching with excitement and heady lust.

"Yes," the man purred, just before he caught her by the backs of her thighs and hefted her with effortless strength. "He knows."

"Condom?" she gasped. Her eyes met his. His gaze was dark and intent, roiling with mysterious secrets and dangerous desires. She began to pant. With hunger. With fear.

"Hush," he crooned, brushing his lips across hers. She felt the muscles in his buttocks and thighs tauten.

Then he thrust deep.

Her cry was both pained and aroused. He gave her no time to think, to move, to fight. He launched into a hard, pounding rhythm and rode her straight into climax. She writhed and sobbed with the pleasure, her body shuddering violently in his arms. He continued to surge into her, over and over again, stroking through her spasms, spurring her into another violent orgasm. And another.

"No more," she begged, pushing weakly at his shoulders. "I can't take any more . . ."

Holding her with one arm beneath her buttocks, he tore at her shirt, scattering the tiny ivory buttons across the floor and down the cement stairs. He bared her shoulder and watched as she came again, the climax arching her body like a tightly strung bow. He lifted his hand and bared his palm, revealing an intricate tattoo in the center. It began to glow, turning into a white-hot brand.

"Bear the Mark of Cain," he growled, pressing his hand against her upper arm and searing her skin. He took her mouth, swallowing her screams, rocking into her, his tempo unfaltering.

Eve's nails dug into the flesh of his back, the mixture of intense pleasure and pain overloading her senses, making her see things that couldn't be real.

Her lover appeared to change, illuminating from within, his clothes falling away to reveal a muscular body and rich golden skin. His dark eyes changed to swirling amber as he threw his head back and roared.

His powerful neck corded with strain as he came hard and long. Deep inside her.

It was a nightmare and a wet dream rolled into one, hurling her into an experience that stole her sanity. Huge white feathered wings unfurled from his back and embraced her.

Darkness followed suit, closing swiftly around her.

CHAPTER 3

*M*s. *Hollis? Ms. Hollis, can you hear me?"*
  Eve's eyelids fluttered, then lifted.
"Ms. Hollis?"

She ached all over and felt hot, but she was shivering, as if she had the flu.

Awareness of her surroundings came to her in lapping waves—the male voice calling out to her, the dozen faces that stared down at her, the glass ceiling of Gadara Tower.

She bolted upright, her head whacking into the chin of a rubbernecker. The man cursed and stumbled backward, but her attention was focused on her clothes. As she took note of the crisply ironed length of her skirt, her fingers drifted down the row of tiny white buttons that secured her pale blue shirt.

"What happened?" she asked, her voice hoarse and raw as if she'd been screaming.

"We're not sure."

She turned her head to meet the blue eyes of a uniformed paramedic. Her gaze dropped to his name tag. *Woodbridge.*

"Have you eaten today?" he asked, his arm strong at her back.

Thinking about her morning, she nodded. "Yogurt and coffee."

Woodbridge smiled. "It's two in the afternoon. That's a long time to go with just yogurt. I think your blood sugar dropped. You became light-headed and passed out."

Two Gadara security guards pushed the crowd back and Eve stood with the paramedic's assistance. She wobbled a moment on her heels, was steadied by strong hands, then fingers pushed into her long black hair and gently felt her scalp. "Does it hurt anywhere?"

She hurt everywhere, but she knew what he meant. "No."

"I don't feel a bump, but I'd like to take you to the hospital as a precaution."

"Sure." She held onto his arm as the room tilted.

As she felt the unmistakable trickle of semen down her inner thighs, blood drained from her face. Her dizziness worsened and her empty stomach heaved.

"Wait. I changed my mind," she whispered through parched lips, her right hand lifting to touch her left upper arm. A painful welt could be felt through her shirt sleeve. "I just want to go home."

Eve stared at her computer monitor and felt an odd, vibrating panic well up inside her.

The Mark of Cain. The mark given by God to Cain

as protection from harm while he wandered the Earth as punishment for killing his brother, Abel.

She'd been screwed within an inch of her life by a religious zealot.

That was scary enough. But what was even more frightening was the familiarity of the design. She'd seen it before, caressed it with her fingertips, her lips, thought it made the man who bore it even more of a rebel. Alec Cain's tattoo had turned her on and spurred a night of sin that haunted her to this day.

Backing her desk chair away from her computer, Eve stood and left her home office. Every step she took toward the kitchen reminded her of the heated encounter in the stairwell. The soreness between her legs made it impossible to forget the feel of her mystery man moving fiercely inside her.

The breath she exhaled was shaky, as was the rest of her.

How could she explain the pleasure she hadn't wanted to feel? The brand on her arm? The intact condition of her clothing? And the wings . . . Good god, the man had wrapped her in soft, white wings.

"I'm losing my mind."

After she'd showered, Eve stared at the burn on her arm, a one-inch wide triquetra surrounded by a circlet of three serpents, each eating the tail of the snake before it. Unlike most deep burns, the intricate details of the mark were clearly visible. She might have thought the design was exotic and pretty, if she'd actually wanted it. Now it was hidden beneath a bandage and a thick coating of Silvadene burn cream.

The doorbell rang, and Eve hurried toward the living room. She reached into the console table by the

door and pulled out her revolver. With quiet deliberation, she unzipped its padded case. She was a single
woman living alone in the heart of a metropolis; it
made sense to own a registered handgun. And since
Eve believed that something worth doing was worth
doing well, she maintained a membership at the local
gun club and practiced often.

"Evangeline?"

The voice was familiar and dear; it belonged to her
next-door neighbor, Mrs. Basso. Eve breathed a sigh
of relief, surprised to find that she'd been frightened
of something as simple as a visitor. She put the gun
away.

Pulling open the door, she found her neighbor waiting for her with a concerned frown and a Tupperware
bowl in her hands. Mrs. Basso wore her customary
Dockers, dress shirt, and sweater vest. Today her ensemble was comprised of various shades of blue.
Pearls decorated her ears, throat, and wrist. She'd been
a raving beauty in her youth. Now she had a stately elegance that was marred only by the slight stooping of
her shoulders.

"Are you okay?" she asked. "You look tired."

"I'm fine," Eve lied.

Mrs. Basso owned Basso's Ristorante and Grille, a
popular Italian restaurant. She and her husband had
once operated the establishment together, but with Mr.
Basso's passing a year ago she'd begun leasing the
business out. This afforded her a steady, reliable income without much work on her part. Because she was
alone, Eve checked on her a couple of times a week.
When she made a run to the store, she always checked

to see if Mrs. Basso needed anything. In return, her neighbor doted on her like a favored grandchild.

"You should get your thyroid checked," Mrs. Basso said.

Eve smiled. "Okay."

Mrs. Basso extended the bowl to her. "I made you some homemade chicken noodle soup. Lots of garlic and a dash of basil. You should eat all of it."

"You didn't have to do that," Eve protested.

"And you don't have to spend your time looking after me," she countered. "But we do it anyway."

Eve accepted the offering. "Come in and eat it with me."

Mrs. Basso shook her head. "Thank you, but a *Buffy the Vampire Slayer* rerun comes on in a few minutes and it's one of my favorites."

"Which season?"

"Six."

"Ahh, the one where Buffy and Spike finally get together."

Mrs. Basso blushed. "That Spike is a hunk. Eat all the soup, you hear?"

Eve laughed. "Of course. Thank you."

"It's the least I can do after all you do for me." With a wave, she moved back down the hall and paused. "There's a new Hugh Jackman movie out next week. He's a hunk, too."

"It's a date."

Mrs. Basso winked and stepped out of view.

Eve stared down the hall for a long time, clinging to the feeling of normalcy. The minute she closed her door it was gone, leaving her with a throbbing in her arm and between her legs, and a desperate need to know what in hell happened to her.

Fetching a spoon from the kitchen, Eve sat on her cream-colored sofa and turned on the television. She watched *Buffy*. A boyfriend had turned her on to the television series in the third season. It was the only thing she remembered about that particular relationship. And that was more than she could say about many of the romances she'd had since Alec Cain. But if she was honest, she hadn't really had a relationship with him either. She'd just been screwed, in more ways than one.

As Buffy and Spike beat the crap out of each other, Eve felt her shoulders and arms tensing to the point of pain. Wild, edgy, aggressive energy pulsed through her veins. Sweat dotted her upper lip and her vision grew fuzzy.

The doorbell rang again and she lurched to her feet. "I ate every drop," she yelled as she moved toward the door. She smiled at the thought of Mrs. Basso following up on her as if she were an errant child.

"Angel."

Eve paused, her steps faltering.

"Open the door."

She retrieved her gun, her hand slipping into the protective case to grip the hilt. Padding quietly to the door, she lifted on tiptoe to peer out the peephole.

For a moment she stood unblinking, unable to believe what—*whom*—she was looking at.

"Come on, angel," he purred, using the pet name only he'd ever used. Evangeline. Eve. *Angel*. "Let me in."

Even through the distorted glass, Alec Cain was breathtaking. Her damned mouth was watering.

Unfortunately, he also closely resembled the man who'd attacked her earlier. Her warning bells were clanging hell for leather. She hadn't listened to them earlier and look where that had gotten her.

Eve backed up silently.

"Angel," he said, softer this time, his voice so clear she knew he had to be resting his forehead against the door. "I know what happened today. You shouldn't be alone. Let me in."

Alec's voice. Hearing it in person, after all these years, stabbed her like a knife. Dark and rich like chocolate, it was decadent. Sinful. It had urged her to relinquish her virginity, an act that was painful for most women, but had been the pinnacle of pleasure for her. She'd fallen head over heels that night. Would have done anything for him, gone anywhere he wanted. *Anything,* if it meant they would be together.

Stupid. Naïve.

Shaking her head, Eve continued to retreat, tears streaming down her cheeks. Her arms were straight and steady, pointing the muzzle directly at the door. She wasn't surprised that he knew what happened to her today. The fact was, Alec always knew. From the beginning, he'd had an uncanny way of knowing what she was thinking and feeling. She was pretty sure that's why he was so damn good in the sack. Before she knew what she wanted, he was giving it to her.

"Eve, listen to me. You can't be alone now. It's not safe."

You're not safe, she thought.

"I'm the closest thing you've got," he retorted, as if he'd read her mind.

No. Go away. She couldn't voice the words. Her throat was too tight.

"I won't, angel. I'm coming in. Keep backing away."

"I-I'll s-shoot you."

Eve could sense him pause.

Then her door burst open in an explosion of splintered wood and bent locks. Three dead bolts. The kind bullets couldn't break.

Her entire body shook violently, but she held the gun level.

He entered her condominium with casual ease, his steel-toed boots thudding heavily on her polished wood floors.

Alec Cain was tall, dark perfection. He wore black from head to toe, from his fitted T-shirt to his leather pants. His inky locks were a bit too long, caressing his nape and falling over his brow. His full lips were drawn tight with strain. His brown eyes were burning. That intensity had done crazy things to her equilibrium when she was a wild child of eighteen. It did crazy things to her now.

The past decade hadn't aged him at all.

"I told you to go away, Alec."

He tossed his leather jacket and helmet onto her sofa as he passed it. "Are you really going to shoot me if I don't?"

"If you don't turn around and get out of my house, yeah."

Alec could stand stock still and be merely gorgeous, but when he moved, all bets were off. There was a sleek, predatory grace to him that was riveting. A woman couldn't help but wonder if he would be as smooth in bed. Eve knew he was. Sex was an art form to Alec, and he was a master.

"I'm not leaving, angel."

Eve's nostrils flared. Then she squeezed the trigger.

CHAPTER 4

The click of the hammer falling was deafening in the quiet room. Had there been a round in the chamber, Alec would be sporting a steaming hole in his chest.

"You can't hurt me," he said softly.

"Don't underestimate me. I always keep the gun stored on an empty chamber. You won't be so healthy when I squeeze off a live round." She gestured toward the door with a hard jerk of her chin. "Get out, while you're still in one piece."

Her home no longer felt like her own. Alec dominated her living room. The darkness of his clothes was completely at odds with the soft champagne colors she'd decorated with. In an odd twist of fate, she and he matched. She wore a black cotton tank top and matching shorts, her comfort clothes.

"I can't." He turned his back to her and pushed the door closed, the protruding dead bolts fitting into the gaping holes in the decimated jamb. He hooked the slender chain into place (the one piece of security she hadn't bothered with before), then grabbed the wooden chair next to the console table and wedged it under the haphazardly hanging knob.

Locking them in together.

He faced her. "That mark on your arm is going to start messing with you."

The damn thing was already messing with her. It throbbed and burned something fierce. "What is it?"

"Both a blessing and a curse." Alec stepped closer, completely unconcerned with the danger her gun presented. "It's a punishment, a form of penance."

"What-the-fuck-ever. I'm agnostic and you're insane. Take your lunatic bullshit and get out of my house."

"You're going to get sick and need someone here."

"Well, it sure as hell isn't going to be you. I'll call a friend. Someone *reliable*."

Outwardly, the dig didn't appear to affect him, but she sensed it had struck home.

"A friend isn't going to be able to help you, Eve. Especially a woman. Not unless you started swinging both ways, which I really doubt. You like men too much."

"No, I only like *parts* of men."

"You liked *all* of me."

"I was a stupid kid." She snorted. "But I learned my lesson the first time." His challenging smile made her breath catch and she stilled, absorbing what he'd said. "Wait. Are you talking about *sex*?"

Eve's eyes widened and her gaze dropped to his groin. The man was rocked, cocked, and ready to go. Every inch of that hard, muscled frame was edgy with tension and arousal. Sudden fury gave her strength, and her shaking stopped.

"No way, Alec. You're insane if you think I'll let you

touch me again. Go find someone else to torment. I'm all stocked up on angst."

The angular lines of his face softened. "Angel—"

"Don't 'angel' me. I'm not your angel. I'm not your *anything*."

"You're everything, which is why I left."

"Shut up." Fire was coursing through her veins making it hard to think.

Alec studied her intently. "The fever's kicking in. Your cheeks are flushed and you're beginning to sweat. You need to lie down."

"Yeah, that'd be convenient for you, wouldn't it? Disarm me and get me horizontal."

"If I just wanted to get laid, why hit up a woman who holds the grudge from hell? I'm not that hard up."

That smarted, the knowledge that he could crook his finger and have whomever he wanted. She should take comfort knowing she wasn't the only one to chase him. But it just made her jealous and cranky.

"If you know what happened," she bit out, "then you know that man looked like you." Although now that he was here in the flesh, Eve saw the differences between them. No one looked like Alec, although the winged man had been awfully close.

But at this point, she didn't care. She just wanted Alec out of her house. She couldn't deal with him. Not today. God, *not ever*. Never again. Even after all these years, he still drove her crazy.

Sweat dripped down her temple and Eve wiped it away impatiently. "This afternoon pretty much ruined me for men with your coloring. Switching teams actually sounds pretty good at the moment."

"Don't," he said tightly, the muscles in his arms flexing. "I'm barely holding it together as it is. I'd hunt him down now, if you weren't about to be extremely sick. You need me here, more than you need me out there."

Her laughter was harsh and without humor. "You're something I *don't* need in my life, especially now."

Alec rubbed the back of his neck. The pose showed off his well-defined biceps to perfection. It pissed her off that she could still find him so damned attractive.

"I'm sorry, angel."

Somehow, he managed to fill those words with a wealth of regret. But she wasn't buying what he was selling. He was one of those guys who never stayed in one place for long and left broken hearts in his wake. The first time she'd been too young to know better. There was no excuse now.

Perspiration gathered between her breasts and trickled down her chest. Eve rubbed at the wetness through her tank top. "It's been a really crappy day, Alec. I need to go to the doctor in the morning. If you would leave and not come back, I'd be super grateful. I might even forgive you for being crazy. Someday."

A sudden flare of heat spread across her skin and made her dizzy. The room spun and she stumbled. Alec caught her, cradling her violently shivering body down to the floor. He pulled the gun from her lax fingers, and set it down carefully beside him.

"Alec . . ." The smell of his skin, achingly familiar, drugged her already confused senses.

"I'm here, angel," he crooned, pulling her into his embrace.

She clutched at his arm and found the raised mark with her fingertips. Turning her head, Eve saw it. The trinity knot and serpents were just like hers, only his brand had another image in the center. An open eye. His looked like an embossed tattoo, while hers was most definitely a blistering burn.

"Dear god," she gasped, her breathing labored as she felt consciousness slipping from her. "What's going on?"

He brushed strands of her hair away from her face. Her skin tingled where he touched her, goose bumps rising. Everything about the way he looked at her exacerbated her fever. There was nothing in the world like being wanted with a primitive desire. The one thing she'd never doubted was that Alec was madly in lust with her.

"You were drawn to *him* because of me, weren't you?" His lips hovered above hers so that their panting breaths mingled and became one. It was as intimate as sex, that sharing of breaths between them.

She didn't have to answer. He knew. He always knew.

His thumb brushed across her cheekbone. He moved to kiss her, but Eve jerked her head away.

"Damn you," she breathed, her nails digging into his skin.

"We're both damned." He pulled her into his lap and tucked her flushed face into the crook of his neck, where the scent of his skin was so strong.

Against her will, she nuzzled him, rubbing her sweat into his flesh. She felt the urge to crawl inside him, to see what made him tick. Her tongue darted out and tasted him. He shuddered in response, squeezing her tighter. Her wound was on the arm facing away from him and she felt his fingertips move, feather light, over her bandage.

Her voice came as no more than a whisper. "I haven't done anything wrong."

"You're right, angel. You haven't." His lips pressed hard to her damp forehead.

"Then why?"

He exhaled harshly. "Because of me. Because I couldn't resist you."

Eve opened her mouth to reply, but weariness pulled hard at her and she sank into darkness.

CHAPTER 5

*T*he deep rumbling growl of a Harley drew Eve's gaze to the parking lot of the ice-cream shop where she worked after school. It was five in the evening and the day was just starting to end. The horizon was the color of a tangerine tinged with burgundy.

She walked to the end of the counter to catch a glimpse of the Heritage Softail that lounged in front of the Circle K convenience store next door. It was a black and chrome beauty, boasting custom saddlebags and a well-worn seat.

"What I wouldn't give for a bike like that," she whispered, "and the freedom of the road."

Not that she was unhappy with her life, because she wasn't. It was just . . . ordinary.

Sighing, she looked over her shoulder at the clock and silently begged it to tick a little faster. Her shift was over at six. The final football game of the season started at seven fifteen. While her high school was across the street, the field they played on was a few miles away.

"Hey. Are we going to Chad's party after the game?"

Eve glanced at her friend Janice and shrugged. "I'm not sure. Depends if Robert's going or not."

Shaking her head, Janice went back to work wiping off the counters, her long, blonde ponytail swaying with her exertions. "You can't avoid him forever."

"I know. And I know he'll stop talking shit about me when he hooks up with someone else, but in the meantime, I just want to stay out of his way."

Crouching down, Eve opened the doors beneath the display case. She pulled out the glass cleaner and a roll of paper towels.

"He's an asshole," Janice muttered. "I'm glad you didn't screw him."

"Yeah." Eve stood. "Me, too."

She tossed one last longing glance at the Harley and froze. The owner was shoving a paper bag into one of the saddlebags. Then he tossed one leg over the bike and settled into the seat.

Wow.

He was tall, dark, and dangerous. His long legs and fine ass were draped in loose, low-slung blue jeans, his powerful biceps bared by the fitted white tank top he wore. His jaw was square and bold, his lips firm but sensual. Wicked. The lines that bracketed them only emphasized how gorgeous he was.

Completely unaware of her fascination, he turned the key and revved the engine, his black leather boots resting firmly on the asphalt, ready to push the bike back. The anticipation of his departure made her shiver.

Then he turned his head and saw her.

Eve knew the exact moment he became aware of her stare because he stilled, his large frame visibly tensing.

The hand on his thigh reached for his sunglasses so he could push them up. As they lifted, they caught the overly long lock of glossy black hair that fell over his brow and took it with them.

Their eyes met. Electricity arced through the space between them. She shivered. The bottle of glass cleaner fell from her nerveless fingers and thudded on the linoleum floor.

"Wow . . ." Janice's voice breathed the awe Eve felt. "He's got to be famous."

Eve didn't break eye contact. She couldn't. "Why?"

"No normal guy is that fucking hot." Janice blew out her breath. "Hey!"

Fingers snapped in front of Eve's face.

"Huh?"

"Stop staring at him. You're going to give him ideas."

"Maybe I want him to have ideas."

Janice yanked her around and glared at her with narrowed green eyes. "Evie, no. First off, that guy is way out of your league. Second, he's too old for you. Third, everything about him screams bad news."

The rumble outside stopped and Eve looked back over her shoulder. He stood beside the bike—watching her.

"Listen, Eve. You have the worst luck with guys, worse than me, and that's saying something. But this guy—hunky as he is—is serious trouble. Look at him. Men that look like that . . ." Janice snorted. "I see him, and I see teen pregnancy and welfare."

That's not what Eve saw when she looked at him. She didn't know what it was, but something inside her was so drawn to him that she felt an invisible string

*pulling her, urging her to close the distance between
them.*

Hi, *she mouthed, trying to smile, but failing. There
was nothing to smile about.*

*His jaw tensed, his hand fisting at his side. His dark
gaze was hot. Burning. No man had ever looked at her
with that level of intensity. As if nothing in the world existed but her.*

Biting her lower lip, she willed him to come closer.
Talk to me. Come on.

*She saw the nearly imperceptible shake of his head.
He yanked his shades back down, shielding his eyes.
He ignored her as he remounted his bike and restarted
the engine. But she knew he still felt her stare.*

*He rode away without another glance in her direc-
tion.*

*The feeling of inexplicable loss stayed with Eve for
days after he left.*

A wet cloth swiping over Eve's skin brought her to a
distant awareness. The whirring ceiling fan blew air
across the lingering dampness, cooling her fevered skin.
Her tongue felt thick in her mouth and her hand lifted to
her parched throat. As her forearm crossed her chest,
she realized she was naked and groaned, hating the feeling of helplessness.

"Here." A thickly muscled arm slipped beneath her
shoulders and raised her to meet the edge of a drinking
glass. Her lips parted gratefully and ice water filled her
empty stomach, causing her to shiver. Burning hot outside, freezing cold inside.

Inhaling a spicy exotic scent that was unmistakable, she croaked, "Alec?"

"In the flesh." He mantled her body, his hip pressed to hers as he sat on the edge of the bed.

"I-I don't want you to see me . . . l-like this. Go away."

Pressing a kiss to her brow, Alec followed her down to the pillow. Silken strands of his hair stroked over her hypersensitive skin. Pleasure flowed through her. Familiar pleasure. Longed-for pleasure. Contradicting her order to leave, her hand lifted to his thick hair. Her fingers slid deep into the glossy locks, her palm cupping the back of his head to keep him close.

"I feel like shit," she muttered.

"I know. I'm sorry, angel. Women always take the Change hardest."

"What . . . what change?"

"Hush," he soothed, wiping her forehead with the wet washcloth. "Sleep now. I'll take care of you."

Her nipples throbbed as if pinched by clamps, the ache boring deep. Her hands moved to them, covering the puckered tips with her palms. A large, warm hand surrounded hers, then pulled them away. At eighteen, she hadn't been this curvy, less than a handful. She was much fuller now, a fact he seemed to appreciate if the rhythmic kneading of his hand on her breast was any indication. She whimpered, finding relief in the pressure of his touch.

Her fingers drifted along the length of his side, feeling hot, smooth skin stretched tight over lean, hard muscles. The image of Alec bare-chested flashed behind her closed eyelids, followed by heated remembrances of the last time he'd handled her so intimately.

Sick as she was, her body still hungered for him. How the hell could she be horny at a time like this? "Alec . . . What's happening to me?"

"You're becoming like me."

"Oh god." As the burn on her arm heated painfully, she whimpered. "Shoot me now."

"Just a few more days, angel. You're strong. You'll be even stronger when you get through this."

"Few days? How long have I—?"

"Three days."

Three days?

And he was still here.

She fought to stay awake, but she lost the battle and drifted off.

As soon as Eve exited the ice-cream shop to the back alley, she knew he was there. She closed her eyes and sighed, then straightened her shoulders and locked the door.

"What do you want, Robert?" she asked wearily, loose bits of old asphalt crunching beneath her Vans. "I've had a long day and I really want to go home."

Her ex leaned against the hood of his white '67 Mustang, arms and legs crossed. He was arguably the most popular guy at Loara High and it was obvious why. A California blond with blue eyes, he had a great body from both surfing at dawn at Huntington Beach and afternoon football practice. But his looks hadn't been enough to tempt to her out of her virginity.

At eighteen, she was the oldest girl she knew who still hadn't had sex. Sometimes the peer pressure was fierce, but mostly she was fine with waiting for more than a quick, painful screw in the back of some guy's car.

"I thought you might want a ride to Jason's party," *he said with a half-smile.*

Eve shook her head. "Thanks, but I'm not up for it tonight."

Her uniform of bright red shorts and a white polo shirt with "Henry's Ice Cream" embroidered on the breast was irritating her. She wanted nothing more than to toss it in the hamper and watch the latest episode of 90210 in a pair of baggy sweats.

"I've got a cooler in the car and a dime bag," he coaxed. "We can skip the party and drive out to the tracks."

"Give it a rest." She started walking. "I'm not doing it, okay? You broke up with me and told everyone I'm a bad lay. Everyone thinks I put out. We're done."

Leaping to his feet, Robert stepped into her path. "Come on, Evie. I know you're scared, but I'll make it good for you. Other people are starting to talk about how cold you are. Your rep as a hottie is slipping, baby."

"Whatever. Like I care."

His voice lowered and became cajoling. He gripped her upper arms, and rubbed up and down. "A couple beers and a joint, and you'll be nice and relaxed when I pop your cherry. You don't want to be a damn virgin forever."

She opened her mouth to take him down a notch.

"Who said she's still a virgin?"

Eve quivered at the sound of the deep rumbling voice. She knew it was him. *Hell on wheels.*

"Who the fuck are you?" Robert challenged, pushing Eve to the side.

The sudden illumination of the Harley's headlight gave away his position. "You ready to go, angel?"

The nickname startled her and she hesitated. Then one foot stepped in front of the other. The next thing Eve knew, a helmet was in her hands. She pulled it on quickly, her body instantly reacting to the exotic male scent that permeated the inside of the protective gear. Her nipples peaked hard and tight, her breathing altered.

She wanted him. Like she'd never wanted anything or anybody in her life. All the raging teenage hormones in her body went haywire around him. She'd had heavy petting sessions that hadn't made her this hot, and all she'd done was smell him.

"This is bullshit, Eve," Robert snapped. "We dated for months. You owe me."

Eve flipped him the bird and climbed onto the back of the bike, her arms wrapping around her mystery guy's lean middle. He smelled spicy. Exotic. Delicious. She pressed her nose to his back and breathed him in. Unable to fight the temptation, she stroked her fingertips over his six-pack abs, shivering when tingles spread up her arms and pooled in her breasts, making them swell and ache.

His hand slapped over hers, halting her explorations.

"Hang on," he growled.

The hog rumbled to life and they roared off into the night.

Eve jerked to consciousness.

Desire burned through her veins. She writhed in torment, her head tossing, her limbs flailing, her breasts swollen with the need to be touched and caressed.

The scent of lavender and vanilla filled her nostrils. Reality hit her hard enough to force the breath from her lungs.

Her fabric softener. She turned her head and breathed in the smell. Clean sheets.

She was home. Alone. It had all been a dream.

"Alec . . . ?" She thrashed, her skin so hot and tight she felt as if it might split open.

Her nipples were hard and aching again, but now the flesh between her legs was plump and slick, the brand on her arm burning. Throbbing.

"Alec!" she cried again, with all the strength of a mewling kitten. Her mouth felt as if it were filled with cotton. Her body quaked with hunger and unable to do otherwise, she spread her legs wide and thrust her hand into the damp curls between her thighs. She'd never been so aroused in her life; the need for sex was more powerful than her need to breathe. Her other hand cupped a swollen breast, squeezing it, praying for relief from her sensual anguish and the goddamn heat. She felt like she was melting from the inside out.

Through her panting breaths she heard the padding of bare feet upon her hardwood floors. The steady, confident stride was familiar and deeply comforting.

Closer. Closer.

The footsteps stopped abruptly in her bedroom doorway.

"Alec." Her fingers parted the tender folds of her sex, exposing her burning flesh to the fan's soft breeze.

"Christ," he whispered, his voice a deep lustful rasp. "Have mercy."

She moved sinuously upon the cool satin sheets of her bed. Were they purple? Or would he be sentimental and choose the white? Much as she wanted to open her eyes and see, she couldn't find the strength to lift her heavy lids.

"Alec." She pushed two fingers inside her, but it wasn't enough to fill the emptiness. She was soaked, desperate. "What's happening to me?"

Her words left her on a sob, hot tears leaking out from the corners of her closed eyes. Her body was no longer her own; the sexual hunger was an alien force, clawing and biting her in its quest for freedom.

Alec. It wanted Alec. And after a decade of starving, it wasn't willing to wait a moment longer to have him.

His breath hissed out between clenched teeth. She heard him step toward her, then the bed dipped slightly as he sat. His hot, open mouth pressed against her calf. "I knew what the Change would do to you."

As his tongue dipped behind her knee, her free hand left her breast and slid into his hair.

His teeth nipped at her inner thigh and she gasped in surprise. "But I didn't know what it would do to *me*."

Grasping her pumping wrist, he stilled her movements and pulled her hand free. She cried out when she felt his tongue licking her fingers, a rough sound of pure male satisfaction filling the air as he tasted her desire. Warm, wet heat engulfed her to the knuckles, then he was sucking in long deep pulls until there was nothing left to consume.

"Damn it." He lunged for the pulsing flesh between her legs, covering it with his open mouth. Eve jerked violently, her senses overloaded with the feel and smell of him. Her heart raced at his nearness and the growling sounds he made as his tongue flicked desperately. Her knees bent and her feet pushed into the mattress, lifting her hips. He rumbled a warning and pinned her down with his large hands. "Stay still."

He held her open with his fingers, nuzzling his lips against her, his hair sweeping across the sensitive skin of her thighs.

She struggled against his hold, but he was too strong and she was too weak. *"Please . . ."*

Alec tilted his head and pushed his tongue through the spasming muscles, the rough texture both soothing and abrading the sensitive tissues. She keened softly at the teasing fullness, nowhere near as thick and long as she needed, but wonderful nevertheless. In and out. Piercing her hard and fast. His groans were animalistic, base and raw, as if he'd gone too long without having her this way. As if he'd missed it.

"Not enough," she breathed, twisting and arching, burning up. Losing her sanity. "It's not *enough*."

Alec's mouth surrounded her, gently suckling. His tongue fluttered in a wicked back-and-forth tease.

As she climaxed hard, she cried out, her legs trembling. The relief was so intense she couldn't catch her breath, every follicle and nerve ending prickling with acute, near-painful pleasure. His lips closed, pressed a soft kiss against her, and then opened again. His approach gentled, and he licked her in a patient, loving rhythm.

Eve reached for his shoulders and found his warm skin covered in soft cotton. She tugged ineffectually at the material. "Naked."

Alec pushed up and the mattress jerked with his violent movements, then he was coming over her. Bare skin to bare skin. He caught her wrists in one hand and pulled them gently over her head.

She found the strength to open her gritty eyes. Dark hair fell around his flushed face. His brown irises were swallowed by his dilated pupils, roiling with violent need.

He pressed his cheek to hers. "Don't hate me for what's happening to you."

Kneeing her legs open, he pushed inside her. A violent shudder coursed the length of his frame. "Angel . . . You're burning me up."

He was so long and hard, built for a woman's pleasure. She knew he would fill her completely, the stretching sensation incredible and addicting.

"Deeper," she coaxed, raising her hips.

The instant he sank to the end of her, the pain eased, leaving only drugging, drowning pleasure behind.

He murmured hoarse praise, clutching her close, beginning to move.

She sobbed, her fever breaking, sweat dripping from every pore and soaking her hair. The bed. Him.

His powerful thighs flexed against hers as he kept her pinned and rode her skillfully. Slow. Rolling his hips. She watched him with heavy lidded eyes, watched him watch her as he pumped into her, his abdomen flexing and rippling with his thrusts. Watched his eyes burn as she writhed and whimpered his name.

Alec was inexhaustible. He would climax with a clenched jaw and deep, stifled groans, but he never softened completely. Her keening cries as she came made him hard again. She could feel him thicken inside her as he rocked in and out. Ready for more.

No other man could compete. He'd ruined her from the very first. No one touched her the way he did. No one looked at her the way he did, studying every nuance of her response and adjusting his movements so she kept coming. And coming. No one had that wickedly dark voice that goaded her. Whispering how she felt to him, how she pleased him, how much he loved to be inside her.

They had sex for hours, moments melding into each other, Alec thrusting between her spread thighs in that lazy, sensual rhythm that said, *Feel that? Feel me? I'm in you. Inside you.*

The room grew dark as the sun set.

Sick as she'd been, she shouldn't have been able to take him, but she grew stronger with every moment that passed, the dull throb of the burn on her arm pumping a wild, edgy power through her veins until she was abandoned. Scratching at his back, biting his neck, spurring him on with her heels in his flexing ass.

Through sheer mulish determination, Eve broke through Alec's steely control, grabbed him by the throat and balls, and rocked his world. As she pleasured him ruthlessly, his guttural cries filled the room, swelling up through the vaulted ceiling of her condominium.

"Getting ready to leave again?" she asked harshly, clinging to his straining, sweat-slicked body with arms made powerful by the energy inside her. "Storing up future memories?"

He grunted and licked the side of her face. "Making up for lost time. You'll cover the future in daily installments."

"You wish." She nipped his ear with sharp teeth, making him curse. "Enjoy the ride while it lasts."

His head lifted, revealing glowing eyes that sent violent shivers down her spine. Resting one hand on the mattress, he drove powerfully into her. Eve was so focused on the pounding of his hips against hers and the impending orgasm that she failed to register the danger until it was too late.

Alec lifted his free hand, revealing the white-hot image of an eye in the center of his palm.

"Oh, hell no!" She shoved at his shoulders.

"Set me as a seal upon thine heart, as a seal upon thine arm—"

He gripped her branded deltoid and burned her anew.

Eve bit out a curse and belted him square in the jaw.

CHAPTER 6

E *ve frowned as the Harley rounded the corner of*
her street and pulled over to the curb several houses
up from her own. Her dad would be dozing on the couch
now, her mother upstairs in bed reading a romance
novel, and her little sister chatting on her private phone
line instead of sleeping. It was home and she loved it,
but she didn't want to go there now. The thought of be-
ing separated from the man in front of her made her
feel panicky.

"Did we have to come here right away?" she asked,
regretting answering honestly when he'd asked for di-
rections.

As he turned off the engine, she laced her fingers to-
gether to keep him close. He was so warm, so solid, so
big. Nothing like the boys she went to school with.

He gently pried her fingers open. "Yes, it's better for
you, angel."

"Can't we go somewhere else? It's still early."

"No."

"Why? Why did you come tonight if you didn't want to hang out with me?"

She felt him sigh. "I don't 'hang out,' and even if I did, I couldn't hang out with you."

"Because of my age?" God, she was so sick of being treated like a kid.

"Among other reasons."

His head turned slightly and the glimpse of his profile, even under the weak illumination of the streetlights, took her breath away. Her heart thudded in an elevated rhythm, her breathing was quick and shallow. His lean hips were cradled between her spread thighs, her breasts pressed to his back. She knew he felt some of the pull she did or he wouldn't have been waiting for her tonight.

But she wanted to prove it, so Eve shimmied her torso, rubbing her erect nipples against him.

His breath hissed out between clenched teeth. "Get off the bike."

The tone of his voice brooked no argument so she dismounted with a moue. "What's your name?"

There was a long silence while he stared at her with that hot, intense stare. She could tell he was debating whether to tell her or not. Finally, he said, "Alec Cain."

Eve nodded and adjusted the strap of her bag. "Thanks for the ride, Alec."

She set off toward her house and a moment later the hog rumbled to life. Though the urge to look back was nearly overwhelming, her pride was stronger.

She knew if he felt anything like she did when they were together, he would be back.

* * *

Eve rested her right hand on the tile and stood with head bent beneath the pummeling water spray of her shower.

Seven days. Seven days of her life gone.

She knew something drastic had happened to her during that short time. The brands on her left arm were completely healed and settled into something that resembled a tribal tattoo. Exactly like Alec's. After nearly a week without food and very little to drink, she should be weak and dehydrated. She was neither. Instead she felt like a million bucks, her foot tapping impatiently on the stone shower floor because she couldn't contain all of the restless energy inside her.

Shutting off the tap, Eve grabbed the fresh towel she'd set atop the lid of her hamper. She dried her skin quickly, then wrapped her wet hair into a turban and padded out to the bedroom.

There was no way to ignore the naked man sprawled facedown across her bed. Alec had chosen the white sheets, a selection that set butterflies loose in her stomach. It made her bed look like a cloud. His dark masculinity upon that backdrop made him look like a fallen angel.

She would never forget the night she lost her virginity. He'd lain beneath her like a wicked fantasy upon white sheets, urging her on with hoarsely voiced encouragements.

Sighing, her gaze moved from his face down the muscular expanse of his back to the dimples just above his perfect ass.

"Have mercy," she whispered, repeating the words he'd used the night before.

Eve tore her gaze away and looked around the room, noting the washcloths on her mahogany nightstand. She imagined what the last week must have been like for him and the intimacy involved in caring for her. The man she couldn't trust to stick around at all had been dependable in her most dire hours. What was the sense in that?

Her jaw clenched. Alec knew exactly what had happened to her a week ago. Then he'd done the exact same thing to her last night. Because of him and the winged mystery man, she was altered. Physically. Mentally. In every way. She could feel the Change like a narcotic slipping through her veins.

Pivoting on her heel, Eve snatched up the short silk robe that hung on the back of the bedroom door and left the room. She went to the kitchen for much-needed food and coffee, knowing she was going to need plenty of both for the confrontation to come.

Alec watched Evangeline Hollis leave the high school parking lot, crossing Euclid Street to reach the Circle K convenience store. His gaze drank in every nuance of her figure—the long, lithe legs, slight but luscious curves, golden California tan, and hair of long black silk. She walked with three other girls, but she didn't fit in. Not because she was Asian, but because she was above them, beyond them. Every delectable inch of her body was ripe with sexual promise and a confidence he admired.

At times he cursed the sudden urge he'd had to grab a bottle of water from the convenience store the day he first saw her. If he'd kept on riding, he wouldn't be in this predicament. But he knew fate and coincidence were mortal concepts. A divine plan was at work, and somehow this angel fit into his. Unfortunately for her.

Wanting to protect her, Alec had fought the compulsion to meet her and fled via Interstate 5 on his way to San Diego. Another city in an endless string of cities he visited in the course of his nomadic life. His bike roared past 1313 Harbor Boulevard: Disneyland—The Happiest Place on Earth.

Then he realized the source of the pull he felt toward her. When she'd mouthed "Hi" with those glossy red lips, he'd felt the first stirrings of connection, something he hadn't experienced in so long he had almost forgotten what it felt like.

Why her? *he despaired.* She's so young. Too young. *Centuries younger than he was.*

But Alec knew the answer. She was his forbidden fruit. Set out to tempt him with what he could never have. One taste and Eve would be his, but the price she'd pay would destroy them both.

Yet, despite knowing the consequences, Alec had found himself exiting the freeway and backtracking to her. Now, two weeks later, he watched her from the shadow of a large tree and ached for the feel of her arching beneath him.

One taste. He was starved for it.

He couldn't forget the feel of her breasts against his back, her curious fingertips drifting across his stomach, the sound of her voice coaxing, Can't we go somewhere?

Yes, *he'd wanted to say.* Let's go and never come back.

Temptation. God's most oft-used test.

But Alec wasn't going to fail this one. He was leaving today if it killed him. He'd come to see her one last time, then he would go, finding strength in the fact that he'd resisted his own needs in favor of hers.

Alec was about to turn away, finally prepared to get on his hog and leave her behind, when Eve paused on the corner, her head turning in his direction. He stilled. Waiting. Wondering if she saw him.

She arched a brow, staring. Then she blew him a mocking kiss and flipped him off, before turning on her heel and sauntering away.

Eat your heart out, *her actions said.*

Taunting him. Tempting him. Not understanding that he was afraid for her, *not himself.* She *would pay the price for his infraction. His punishment would come from knowing that he was the cause of hers.*

His jaw clenched so tight his teeth ground together.

Sliding his sunglasses back on, he walked to his bike and hit the road.

Pausing on the threshold between the living room and the hallway, Alec carefully studied the set of Eve's shoulders. She was clad in a blood-red, knee-length silk kimono robe. Her black hair tumbled halfway down her back, the thick strands swaying with the salt-tinged breeze drifting through the open balcony door.

She looked relaxed, her hip leaning into the jamb of the sliding glass door, her hands filled with a steaming cup of coffee as she stared at the ocean view. But he knew her senses were alert, her hearing more acute, her sense of smell inhumanly accurate. When she reached full strength, her speed and stamina would make Olympic athletes weep in envy . . . if she ever moved slowly enough that they could see her. She was a hunter now, a predator.

Tightening the towel he had wrapped around his waist, Alec crossed the vast space, admiring how well she'd done for herself. She had a gleaming new Chrysler 300 in her garage downstairs and she was so close to the beach that her living room balcony hung over the sand.

She was going to hate him for ruining her perfect life.

"Good morning, angel."

Eve spun to face him. Despite hours of hard sex, she looked none the worse for wear. Her dark eyes, almond shaped and framed by thick sooty lashes, were clear and bright. She would heal with remarkable speed now. At least on the outside. As for the inside . . .

He ran a hand through his damp hair. Would she understand when he explained? And even if she did, would it mitigate the fact that he was the reason this had happened to her?

She held up a hand, halting his advance when he was a few feet away. "What am I now?"

"You're a Mark." He spoke calmly, while inside he felt far from it. "You're stronger, faster—"

"Better, stronger, faster?" Her laughter was harsh. "I'm the fucking Bionic Woman? What the hell was that fever I had?"

Alec crossed his arms over his bare chest and decided to take the high road. She had every right to be pissed and confused. "Punishment. Women's sexuality has been used against them since my mom ate the forbidden fruit. Why do you think childbirth is so painful?"

"Are you *insane*? What does childbirth have to do with me?" She made a slashing gesture with her hand. "On second thought, don't tell me. Just explain what I'm being punished for."

"For tempting me."

"I haven't seen you in ten damn years!" she snapped. "You got your rocks off and left."

Eve had never been able to hide anything from him. She was hurt. The knowledge tightened his throat and made him speak gruffly. "I love you."

A visible shudder moved through her. She reached out and gripped the door frame. "Screw you."

"Evangeline—"

"Go to hell."

"My job is to send demons back there. Now it's your job, too."

"You're nuts. You need help." She jerked her chin toward the door. "There are lots of shrinks out there. Go find one. I'll even let you take the Yellow Pages with you. For old time's sake."

"Did he show you his wings, angel?" Alec stepped closer. "Did he spread them wide? Intimidate you with them?"

Her fingers gripping the jamb were white, as were the edges of her lips.

"I bet he made a great show out of the marking, didn't he? How did he say it?" He deepened his voice, then growled, "Bear the Mark of Cain!"

The coffee cup fell from her fingers and shattered on the hardwood floor, coffee exploding outward in a wide splatter. Her knees buckled and Alec lunged forward, catching her.

He carried her to the sofa and sat, cradling her in his

lap. Tucking Eve's head under his chin, he rocked her, taking comfort from her embrace even as he gave the same to her.

"What about you tempting me?" she accused, her breath gusting across his throat. "How was I supposed to resist you? A girl my age . . . a guy like you—"

A soft sob escaped her. Alec thrust his hand into her hair and held her tight against him.

That night haunted him. He'd rented a suite, bought every beautifully scented flower he could find at the florist's, and lit the room with a profusion of candles. He took her virginity on white satin sheets covered in rose petals.

"I couldn't have done anything differently," he said softly.

"You knew you weren't going to stay before you seduced me."

He spoke with his lips pressed to the crown of her head. "I tried to spare you any suffering by leaving. I hoped that if we separated, you could still have the same future you would have had before you met me."

Eve struggled out of his embrace, fighting him with such fervor she fell on the floor. "You're an asshole." Rising to her knees, she slapped him.

Alec clenched his jaw and turned the other cheek.

She cursed and pushed to her feet, her robe askew. He stood with her, securing his towel while facing her head on.

"Spare me any suffering," she scoffed, glaring at him. "That's lame, Alec. You have to do better than that."

"What do you want me to say?"

She ran both hands through her hair and growled.

"Something that makes sense. Something sincere and believable."

"I'm sorry, angel."

Pausing midstep, Eve gaped at him. "That's it? You're *sorry*?"

"Would it be better to say that I would do it again?"

She looked away. "Don't do that."

"Don't do what?"

"Look at me like that."

"You love me." Alec smiled wryly.

They stared at each other across the few feet that separated them.

"Hate to burst your bubble," she said grimly, "but I have more important things in my life than you. You're expendable."

"Actually, I'm not, but we'll get to that later. In the meantime, you can't ignore what happened last night."

"It doesn't mean what you think it means." She walked past him to the kitchen.

He followed. "It means we're in a lot of shit. It also means getting you out of this mess just got a hell of a lot more complicated."

She grabbed two mugs from her cabinet and changed the subject. "You want to explain the winged man?"

"Yes, brother, *would you like to explain me?"*

Eve turned at the sound of the voice she would never forget. He strode in from the balcony as if he owned the place. The man who'd screwed her into unconsciousness in the stairwell. His smile was sensual and slightly cruel, and it made her shiver, not entirely with fear.

Alec snarled and vaulted across the room with a ferocity and speed that frightened her, hitting his brother in the midsection with a brutal tackle. The ensuing scuffle was far from brotherly tussling. It was a fight to the death, and the sounds and sights of the battle did something strange to her. Made her mark burn, made her pulse race. The scent of blood in the air caused a physical reaction that she likened to blood lust. A rough growl rumbled up from her chest.

Alec lifted his brother into the air like a WWE wrestler and smashed him onto her glass-topped coffee table, destroying it. A moment later, he finished off the job by braining his brother with her Waterford crystal candy bowl.

The sickening crunch of a crushing skull should have horrified her, should have made her vomit, and she was in fact stumbling toward her sink to do just that when Alec disappeared.

Vanished into thin air.

One moment he was pushing to his feet, his bare body sheened with sweat and high-velocity blood spatter. The next he was gone.

Eve paused, unblinking, her body's natural response seized by shock. Her gaze dropped to the dead man on the floor.

Then she spun to the sink and wanted to retch, but her body wouldn't cooperate.

"Oh my god," she gasped, hanging on to the curved granite edge to remain standing. As her mark sizzled within her skin, a sharp sound escaped from her throat.

"Yeah, that's where he went," came a dry voice from the living room. The corpse on the floor rose to its feet, its disfigured head restoring before her very eyes, the dent slowly filling like a balloon. Wings sprouted from the man's back and he shook them out, testing each side with a quick flap before retracting them.

"Cain never learns," he said, winking at her, once again looking like the Armani-clad businessman from Gadara Tower.

"I'm insane," she gasped. "Certifiable."

Alec's brother laughed. "Don't get your panties in a twist, babe. He'll be back, and in one piece, too."

"You're dead," Eve muttered, "and I'm going to pass out."

"You're too healthy for that. All the physical reactions you used to have to stress won't happen anymore."

"*What* the hell are you?"

He smiled, the arrogant curve of his lips a faint echo of Alec's.

Brothers.

She could see it now. All the hints of Alec that had drawn her to him the other day *were* Alec. His blood. His genes. His traits. But all the warmth and love that shone in Alec's dark eyes were absent from this man's. His gaze was filled simply with mischief and male appreciation.

Somehow that was easier to bear right now.

"I'm the guy who fucked you into three screaming orgasms, babe."

"I see asshole runs in your family." The full reality of talking to a stranger she'd screwed in a public place, *on camera,* a stranger who happened to be Alec's brother, and had *wings,* and had been a *corpse* a minute ago, hit her hard and she leaned heavily on her countertop. "I could use a good bout of unconsciousness right about now."

"Reed," he said more softly, his leer fading into something more sincere. "My name is Reed, Evangeline."

"What did you do to me?"

"Did Alec tell you that you're marked now?" Reed settled onto a barstool and picked an apple from the fruit bowl. "Damned to hunt the scourge of the earth and make the world safer for everyone?"

"I got the damned part. *Who's* doing the damning is a bit murky."

"Let's just say you should reconsider being an agnostic."

Eve turned on the faucet and splashed water over her face. "Christ . . . Shit!" she hissed, as her mark burned.

He grinned. "You're getting warmer."

"Ha-ha." Forcing herself to act normal, she retrieved one of the mugs she'd set out earlier and filled it with steaming coffee. "Why now? It's been ten years."

"The wheels of justice turn just as slowly up there as they do down here."

"How does Alec fit into all of this?" She shot a worried glance over her shoulder. "Is he okay?"

"He's fine. It's not the first time he's killed me. As for how he fits . . ." Reed shrugged. "He could have spared you if he'd kept his dick in his pants."

Grabbing creamer out of the fridge, Eve poured a liberal splash into her mug. "I understand that part. Is he under some sort of vow of celibacy?" She liked the thought of that.

Reed laughed. "That's rich."

Scowling, she returned the creamer to its spot in the fridge door and shut it with more force than necessary.

"Sweetheart, your name may be Eve, but in this lusty

tale, you play the apple. 'Look, but don't touch.' " Reed took at hearty bite of the Red Delicious in his hand.

"That's sick. Who tortures people like that?"

"Free will," he said, chewing with obvious relish. "You always get a choice, but sometimes it's obvious which choice you're supposed to make. If you decide to do your own thing, you pay the consequences." Reed licked his lips. "If Alec had made the right choice, you'd be married now with two kids. Happy as a clam."

Eve stared into her coffee and wondered what that life would have been like.

"So what's the mark for?" she asked finally.

Studying Reed over the rim of her mug, Eve noted that his hair was much shorter than Alec's, his lips thinner, the air about him more intense. Unlike Alec's grungy attire, Reed's garments were perfectly tailored. Today he sported fitted gray slacks and a black dress shirt, worn open at the collar and rolled up at the sleeves.

"Well, the mark has several uses. It originally put you in line for a hearing. The court docket is full and it's important to get penciled in as soon as possible."

"A hearing?"

"Everyone gets a hearing, babe." His smile affected her; there was no getting around it. Fact was, it wasn't just his similarities to Alec that were attractive. "Alec's contribution to the mark waived the hearing and acts as somewhat of a plea bargain. Instead of arguing your case, you get to earn your indulgences in the field."

"Why doesn't that sound as if he did me a favor?"

Reed shrugged. "Depends on how you look at it. It was the only way to guarantee that he would be with you all the time. If you'd gone to trial, you would have been assigned to whichever position was next in the queue that you were best qualified for. Not all positions require mentors and not all positions are in the field." His gaze narrowed as he considered her. "This way, he's certain to be with you."

"And what am I supposed to do in the field?"

"Hunt demons, feral fey, rogue interdimensional be-ings, warlocks, and various other nasties. You're going to have to work for absolution just as Alec has been doing for centuries."

"Centuries?" She was in lust with a man who was *centuries* old? Eve set her coffee down before she dropped it again. "He's immortal?"

"Almost. Marks heal quickly, so it takes a lot to kill one. There's no time limit on how long you have to prove your worth, and the whole 'sevenfold vengeance' protection has a way of scaring off most hazards to your health."

"Sevenfold vengeance?"

"It's mentioned in the book of Genesis. 'And the Lord said unto him, therefore whosoever slayeth Cain, vengeance shall be taken on him sevenfold. And the Lord set a mark upon Cain, lest any finding him should kill him.' You've got the mark. You get the protection."

"How bad is that? The sevenfold stuff."

"Whatever the demon does to the Mark, they get the same in return. Seven times over."

Eve's brows rose. "That could be bad, I take it."

"Usually so. As I said, it works as a deterrent most of the time. Only the most evil, wretched, and insane creatures don't care."

"Lovely."

He stood and rounded the kitchen island. There was no mistaking the change in his focus.

She lifted her chin. He caged her in with the counter at her back. "In addition to learning how to kill and dealing with a fear of all things evil, you've got Alec to manage, and your feelings about what happened to you because of his lust." He held up the half-eaten apple between them. "Then there are the apples."

She arched a brow, hoping to hide how her body responded to his nearness. Her senses remembered him—his smell, the power and heat of his large frame, the near brutality of his passion. The orgasms he'd wrung from her body.

"The apples?" she asked softly, focusing on his lips as they curved into a feral smile.

Reed ran the bitten side of the apple from the hollow of her throat down to her cleavage. Shivering, Eve reached behind her and gripped the edge of the counter. He lowered his head slowly, watching her, giving her time to pull away. His tongue touched her skin and slid up the trail he'd made in a long, slow glide. His teeth nipped at her chin, then he moved to take her mouth. She turned her head away.

His warm chuckle filled the electrically charged air between them. Then he changed tactics, sliding his hand into her robe and cupping her breast. As his fingers found her nipple and pinched roughly, his tongue slid along the shell of her ear. "Apples, baby. Temptations. The exercising of your free will."

Reed's hips pressed against hers, his knees bending so that the hard ridge of his cock notched into the softness of her sex. He thrust gently, nudging her. She gasped, but kept her hands on the counter. Her body was so tightly strung the slightest provocation had her ready to tear of her clothes. Anytime. Anywhere.

"I wondered," he breathed, his lips to her ear, "what you had that twisted Cain up in knots." His other hand cupped her ass and urged her to rock into him as he tugged and rolled her nipple, sending shockwaves down to the aching flesh between her legs. "Now I know."

"Back off."

His tongue thrust into her ear and her knees buckled. "Hottest, tightest fuck I've ever had. Your slick pussy sucking on my cock. And those sounds you make . . . those little whimpers . . ." He growled. "I want to take you right now. Hard and deep. Pound my dick into you and watch you come until you can't take any more." His hand on her ass slid lower, lifting her leg to anchor it onto his hip. His thrusts grew bolder, more fervent, his chest rising and falling with his harsh breathing. "You're a predator now, Eve. And predators like to fuck."

"Back off!" Eve's hands went to his shoulders and pushed. He flew across the room and landed in a heap on her living room rug.

"Oh my god," she breathed. The damn mark seared her skin anew and made her dizzy.

Reed threw his head back and laughed, rising to his feet with an easy grace. "See? You're beginning to catch on already."

He reached down and adjusted himself, drawing her attention to the obvious wet spot on his pants where she'd been rubbing against him. "Watch out for the apples, babe."

With a rakish wink, he disappeared—vanished—just

as Alec had, and a moment later Alec was back. Still naked, but minus the blood, his handsome face marred by a fierce scowl.

Eve picked up the apple and threw it at him.

CHAPTER 7

Alec caught the apple and crushed it into a juicy pulp with his fist.

He was a successful hunter because of his patience. Unlike most Marks, his goal wasn't quantity but quality. Infernals were like all parasitic organisms. They learned, adapted, mutated. As they survived repeated attempts on their lives, they grew stronger and more formidable.

When Alec was summoned to make a kill, he was prepared to wait for days, weeks, months, or even years to strike. Long, protracted battles were wearisome and drew too much attention. He preferred a quick assassination, and he bided his time until that opportunity presented itself.

That was why he was frustrated by his inability to be patient with Abel. His brother was like fingernails on a chalkboard. Alec couldn't ignore him or forgive him. The grudge he carried was too deeply ingrained.

With a quick stride, he moved to the kitchen and

opened the trash compactor. He unclenched his fist, releasing the destroyed apple to thud to the bottom of the lined basket. Sticky juice coated his fingers and he watched, detached, as it dripped. Drop after drop.

Eve made a small noise and he glanced at her. She stood nearby, flushed and bright eyed. Aroused.

Alec growled low in his throat. "Stay away from him."

Her chin lifted. She looked prepared to argue, then she turned around and lifted to her tiptoes, pulling open a cupboard and reaching for a bottle of Baileys Irish Cream.

"If you're looking for a buzz," he bit out, "you won't get one there."

She paused midmovement.

"Your body doesn't process alcohol—or any mind-altering substance—the same way it used to."

Her hand fell as a fist into the counter. She faced him, her sloe eyes narrowing with flaring anger. "Are you saying I can't get high?"

"You can orgasm from here to eternity," he said roughly. "That high enough for you?"

"Fuck."

"I'm happy to oblige."

"Oh, shut up!" she snapped. "This is entirely *your* fault."

"Is that all you've got?" he taunted, his blood hot and his temper high. He'd been punished for killing his brother *again*, which left Alec spoiling for a fight. Or a hard, raw screw. Since the latter was what had gotten Eve in trouble in the first place, he would be better off settling for the former. "Your life just blew up in your face and 'shut up' is the best you can do?"

Her fists clenched, and he felt a surge of satisfaction. If she was pissed off at him, she wouldn't be thinking about Abel.

"I don't know," she retorted. "I'm feeling like a superhero. I might be able to kick your naked ass. Maybe we'd both feel better if I did."

Alec laughed and moved to the sink to wash his hands. "You can say that after watching me kill a man? You've got balls, angel. Thank God, 'cause you'll need 'em."

"Don't make light of this, Alec."

Turning off the tap, he crossed over to her. His hips pinned her to the cupboard while his wet hands caressed her cheeks. "I'm not."

"I feel like I've lost my mind."

"You haven't lost anything. You're still the same smart, sexy woman I remember."

"I wasn't a woman then," she grumbled.

He smoothed her eyebrows and followed the curve of her cheekbones. "You gonna argue with me about that, too?"

Eve sighed and rested her cheek into his palm. "You killed him."

"Yeah."

"Explain that to me." Her dark eyes gazed up at him with a mixture of revulsion and wary fascination. "He said it wasn't the first time."

" 'Am I my brother's keeper?' " he recited softly.

Eve blinked up at him, a frown marring the beauty of her face. "You're going to quote scripture at a time like . . ."

As her voice faded, Alec watched her confusion turn into a slowly dawning comprehension. She had never been able to hide anything from him, but she'd have to learn to don a poker face now. Infernals would take advantage of any perceived weakness.

"The Mark of Cain," she whispered. "Alec *Cain*."

"I know it sounds fantastical," he began tightly.

"I believe you." She made an impatient gesture with her hand and barked a little laugh. "I'm not even all that surprised. Not after the last week.

"Seven full days. Shit . . . I suppose that's not a coincidence."

"There's no such thing as coincidence."

"What's going on?" Her hand covered the spot on her arm where the mark rested. "What does this mean?"

"It's a calling, angel. A—"

"I thought it was a punishment."

"It serves that purpose, too."

The way she bit her lower lip was an added sign of her distress, but the inner core of steel that had first attracted him to her did not fail. "Killing demons and fairies? Look at me, Alec. Do I look like I can do that?"

"You're capable of anything that needs to be done. Far more so than most Marks."

"*Most* Marks?" Her eyes widened. "There are *more*?"

"Thousands."

"Jesus . . . Ow, damn it! This thing keeps burning."

"Because you're taking the Lord's name in vain. You'll have to get over that."

Her mouth took on a mulish cast. "This is bullshit. Why me? *Why*?"

He exhaled harshly, his breath ruffling the hair atop her head. There was no way to deny his culpability in her downfall. But he wasn't going to keep pointing it out.

"After my father was created," he said instead, "the

angels were commanded to prostrate before him, because he was created in the image of the Lord."

Eve snorted. "God's not at all full of himself, is he?"

"Watch it," Alec warned, shaking her a little. "That mouth is going to get you in trouble."

"That's not the only troublesome part of me."

"Some of the angels refused, insisting they were superior to man—"

"I have a tendency to agree with them."

"Those who opposed God's will were banished from the heavens. They fell to earth, where they mated with man and produced nephilim—half-angels who felt animosity toward the Lord. My family began to lose its position in the food chain."

"So God drafted you?"

He laughed softly, humorlessly. "He said sin crouched at our door and it was my duty to master it. If I did well, I would be forgiven the death of my brother. If I didn't, the Infernals would kill me."

"Why doesn't anyone know this part of the story?"

"It's in the Bible, angel. The order of events is a bit skewed, but it's mentioned."

"So you had no choice."

"We are always given a choice. It was my brother Seth who urged me to accept the offer. Since I had . . . *experience,* it made sense. In the end, I was grateful to be given a purpose. I'm good at what I do."

"You have *another* brother?" She was clearly horrified by the thought.

"Thirty-two of them, and twenty-three sisters. Not all are still here on earth. Many have already ascended."

"Oh, jeez . . ." She winced. "Your poor mother."

"You have to consider that without television, radio, and sporting events, sex was the best form of entertainment there was."

"I'd abstain, if it saved me from birthing that many kids."

"No, you wouldn't," he teased, achingly aware of her simmering state of arousal. Beneath Eve's fear and confusion Alec scented the underlying spice of pure desire. Combined with the salt-tinged sea breeze coming through the open sliding glass door, it was potent and alluring. Eve, by nature, was a sexual creature. That proclivity would be enhanced now.

"Go back to your explanation," she said. "You started killing the nephilim?"

"Yes, which angered Sammael."

"Sammael?"

"Satan."

"Oh, gotcha."

"As the nephilim began to interbreed with other nephilim and the fallen, Sammael trained their offspring, instilling in them a hatred for everything but him. I couldn't handle the job alone. There were too many to kill, too many variations and mutations."

"So God started marking other people?"

"Sinners. Giving them a chance to work off their offenses."

"I'm not a sinner. And the whole setup is totally jacked. There are millions of religious zealots around the world who kill in his name every day, but why use them, right? That would make too much sense. Better to draft unwilling suckers like me. That's more fun. Put the screws to them, watch them squirm."

"Evangeline . . ." Alec's stomach knotted. "You

don't have to like Him, but you're going to have to respect His power."

"What more can he do to me?" She pushed him away.

He briefly considered resisting, then thought his state of undress might give him an advantage. He was a hunter by nature, a predator. He knew he would have to approach her with caution. He would have to maneuver skillfully, bending and adjusting as necessary in order to keep Eve close. She would have to see him coming, because surprising her with a pounce would shatter her trust further, and she needed to trust him. Otherwise he had no hope of keeping her alive.

As if she sensed his intent, Eve shot him an arch glance and tightened the belt on her robe. "You went to see him like that? With it all hanging out?"

He shrugged. "It's not as if I had a choice."

"I can't do this, Alec. You got me into this, you get me out of it."

"I'm trying."

"Try harder." She gave a little growl, like a pissed-off kitten. "Listen. I can't watch horror movies. I get freaked out just walking alone through parking garages. Being the Bionic Woman isn't going to change the fact that I don't have it in my programming to kill things."

"This is coming from the woman who met me at the door with a loaded gun?"

"Self-defense is a different story," she argued, turning her back to him and guzzling her neglected coffee.

"He wouldn't have marked you if you couldn't handle it."

Eve choked and glared at him over her shoulder. "We're talking about the god who promised Moses he'd go to heaven if he worked like a dog and ruined his life, then at the last minute reneged on the deal."

Alec's jaw clenched as he linked his fingers behind his back. "I'm starting to think He picked you not because of *me,* but because of *you.* You've got a lot to learn."

"Whatever. Your brother said I could have a trial. I want one."

"It's too late for that."

A terrible stillness gripped her. "Because of what you did?"

He nodded, hating the unfamiliar feeling of dread weighting his gut. Eve had to trust him, implicitly. And now she had every reason not to. The battlefield was not a place to doubt the person watching your back. "I can't help you if I'm on the other side of the world. I had to do what I did to stay with you."

Eve walked away, departing the kitchen and heading down the hallway to her bedroom.

He followed. "Where are you going?"

"You're not my favorite person right now."

"Angel . . ."

Eve spun about in a flurry of ebony hair and blood-red silk. The movement was agile and inherently grace-ful. Sensual.

"I *will* get you out of this," he said, struggling against his body's reaction to the sight of her. He was so hard it hurt.

Her gaze dropped and her lips parted on a silent gasp. She pointed viciously at his erection. "Put that thing away! It's gotten me into enough trouble as it is."

She entered her room and slammed the door.

"My gear is in there," he called after her, smiling.

A heartbeat later his jeans and shirt flew into the hall and hit him square in the chest.

"You prefer me to go commando?" he asked.

"Shut up and get dressed." But there was a hitch in her voice that told him she wasn't unaffected by the idea.

"We're not done talking."

"Give it a rest, okay?"

He moved to the guest room, his bare feet on the polished hardwood creating a mournful tempo. The extra bedroom bore the same sparse modern styling of the master bedroom and was nearly equal in size. Massive slabs of polished, lacquered pine hung from metal tracks on the ceiling and acted as doors for the floor-to-ceiling closets that occupied the entire right wall. The matching wood floor was littered with several fluffy white rugs cut in irregular shapes. A built-in system of shelves decorated the bottom half of the rear wall, while the top half was covered in black-and-white photos in silver frames.

The bed was to the left. It sat low to the ground and was quite large. A California king, Alec guessed. It was covered with a chocolate satin duvet and cream pillows with brown and rust-colored trim.

The sight of the perfectly made bed both lured and depressed him. He was exhausted. While Eve's body had been changing and storing up energy, his had been drained by worry, guilt, and lack of sleep. If he had a choice, he'd be curled up with her, not fighting the urge to crash. Alone.

He was tired of being alone. Which added to the whole fucked-up situation he found himself in.

His desire to do what was best for Eve—get her life

back—was in direct opposition to his long-held need to cease wandering. His mentorship gave him the opportunity, for the first time, to prove that he could play well with others.

Finally, after centuries of nomadic living, he'd been assigned to a home base. Through his mentorship of Eve, he could learn what he needed to know to achieve his ambitions. If he absorbed all the layers of the mark system well enough, he had a shot at pleading his case for stability. He could teach others to perform as well in the field as he did . . . if he had a cadre of handlers and Marks at his disposal.

It had been his long-held dream that one day he would convince Jehovah that by running his own firm he'd be more productive. Everyone knew that expansion of the mark system was long overdue. He wanted to be the one to step into play when a new firm was created. No one had the field experience that he did.

As usual, the choices given to him were damned if he did, damned if he didn't. He needed Eve to get ahead. But he wasn't what *she* needed.

His eyes went gritty with exhaustion.

"Don't do this to me," he bit out, glancing skyward. "You know damn well it's not a good time for me to fall asleep."

But his wishes were ignored, as usual. He was due for a punishment because of killing Abel, and Jehovah had kept the method of chastisement on retainer. Benching him in the heat of the game was an easy and effective way of putting him in his place—behind the curve.

Alec collapsed face first into the mattress and lost consciousness despite his best efforts.

When he awoke a few hours later, his anger surged as if it had been simmering throughout his forced nap. Through the open doorway to the hall, the cries of sea-gulls and the sound of waves crashing against the beach reminded him of a thousand other awakenings. Too many days of his life all the same, blending seam-lessly and unremarkably into each other. He wanted a different life, one he shared with someone. He wanted Eve, but he couldn't have her.

He would have to find a way to free her, then let her go. Again. He had no idea where he would find the strength to walk away a second time, but he'd do it. Even if it killed him.

"Eve!" he shouted, running his hands through his hair before pushing to his feet.

She was gone. He sensed it. Her absence from the house left a chilling void. It was also life threatening. An untrained Mark was a susceptible and irresistible target for Infernals.

Cursing under his breath, Alec yanked on his clothes and raced out of the house.

Taking a deep breath, Eve pushed open her car door and stepped into the Southern California sunshine.

She paused a moment to run her hands over her Knott's Berry Farm T-shirt. If she'd turned her brain on, instead of running on instinct, she would have found something more suitable to wear to church than sweat-pants and a faded T-shirt. Although she didn't believe in organized religion, she respected the beliefs of those who did. But she hadn't planned to come here.

Her gaze moved over the roof of her car to the contemporary, almost-southwestern style of the new Catholic church. In her opinion, it looked more modern Christian than old-world Catholic, but what the hell did she know?

Which was exactly why she was here. She never tackled any project without exhaustive research first. As a child, her Southern Baptist parents had exposed her to religion, but her recollection of those early Bible classes was weak at best.

Eve rounded her car and crossed the massive parking lot, heading toward the carved wooden doors that protected the interior. There were a few vehicles near the front. Some had religious stickers or emblems on the back, but for the most part there were no outward indicators of devotion. The sort of devotion that could drive someone to visit church in the middle of a workweek.

Gripping the handle, she pulled open the door and entered the cool, quiet interior. Like the outside, the inside had a clean minimalist design. The ceiling arched thirty-plus feet above the center of the worship hall and boasted exposed wooden beams in an intricate pattern. Straight ahead, a bronzed statue of the Crucifixion protruded from the wall and shimmered under the glare of a massive spotlight. Eve shivered at the sight, finding the depiction of eternal torment creepy rather than inspiring.

As always, she paused within the threshold, searching inwardly for any sense of awe or contentment. So many people described a sense of homecoming when they entered a house of God. She felt no different than she would entering a convenience store.

The low drone of voices off to her right turned her attention toward a recess filled with a life-size statue of the Virgin Mary and a profusion of lit votives. Two people knelt there, a woman and her child, their heads bent in prayer.

"Can I help you?"

The warm huskiness of the masculine voice froze her in place. The timbre was that of a phone sex operator, which put it seriously out of its element in a church.

Curious, Eve pivoted to face the source.

She was startled to discover a portly balding man in a priest collar. "Hi," she managed through her stupefaction.

"Hello," he replied.

Not the same voice. She frowned.

"I'm Father Simmons. This is Father Riesgo." The priest gestured behind her and Eve canted her body to see whom he referred to.

She almost gaped, but caught herself in time. "Father."

Younger than Father Simmons by a good two decades, Father Riesgo looked so fish-out-of-water in the collar that it seemed more of a costume than anything else. His features were rugged and blunt, his green eyes extraordinary, his cheek marred by a scar she guessed came courtesy of a knife blade. With his dark hair slicked back in a short tail, he seemed more renegade than missionary.

"Hello." He smiled, revealing perfect white teeth. "How can I help you?"

"I need a Bible."

Both priests blinked, as if taken aback. She inwardly kicked herself for being an idiot. So her father didn't own a Bible and her mother's was written in kanji. She should have headed to the bookstore, not driven around aimlessly until she found a church in which to give her moronic tendencies free rein.

Father Simmons set his hand on Father Riesgo's shoulder and said, "I will begin preparations."

As odd as her day had been so far, the fact that she'd been left to the care of Father Riesgo was not inconsequential. Perhaps they thought she was a nut who might require some muscle to get rid of. Eve couldn't decide if that was funny or sad.

Riesgo nodded and waited until the other priest had moved out of earshot. Then he returned his attention to Eve and studied her for a long moment. "What's your name?"

She winced and extended her hand. "Sorry. Evangeline Hollis."

"Ms. Hollis. It's a pleasure to meet you." His grip was strong and bold, like the rest of him. He gestured to the nearest pew, but she shook her head. "Okay," he agreed, in that sinful voice. "Are you a member of this parish?"

"To be honest, Father, I'm not even Catholic."

"Why come here, then? To St. Mary's?"

She hesitated a moment, reluctant to display any further stupidity. Riesgo was the kind of man one approached without facetiousness. His green eyes seemed to take in everything with a laserlike intensity, and the set of his square jaw warned against subterfuge. But in the end, Eve went with the truth simply because that was her nature. "I'm not sure. I'd like to refresh my memory about some biblical stories, particularly the one about Cain and Abel, and I realized I don't own a Bible. This building just happened to cross my path at the wrong time."

"Perhaps it wasn't wrong."

Eve took a tentative sidestep toward the door.

Riesgo stepped as well, keeping abreast of her. "We offer classes, Ms. Hollis. The Rite of Christian Initiation. We would love to have you participate. For many, the Bible is a journey that needs a guide. I wouldn't want you to feel lost or overwhelmed."

"I appreciate the offer, but I'm not interested in joining the church. I just need a research source."

Riesgo's smile returned. "Wal-Mart sells Bibles. They're priced around five dollars, I believe."

"Of course." She mentally kicked herself. "I should have thought of that. Thank you."

Eve continued to edge her way toward the door.

Father Riesgo kept pace, grinning. "Ms. Hollis?"

"Yes?"

He reached into his pocket and held a business card out to her. "If you have any questions, please feel free to contact us here."

"You're too kind." She accepted the card only in the name of politeness. "There are churches closer to me, so I doubt I'll be bothering you again."

Father Riesgo was disconcerting by nature, but when his focus narrowed, the intensity was arresting. He wasn't handsome by standard definition, but charisma . . . he had it in spades. Combined with the husky voice, he probably lured a ton of women to mass.

"Hmm . . ." His skeptical hum made her slightly defensive.

"I have a bad sense of direction."

He shook his head. "I don't think so. You're looking for answers, and your search brought you here. Would you mind waiting a moment? I have something for you."

"I'm in a hurry," she demurred, fearing a long lecture and hard sell ahead of her.

"A minute only. I'll be quick."

He set off at a lope down the center aisle. She watched in fascination, absently noting that the severity of his black garb did nothing to detract from the grace with which he moved.

"Go," she ordered herself.

Eve retreated toward the door. She figured if she made it to the parking lot before he came back, her escape was meant to be.

There was a padlocked tithing box on the wall near the exit. She dropped his business card into the slot and reached for the door handle.

Her hand had barely made contact with the cool metal when Riesgo reappeared at the end of the aisle with a dark red bag in his hand. Her often lamentable curiosity kicked in with a vengeance. The priest looked both excited and impassioned, making it impossible for her to turn away.

He reached her in no time and began to speak in a rush. "Last week, I was compelled to buy this—" he reached into the bag and withdrew a book "—although I didn't know why. My sister owns a Bible that's been passed down in my family for generations and my mother is no longer with us."

Eve accepted the proffered Bible with tentative hands. It was covered in satin-soft burgundy leather and trimmed with ornate, feminine embroidery of floral vines and colorful butterflies. Such craftsmanship was costly. She stared at it in confusion.

"It's yours," he said.

Her stunned gaze lifted to meet his. "I can't accept this!"

"I bought it for you."

"No, you didn't."

"Yes," his eyes twinkled, "I did."

"You're nuts."

"I believe in miracles."

She thrust it at him. "Take it back."

"No."

"I'm going to drop it," she threatened.

"I don't think you can."

"Watch me."

"Borrow it," he suggested.

"Huh?"

"You need a Bible. I have one. Borrow it. When you're done, bring it back."

Her nose wrinkled.

His arms crossed, making it clear he wasn't budging.

"You're wrong about me," she said. "I'm not a lost soul looking to be found."

She'd already been found. That was the problem.

"Fine," he countered easily. "Do your research and bring it back. The Good Book should get some use, not sit in a bag in a desk drawer."

When Eve stepped out of the church a few minutes later, she couldn't believe she had the Bible in her hand. Frustrated by the bizarre twists that were marring the once steady course of her life, she paused on the sidewalk at the edge of the parking lot and groaned.

"I don't like this," she said aloud, figuring the proximity to the church couldn't hurt her chances of being heard by someone upstairs.

A drop of water hit her cheek. Then another splattered on the end of her nose. Frowning, she looked up at the cloudless blue sky. A droplet hit her smack in the eye and stung.

"Ow! Damn it."

High pitched chortling turned her gaze back to the church. She rubbed her eyes and searched for the source. Just as her vision cleared, a stream of liquid hit her dead center on the forehead.

Eve jumped back and swiped the back of her hand across her face. Her gaze lifted to the archway above her.

"Ha-ha!" cried a gleeful voice.

Her eyes widened when she found the source, then narrowed defensively when she realized the water spraying her was urine.

Gargoyle urine.

The little cement beast was about the size of a gallon of milk. He sported tiny wings and a broad grin. Dancing with joy, he hopped from foot to foot in a frenetic circle that should have toppled him to the ground.

"Joey marked the Mark! Joey marked the Mark!" he chanted, pissing all the while.

"Holy shit," she breathed, pinching herself.

A sharp whack to the back of her head knocked the bag from her hands and confirmed that she wasn't having a nightmare.

"Shame on you!"

Clutching her skull, Eve turned to face her attacker— a stooped elderly woman brandishing a very heavy handbag.

"It's not what you think," Eve complained, rubbing at a rapidly swelling knot.

"Whack her again, Granny," suggested the angelic-looking heathen at her side.

"Beat it!" the woman ordered with a menacing shake of her bag.

Eve debated the merits of laughing . . . or bawling. "Give me a break, lady."

"Sinner," the heathen child said.

"I am *not* a sinner! This is not my fault."

A large, warm hand touched Eve's shoulder, then the dropped bag came into her line of vision. "Here."

Father Riesgo. The voice was unmistakable.

Eve glanced at the archway behind them. The gargoyle was gone. The Gothic creature had been out of place on the modern exterior of the church.

"Father," the purse-wielding woman greeted sweetly.

"I see you've met Ms. Hollis." He glanced at Eve. "Don't give up on her yet, Mrs. Bradley. I have high hopes."

Accepting the bag, Eve stepped away in a rush. "Thanks. Bye."

As she hurried to her car, she ignored the fulminating glare from Mrs. Bradley that was burning a hole in the back of her head. But she couldn't shake the feeling that she was being watched by a darker, more malevolent force.

The sensation scared the hell out of her.

After sliding into the driver's seat, Eve locked the doors and released the breath she hadn't realized she was holding.

"I'm getting out of this," she promised whoever might be listening. She reached into her purse and withdrew the hand wipes her mother, a retired nurse, insisted she carry.

After she scrubbed her face and hands, Eve turned the ignition. Then she drove around the block, looking for "Joey." She had no idea what she'd do when she found him, but damned if she'd let herself get pissed on and not track the little shit down.

CHAPTER 8

An hour of fruitless searching later, Eve parked her car in her assigned spot in her condominium complex's parking garage. With her hands wrapped around the steering wheel, she refused to look at the empty space where Alec's Harley had been when she left. He might be gone for five minutes or five years or forever.

The first time they made love, he'd disappeared before she awoke. She'd waited in their hotel room all morning. Tired. Sore. Madly, stupidly in love. She had believed he intended to come back for her. No man could hold a woman as he'd held her and not return.

In the end, she'd left only when the maid told her she would have to pay for another night if she didn't vacate.

Days of waiting and hoping and heartbreak followed. Weeks passed, then years. She wanted to kick herself for being in the same spot, feeling the same pain ten years later. Smart people learned from their mistakes; they didn't keep making the same ones.

A sudden rapping on her car window jolted her out of her musings. Frightened, she looked out the window and found Mrs. Basso leaning over with a frown.

"Eve? Are you okay?"

Her tense shoulders sagged with relief. She pushed open the door. "You scared me."

"You're jumpy today." Mrs. Basso held mail and keys in her frail hands. The mailboxes were all located on the ground floor, just a few feet away from the parking garage.

Climbing out of her car, Eve managed a reassuring smile. "I have a lot on my mind."

"I bet part of it is six foot two and around two hundred pounds."

Eve blinked.

"He was looking for you," Mrs. Basso said. "Seemed really concerned that you were gone."

"Did he say where he was going?" *Or if he'd be back?*

"No. He had a duffel bag with him though. Don't fret. If he's got a brain, he'll be back. You're worth it."

Touching Mrs. Basso's shoulder gently, Eve kissed her wrinkled cheek. "Thank you."

"Come on, I'll walk up with you."

Depressed by the prospect of returning to her empty condo, Eve briefly considered heading to her parents' place but didn't think she could deal with her mother at the moment. Some days, her mom's quirkiness was just what the doctor ordered. Most days, however, it drove her nuts. Since she was already on the edge of insanity, she thought it best to keep her distance for now.

Eve shook her head. "I think I need to walk a bit and clear my mind."

"I would feel better if you came upstairs. You've had a rough week."

Eve laughed softly, without humor. She wished she could explain. Part of her believed her friend would understand. "I won't be gone long. Just a few minutes."

Mrs. Basso sighed. "Okay. We still on for the movies?"

"You betcha."

She watched Mrs. Basso head to the elevators, then left the building through the garage's pedestrian gate.

It was a beautiful day and the number of sunbathers on the beach gave her a feeling of security. Too many witnesses. Which was both good and bad. The exposure that kept her safe also exposed her when she most wished to be private.

As she walked the length of the beach, she kept her head down to discourage interaction. She was too busy thinking to be interested in casual conversation. If she wanted out of this mark business, she'd need something of value to bargain with.

The wind whipped loose strands of her hair across her face and throat. Her heightened senses magnified the sensation until it was almost unbearable. Not in an uncomfortable way, just alien. Disconcerting.

She'd always controlled every aspect of her life, even as a kid. Her mom, a native of Japan, was an eclectic mix of old-world Bushido and 1970s hippy nonchalance, and her Alabama-native dad was so mellow, she wondered if he was awake half the time. A twenty-year employee of the phone company, Darrel Hollis's normal tone of voice was that of a terminally bored telephone operator. In response to her parents' loving indifference, Eve had become self-reliant and responsible to an extreme degree. Everything had its place and could be neatly compartmentalized. Interior design fit beautifully within that structured way of thinking. Assassinating monsters for God didn't.

"Hey, baby."

The catcall drifted across the breeze along with a vile stench. As her nose wrinkled in protest, her head turned to find the heckler. Some were easily ignored, others bolder. She needed to know which class of annoyance this guy was.

She found him sitting in the sand on a black towel, his legs stretched out before him, propped up by canted arms. He was fair haired and blue eyed, and sported arms sleeved in tattoos. His face bore a foreign cast, and his irises were hard and glittered like sapphires. He wore only makeshift shorts cut off crudely below the knee and a leer that made her skin crawl.

"Come sit with me," he cajoled in a gutturally accented voice. He patted the spot next to him in a gesture that was anything but inviting. An indigo teardrop stained the skin at the corner of his eye, distinguishing him as a felon. She was about to look away when he flicked his tongue at her in a lewd gesture.

"Jesus!" she cried, stumbling backward into the lapping water. She was so horrified by the impossibly long and slender forked appendage that had slithered out of his mouth, she barely registered the mark burning her deltoid in chastisement.

A red slash appeared across the demon's face and he hissed like the snake his tongue resembled. *"Du Miststück!"* he spat.

She had no idea what that meant, but it didn't sound good.

As he leaped to his feet, Eve sidestepped to avoid him. "Stay away from me."

"Make me."

The menacing tone with which the words were spoken made her hackles rise. It also sent a surge of heat and animosity through her veins. "Christ, you're a real piece of work."

His head jerked to the side as if struck, and when he looked at her again, his eyes were unnatural. Brilliant and intensely, inhumanly blue. He lunged. She shrieked and pivoted to run, crashing into something warm and rock-hard.

"Leave her alone," a dark voice warned. Masculine arms wrapped around her and Eve struggled briefly before absorbing the familiar scent of his skin into her lungs. It was heaven compared to the stench in the air and she gulped with relief.

"Reed." Her hands fisted in his expensive dress shirt.

"You can't intercede," her tormenter said smugly.

"You'd risk the wrath of your brethren for her?" Reed asked.

"She cut me first."

"I did no—" Eve began, only to find her face pressed brutally into Reed's chest. She briefly considered biting him, but her overactive libido kicked in with a vengeance, mingling with the hair-trigger aggressiveness pumping from the throbbing mark. It was like PMS multiplied by a million.

"She was toying with you," Reed drawled. "Assuming you were big enough to take it."

"Is *she* big enough to take it?"

"Can you take *me*?" Reed retorted. "You're not in the queue; I'm not barred from stepping in."

A stream of unintelligible words that sounded German poured from her antagonist, and Eve wrenched free to face him. She could feel the evil radiating off him, and his tattoos writhed sinuously over his unmoving skin, as if they were alive.

Wondering if she was the only one aware of the man, her gaze surveyed the area around them. The proliferation of beachgoers hadn't diminished, yet no one paid any attention to the tense scene taking place in their midst.

Reed's hand settled at the small of her back, giving her much needed support in a madly spinning world.

"Go away," Reed said. "Let's just forget this happened."

"I won't forget." The man crossed his arms. "We'll meet again," he told Eve.

"You cross that line," Reed warned, "and you'll start a war none of us wants."

"*You* don't want it."

Eve's gaze shot back and forth between the two bristling men, trying to grasp the undercurrent arcing between them. They were doing some kind of manly staring thing, then the blond sank back onto his towel and sprawled in a pose so relaxed it was clearly meant to insult.

You're no threat to me, his posture said.

Reed exhaled slowly and carefully, deliberately stemming his rising ire. Backing down from a challenge wasn't in his nature, but he didn't have a choice. Any offensive move on his part would put the blame for this unauthorized confrontation firmly on his shoulders. He didn't need any more heat right now, not after the upbraiding he'd endured for his most recent fight with Cain.

Cain the hero. Cain the fearless. Cain the invincible. No matter how often he broke the rules, Cain always emerged unscathed, his reputation strengthened by his sheer audacity.

Now Cain had been given his heart's desire and Reed's sampling of her charms was rebuked, his protestations of her willingness disregarded. *He,* who had always toed the line without question, had rarely been given anything he truly desired.

Hands off Evangeline, he'd been told.

Tightening his jaw, Reed reached for Eve's elbow and pulled her away. Damned if he would toe the line in this. If he had to reap his own rewards, he'd start with her.

"What the hell is going on?" Eve queried on a hiss of breath.

"A major fuck-up," he snapped. "Where's Cain?"

"Sleeping. And why do you two have different names? It's confusing."

"Eventually, you will have to change names, too. It looks suspicious if you don't die."

"Screw that."

He led her up the beach. At the last minute, he directed her toward the patio of a Mexican restaurant and cantina. Festive music blared from hidden speakers and the spice-laden scent of food teased his nostrils. He heard Eve's stomach growl and shook his head. "You haven't eaten?"

"I haven't thought about it. By the way, I don't have any cash and the patio is closed to noncustomers."

He shot her an arch glance. "I don't expect my dates to pay when they're with me."

"This is a date?"

"It is now."

"I'm not feeling it. Not after that creep on the beach."

"He was a Nix," Reed corrected. "And you need to watch your mouth. If I hadn't shown up when I did, you'd be dead right now."

"I didn't say anything!" Eve sank into the plastic patio chair he pulled out for her. Their table was in the corner formed by two Plexiglas panels. It afforded them a view of the beach while shielding their food from the ocean breeze and sand.

"You used the Lord's name," he explained, taking the chair opposite her. "It's a weapon against demons. Rarely deadly but always painful."

"How the hell was I supposed to know that? He was heckling me. If he'd left me alone, none of that would have happened."

"You're ripe for the picking. An untried, clueless Mark. I could kill Cain for falling asleep on the job." He snorted. "Irresponsible, as usual."

"What's a Nix?"

He noticed she chose to ignore the dig about Cain, and he smiled inwardly. The first time he saw her, Eve had been dressed for business. Her unbound hair had been the only hint of softness about her. Her "look but don't touch" air had stirred him, but it was the moment their eyes met that his interest went beyond merely pissing off Cain. Whoever said Asian women were shy and reserved had been smoking something at the time.

"A water demon." Reed gestured to a waiter. "The Nix used to be concentrated in Europe, but they've since spread to most coastal cities."

"He didn't look like a demon," she muttered.

"What does a demon look like?"

"Not like that. Aside from the freaky tattoos, he reminded me of a ski instructor, like he should be wearing a turtleneck and sitting near a stone fireplace at a lodge."

"You've got a vivid imagination." His mouth curved. "But those weren't tattoos. They were *details*—markings that tell us about his affiliations and his status within those affiliations."

"Like gang markings?"

"Exactly. Even in Hell there's a hierarchy and it's constantly under threat by warring factions. Infernals most likely passed on the practice of marking symbols into flesh to mortals." Reed looked at the approaching waiter, a young Latino wearing Oakley shades, hoop earings, and an El Gordito apron tied around his jeans-covered hips. "Two Modelos," he ordered.

"And two shots of tequila," Eve added.

"That's not going—"

"To get me buzzed? I don't care." She managed a brief smile at the waiter. "And a taco plate, please. With lots of salsa. The hot kind."

"Make that two," Reed said.

Eve waited until they were alone again before speaking. "The guy's *details* were moving. Writhing."

"He was trying to intimidate you." And it hadn't

worked well, something Reed noted and admired. "Infernals can move them at will, and only others of their kind and Marks can see the show."

"That's why no one paid much attention to him on the beach?"

"Exactly. Some Infernals prefer to keep their details as visible as possible, especially if they're higher ranking. Others prefer to keep them out of sight to maintain a low profile. They can't remove them, but they can put them in places no one wants to look." He shrugged elegantly. "Pointless, really, because they stink so bad you can smell them coming. And when their number's up, it's up. Hidden details or not, once they're in the queue, it's only a matter of time."

"Is that what that smell was? It reeked like a sewer."

"Rotting soul. You can't miss it."

Her eyes widened with such horror, Reed felt a sharp tinge of sympathy . . . even as he appreciated how her inevitable resentment would create a rift between her and Cain.

Eve leaned forward, resting her forearms on the table and staring at him with a grimly determined gaze. "How do I get out of this gig?"

"There's no way—"

"I don't believe that. There has to be a way."

Leaning back, he settled more comfortably into his chair. "Why?"

"Because I feel like a victim, that's why." Her jaw hardened. "And I'm not the type to take it lying down."

"A victim." He stilled at that.

"Wouldn't you feel the same in my shoes?" she challenged.

Maybe. *Probably*.

"You've been placed in a position of power," he pre-varicated, "and given the tools to change the world and make it safer for others. Can't you view this as a blessing rather than a curse?"

"The Mark of Cain is a blessing? You're slick, but not *that* slick. And I'm not stupid."

"Slick?"

The waiter returned with a tray bearing two bottles of beer, two shot glasses, and chips and salsa. Eve sat back to make room. Reed continued to watch her, smiling.

"The clothes. The cockiness." An impatient hand gesture encompassed him from head to toe. "Slick."

"Style and confidence, babe. I happen to like both qualities." His voice lowered. "So do you."

She shook her head, but the look in her eyes gave proof to his statement.

Reed reached over and caught her hand. Her fingers were long and slender, her skin soft as silk. That would change. Wield a weapon often enough and it left its mark with roughened flesh. "You don't have to admit it."

"I won't."

He bared her wrist, then lowered his head. As his lips parted and his tongue stroked across her vein, Eve watched in helpless fascination. He could smell her growing arousal and knew she'd be hot and wet. Her recently acquired hyperactive sex drive was a godsend to his plan to have her again, no pun intended. Restraint was difficult the first few years. The heightened senses and fluctuating emotions were killer until one learned to control or ignore them. The best and fastest way to release all that tension was with long, hard sex. Reed was determined to be the man Eve turned to as a pressure valve.

Straightening, he kept his gaze locked with hers. He reached for the salt with one hand, slowly stroking across her palm with the thumb of the other.

"Where is this going?" Her normally clipped tone was softened by hoarseness.

"To bed."

"Not with me."

He smiled and sprinkled salt over her damp skin. Picking up a shot glass, Reed licked her wrist and tossed back the tequila.

Eve handed him a slice of lime. "You're not here to get laid."

"How can you be sure?" He bit into the tart pulp with relish.

"You're the type who likes to be chased, not do the chasing."

"You don't know me as well as you think. But that'll change."

"I told you, I want out." With an offhand toast, Eve downed her shot and chased it with a long swig of the beer. She growled. "Okay. This sucks. It's like drinking water."

"You can't bargain with God, Eve."

"You can bargain with anyone, as long as you have something they want that they can't get anywhere else." She turned her head, her gaze moving to the strip of street visible from her position.

His glance followed hers. Sport-utility vehicles traveled alongside luxury sports cars. Joggers and in-line skaters weaved in and around each other.

"Are some of those people . . . *Infernals*?" she asked.

"Certainly."

She glanced back at him. "They coexist peacefully with the rest of us?"

"If you call living with greed, depression, murder, and lies 'peaceful.' " Reed tipped his bottle back and drank deeply. "Complete destruction of humanity isn't the goal. They need mortals for entertainment."

"Lovely." She exhaled sharply. "You mentioned a queue?"

"There comes a point when an Infernal crosses the line one too many times."

"They have to cross a line first?"

"We're not vigilantes," he said, chuckling. "We can't go around whacking the bad guys for the hell of it. There's a balance to everything. A yin and a yang, if you will. Orders have to come down. Once that happens, all bets are off."

"And then what?"

"The Mark nearest in location who has the necessary skills is dispatched to take them out."

"Who makes that call? God?"

"The Lord assigns Cain directly. The seraphim manage everyone else."

Her lips pursed and he could practically see her curiosity. When she finally said, "Tell me how it works," Reed's answering smile was indulgent.

"Relating it to the human judicial system might make it easier to understand. Every sinner has a trial in absentia and the Lord presides over every case. Christ acts as the public defender. Clear so far?"

"I watch *Law and Order*."

"Okay, good. If there's a conviction, one of the

seraphim send the order down to a firm to hunt the Infernal."

"A firm?"

"Think of it as the bail bond agency. An archangel becomes responsible for bringing them in—like a bail bondsman. They don't actually do any hunting. The Marks do the dirty work and they collect a bounty, just as a bounty hunter would, only in this case the prize is indulgences. Earn enough and you'll work off your penance."

"Bring them in? As in dead or alive?"

"Dead."

"Blood-and-gore-dead? Or some kind of magical-dead?"

"There's nothing magic about it." He set his hand atop hers, trying to offer what little comfort he could. "Sometimes it's dirty, sometimes it's not. You'll learn the difference. Training is intense and thorough."

"Training in Infernal hunting?" She shook her head. "No thanks."

"Some Marks think the work is glamorous."

"My idea of glamour is drinking champagne and wearing a little black dress."

Reed's mouth curved. "Can't wait to see it."

"How do I get out?"

"Of the dress? I'll help with that."

"Jeez. Not the dress. This bounty-hunting gig."

"Not possible."

"Bullshit. I want to talk to someone else."

His smile turned into a grin. "My superior?"

"Sure. Why not?"

"You'll meet him soon enough. In the meantime,

class should begin shortly. You'll be notified when it's time."

"Class?" Eve stared across the table at Reed and hated the fact that she didn't have a buzz, yet felt light-headed anyway.

Her gaze moved beyond his shoulder. She straightened. "Heads up. We've got company."

Reed didn't even flinch. "About time he showed up."

"What the hell are you doing here?" Alec barked, stopping at their table.

"Waiting for you," she replied, kicking out a chair for him.

Alec caught the back and dropped into the seat. He looked at Reed. "What do you want?"

"Good morning to you, too."

"I want to know how to get rid of the mark," Eve said.

"I haven't figured it out yet," Alec said grimly, "but I'm working on it."

"It's impossible," Reed scoffed.

"Listen." She crossed her arms. "I don't subscribe to the 'impossible' school of thought. Anything is possible. We just have to figure out how."

"You don't even know what's involved with the job yet, babe."

"She's not your *babe*," Alec snapped.

Reed smiled.

Eve glared at both of them. "I know I'm not about to get pissed on and provoked every day of my life. I have a job I love, a home I worked damned hard for, and a life that suits me, even if it's not perfect. I don't want to hunt demons and nasties."

"Pissed *off*," Reed corrected.

"What?"

"You said 'pissed *on* and provoked' not 'pissed *off* and provoked.'"

"I know what I said! And I meant what I said. I was out running errands while Alec was napping and ran across a gargoyle with a rotten sense of humor and a large bladder."

Alec froze. "A gargoyle?"

"What did it look like?" Reed asked.

"Like a gargoyle," she said dryly. "Made of gray stone or cement, small wings, big mouth. This one was kind of cute, with a face like an Ewok."

"No," Alec said. "What did its *details* look like?"

She frowned. "It didn't have any."

"It had to have some kind of designator," Reed argued. "They're marked just like you are."

"Then he hid his details up his ass or something, because I saw every inch of him, even the bottom of his feet. He was bouncing around, spinning circles, and laughing like an idiot."

"Maybe your sight isn't working yet," Alec suggested. "They can't hide their details in body cavities. On the buttocks, genitalia, or even under their hair, yes. But it has to be on the skin."

"I'm telling you, this guy had nothing on him," she insisted. "And I know my 'sight' is working, because I saw the jerk on the beach's details just fine."

"Jerk on the . . ." Alec scowled. "You ran into something else?"

"You can see why taking a nap was a great idea," Reed drawled.

"Screw you." Alec looked fit to kill again. "That was probably your idea."

"Not this time. I was too busy keeping your girl alive."

"You can't even keep *yourself* alive."

Eve stood.

The brothers barked in unison, "Where are you going?"

"Away from you two. I'll take my food to go, then you can fight over which one of you will pay."

"Sit down, angel."

Alec's voice arrested her, the tone of command undeniable. This was a different side of Alec. Even more delicious than the others.

Damned libido.

Angry with her unruly desires, Eve plopped back into her seat.

"Tell me everything that happened," Alec said. "Every detail."

When she finished, the two men exchanged glances.

"What?" Eve asked.

"The tengu went after you," Reed said. "He shouldn't have."

"Tengu?"

"The demon you thought was a gargoyle."

"I feel like the kid in school who has Kick Me taped to her back," she muttered. She looked at Alec. His unwritten sign said Don't Mess with Me. If she had to wear any sign, that was the one she wanted.

"We have to find him." Alec's fingers drummed atop the plastic table.

The server returned with their food and they all waited while the plates were set down. Alec ordered the same meal, then watched Eve closely as she began to eat.

"Why do we need to find him?" Eve asked between bites of her first taco.

"We need to know who he's affiliated with."

"By his details?"

"Yes."

"Fine."

A smile tugged at the corner of Alec's mouth. "You sound grumpy."

"Neither of you believe me. That thing was completely gray from head to toe. Not a speck of color or design on him."

"Your senses probably didn't kick in until you ran across the Nix on the beach," Reed pointed out, wiping his mouth with a paper napkin. "They fluctuate quite a bit for the first couple of weeks."

"A Nix?" Alec swore.

"Is that bad?" Eve glanced back and forth between the two.

"Hell yeah, that's bad. And I bet you riled him up with that mouth of yours."

"There's nothing wrong with my mouth."

Both men's gazes dropped to her lips. They tingled in response. She cleared her throat.

"And the tengu is bad, too?" she asked in order to break the sudden tension.

"Any demon is bad," Reed answered. "But as far as pests go, a tengu is a mosquito and a Nix is a rat. Our resources are strapped, so the tengu fall fairly low on the scale. We don't hunt them as actively as we do some other Infernals."

"We're going to hunt this one," Alec said grimly.

"I'm going, too." Eve wiped off her fingers. "If that thing had details, I want to see them."

"It definitely had details, babe." Reed picked up his beer. "There's no doubt about that."

"Says you," she corrected. She looked at Alec. "What do you intend to do when you find him?"

Alec shrugged. "Shake him down and see what kind of information falls out."

"Unless he has hidden talents, it doesn't seem like a fair fight. He was small."

"It's the demon he works for that concerns me. The tengu are lesser demons who lack initiative and ambition. It's out of character to risk bringing attention to himself. They like to cause trouble, but only indirectly."

"It's not going to be dangerous, is it?"

His gaze softened. "You'll just point him out and get out of the way."

"I can do that." Eve picked up her fork, scooped up some rice, and tried to concentrate on eating. It wasn't as easy as she would have wished.

She was too exhilarated, a response she found more disturbing than exciting.

"Now . . ." Alec's voice was laden with frustration. "Tell me what happened with the Nix."

CHAPTER 9

As Eve unlocked her front door, she took a moment to appreciate the speed with which it had been replaced. But when she stepped inside her condo, admiration gave way to trepidation.

Someone was inside her home.

Alec sensed her hesitation. He caught her arm and pulled her back, taking a defensive position in front of her. Then he sniffed the air and shot her a questioning glance.

She sighed. She didn't need an enhanced sense of smell to recognize the scents of curry and freshly steamed rice. "It's my mother."

An odd look passed over his handsome features. Shock and wariness, perhaps. Then a dawning wonder.

It was the worst possible time for Miyoko Hollis to be visiting. She would view Alec's presence in Eve's house with more significance than Eve was presently prepared to give him. And he knew it, if the sudden mischievous grin he wore was any indication.

"Evie-san?" her mother called out.

"Yeah, it's me, Mom." Eve narrowed her eyes at Alec. She hoped like hell her father wasn't here, because if he was and if he'd seen Alec's belongings in her bedroom, he'd expect there to be a ring on her finger. Despite her traditional Japanese upbringing, Miyoko actually had less old-fashioned views of courtship.

"Behave," Eve admonished.

"Of course." But the gleam in Alec's eyes belied the promise.

Her mother's head peeked out from around the support pillar that anchored the end of the island. The same thick, inky black hair she'd passed on to Eve was permed into tight, short corkscrews that made her look as young as her daughter.

"Oh, hello," her mother greeted, her face brightening at the sight of Alec. She appreciated a good-looking man as much as the next woman.

The rest of Miyoko's four-foot eleven-inch frame appeared, revealing an apron that protected a lime-colored sweater tank and multihued skirt. A tiny, diamond-encrusted cross decorated her neck. The Hollises were Christian—Southern Baptist, to be precise, although they attended the occasional festival at the Orange County Buddhist Church for the food and entertainment. Eve had been baptized as a child, but broke free in junior high, refusing to accompany her family to any further church events. It was still a point of contention between her and the rest of the family. They didn't understand her renouncement of organized religion, but then, they'd never tried to.

Eve made the introductions, her gaze darting to

the end of the couch where two suitcases waited with feigned innocuousness.

"Where's Dad?

"Fishing with his buddies again, near Acapulco."

Damn.

Her mother was a caregiver by nature. When her husband was away, she needed someone to fuss over. Since Eve's sister, Sophia, lived in Kentucky, Eve was the recipient of that fussing.

The whole day had been hell. Now, her mother and Alec were in her house at the same time. Eve cringed inwardly.

"A pleasure to meet you, Mrs. Hollis," Alec greeted her.

"Please. Call me Miyoko."

"*Konichiwa,* Miyoko-san." He bowed.

Eve watched startled pleasure pass over her mother's face, but Alec's charm wouldn't be enough to make up for his bad-boy exterior. The slightly overlong hair, worn jeans, ripped physique, and scuffed biker boots made him unacceptable from the get-go. Her mother had impossible-to-meet standards for her daughters' suitors. Reed's exterior would be closer to passing muster, but his arrogance would never make the cut. In all of Eve's years of dating, she had yet to meet a man her mother approved of for longer than five minutes.

"It smells wonderful in here," Alec praised.

"Japanese curry." Her mother beamed. "Have you tried it before?"

"Yes. It's one of my favorites."

For a moment, Eve was startled by the statement. Then she considered how long Alec had been living and how far he'd traveled.

"I made two flavors," her mother said, returning to the kitchen where onions, carrots, and potatoes were in various stages of being peeled and cut. "Hot and mild."

"Why mild?" Eve asked, going to the fridge for a can of soda. She lifted one up to her guests in silent query. They both nodded, so Eve pulled out three and kicked the door closed.

"I invited Mrs. Basso to have dinner with us. Poor dear. I can't imagine living alone."

"I'm glad she accepted." Eve set the sodas on the counter and opened the dishwasher. It was empty.

"You shouldn't live out of the dishwasher," Miyoko admonished. "I put the dishes away for you."

"You didn't have to do that. I can take care of myself."

"I don't mind."

Maybe her mother didn't mind, Eve thought, but she'd never let Eve forget that she'd done it.

Eve turned to the cupboard that held her glasses and found Alec there before her, pulling them down. He handed her one, then pushed the other two—one at a time—under the fridge's ice dispenser.

She watched with a mixture of horror and pleasure. This was the man who'd taken her virginity ten years ago. It seemed impossible that he was in her home, moving around as if he'd lived with her the whole time.

Their gazes met and held.

"How long are you visiting, Alec?" her mother asked.

"Actually, business has brought me into the area indefinitely," Alec replied, setting both ice-filled glasses in front of Eve, and taking the empty one from her hand.

"Oh?" Wariness crept into Miyoko's tone. "What do you do?"

"I'm a headhunter."

"For what company?"

Alec smiled. "For Meggido Industries. We specialize in disaster avoidance."

"How interesting." Her mom's eyes lit up.

As her mother reassessed Alec, Eve could practically see the wheels turning in her head. It wouldn't go well if Miyoko researched Alec's company and found it to be a fraud.

"How did you meet Evangeline?"

"It was years ago, when she was in—"

"—college," Eve interjected, before gulping down her soda.

Miyoko paused in the act of scooping up vegetables. She frowned. Alec rested his hip against the counter and smiled.

"I need a shower." Eve set her empty glass on the counter.

"Don't leave that there," her mother scolded.

"It's my house, Mom." But she picked up the cup and carried it to the sink.

"Can I help with anything?" Alec asked as Eve left the room.

"Would you mind cutting the onions?" Miyoko asked. "They make me cry."

As she traversed the length of the hallway, Eve forced herself to shake off the feeling of being invaded. Her mother had obviously been in her house for a while. The washing machine was running and the air smelled like floor cleaner, which made her wonder how long Alec had been out looking for her.

You're lucky you're not dead, he'd said when she finished telling him about the Nix.

She couldn't imagine living a life where a walk on the beach was a death wish waiting to be fulfilled. Even church wasn't sacred. Nothing was safe. A shiver moved through her.

After a very hot, very long shower, Eve felt slightly better. She pulled on a merlot velour jogging suit and left her hair down to dry naturally. When she exited to the hallway, she ran into Alec as he was stepping out of the guest bedroom. He had changed into a button-down shirt and loose slacks. He looked respectable and edible. She stared.

The corner of his mouth lifted. "I have many sides that you haven't yet seen, angel."

"Not *my* fault."

"No." He stepped closer. "It isn't."

The scent of his skin intoxicated her. "I'm becoming a nymphomanic."

"I'm available."

"For how long?" she challenged. "I keep wondering when I'm going to look around and find you gone."

"I'll be with you until we find a way to free you."

"So you're temporary."

"Do you *want* permanent?" His gaze was hot.

Eve debated that question for a long moment, then offered a weak shrug. She didn't know what the hell she wanted. A week ago she would have said a successful career, a loving husband, two kids, and a dog. Normal. Comfortable.

"My mom is planning on staying the night," she said instead.

He nodded, but his intensity didn't diminish. "I noticed. I offered to find a hotel, but she absolutely refused the guest room. She says the futon in your office is fine."

Eve sighed. "She doesn't like sleeping in a big bed without my dad. She doesn't even pull out the futon, she sleeps on it like a couch."

"A wife after my own heart."

"I can't see you ever getting married."

"Just because it didn't work the first time, doesn't mean it won't ever work."

She stilled.

"I told you," he murmured, watching her with heavy-lidded eyes. "There's a lot you don't know about me."

"I never got the chance to learn."

"You have one now."

Eve leaned back against the wall. Alec moved in, stepping closer and caging her with one hand beside her head. Memories of their recent night together flooded her mind. The desperate consuming lust. The gnawing hunger. The skill and passion with which he slaked both.

With only centimeters between them, she could feel the heat of his skin and if she listened with her new hearing, she could make out the steadily increasing beat of his heart.

"Your heart is starting to race," she whispered.

"Because I'm with you. Sex is one of the rare times when we're capable of experiencing the full force of our physical responses."

"We're not having sex."

"In my head we are."

Eve's lower lip quivered. It would be so easy to turn to him for comfort and support, but that was what had landed her in trouble in the first place. And when she managed to shed the mark, he would leave along with it.

That didn't stop her from wanting him. Badly.

Her stomach growled, breaking the moment.

"I cannot believe I'm hungry already," she whispered, grateful for the intrusion, however embarrassing. "Those taco plates usually fill me up all day."

"Your body is going through some pretty drastic changes. It requires fuel to manage it all."

"Will my system revert when I'm . . . free?"

Alec sighed, his breath flowing across her lips like a feather light kiss. "I don't know, angel. I've never met a former Mark."

"Really?" She bit her lower lip.

"Really." He pressed his temple to hers. She could sense his sexual hunger in the underlying tension of his powerful frame.

"I'll find a way," she promised, as much to herself as to him.

"I'll help you."

The doorbell rang, and they broke apart. She looked away first.

"What about the gargoyle?" she asked, as they moved into the living room.

"We'll catch up with him tomorrow." Alec noted her questioning glance and explained, "He can't go far. Tengu draw their energy from the inhabitants of the building they decorate. They stir feelings of anxiety and unhappiness, and feed off of them. Straying too far is like starving."

"That's fascinating."

"All Infernals have their preferences and vulnerabilities. The Nix have to stay near water, as do kappas. Trolls live near woods. When you start your classes, you'll learn the vagaries of each branch. Knowledge is power. Exploiting a weakness can save your life."

Eve reached for the doorknob. "How many branches are there?"

"A few hundred. But each has subdivisions that can number into the thousands."

"Oh my G—" She caught herself.

"Watch it."

She growled. "I'm trying."

Pulling open the door, Eve felt her mood improving when she found Mrs. Basso on her doorstep. Tonight her neighbor wore olive slacks with a matching sweater vest and emerald necklace. A loose white blouse kept the ensemble feminine and casual.

Eve hugged her.

"You look gorgeous," Mrs. Basso said.

"So do you," she returned. Then she introduced her to Alec.

Mrs. Basso held a brown paper bag and a bottle of Chianti in her hands. Eve offered to take both from her, but she declined with a curious blush staining her cheeks.

"Evie-san!" her mother called out. "Can you set the table?"

"Yes, Mom." She looked at Alec. "The remote is on the coffee table, if you two would like to watch TV."

As she moved to the kitchen, Eve heard the low drone of subdued voices behind her. She strained to hear, curious about Alec and the way he interacted with others. He was right. She didn't know anything about him beyond the combustible attraction her body felt for his. Maybe she should learn, if only in the hopes of discovering something that would turn her off enough to get over him.

As she opened the cupboard that held her plates and withdrew four, the voices in the living room grew in volume. Not because Alec and Mrs. Basso were moving closer or talking louder, but because Eve's hearing was sharpening. Every noise seemed suddenly amplified, as if her ears had an adjustable volume knob and someone had cranked it higher.

"I brought this for you, Mr. Cain," Mrs. Basso said.

Eve heard the paper bag exchange hands.

"Thank you." The surprise in Alec's voice made her smile.

"It was one of my late husband's favorite recipes. I included some of the spices that are sometimes harder to find."

Leaning around the support post, Eve craned her neck to get a look. They stood in the living room, the recessed lights bathing both of them in a white glow. Alec stood a foot taller than Mrs. Basso, giving the impression of a man speaking to a child. He was looking into the bag, and the perplexed frown on his face intrigued her.

"Add a cup of the Chianti to the sauce just before serving," Mrs. Basso said, "then enjoy the rest by the glass. You'll find the meal creates a mellow, luxurious mood."

"Mellow mood?"

Eve set the plates down quickly, fighting a building surge of humor.

Mrs. Basso cleared her throat. "Evangeline is so like me in some ways." Her face flamed with color. "We can appear tougher than we are. I think a quiet, romantic evening with good food will please her greatly."

Alec's head turned to find Eve and she faced forward swiftly, moving toward the silverware drawer in feigned ignorance of his conversation. She felt Alec's gaze on her back and bit her lip. Listening to Mrs. Basso give seduction pointers to Alec was priceless.

"Don't forget the forks," her mother chastised, pouring the curry from the pot into a serving dish. "Even when you plan on using only spoons, you should still set out forks."

"Hush, Mom," Eve said, waving her hand in an impatient gesture.

"Why are you whispering?"

"Uh . . ." Alec coughed.

"I worry about Evangeline." Mrs. Basso's voice strengthened. "A young, beautiful woman living alone. It's never been completely safe, but these days . . . These are rough times."

"You're right about that," Alec agreed grimly.

"She's such a lovely girl, inside and out. I would like to see her find someone special and this afternoon when you left . . . Well, she looked a bit lost. I think there's something there."

"Mrs. Basso—"

"I hope things work out between you, that's all. I won't embarrass you anymore. I feel like a meddling old woman as it is."

Eve caught the edge of the drawer and blinked back tears, deeply touched. It was then that she saw the large, clear glass bowl on the counter filled with water and a single, beautiful white water lily.

Her mother was an amateur horticulturist with an impressive green thumb. She often brought over plants and flowers from her garden. But she'd never brought over anything like this.

"The water lily is beautiful, Mom." Eve sniffled, arrested by its perfection.

"Isn't it? I am still reserving judgment on your Alec, but such thoughtfulness is a good sign—if he keeps it up. Men always try hard in the beginning, then they slack off. Anyway, you should put it on the table as a centerpiece."

"Alec brought that?" Eve glanced over her shoulder at the living room. He was seated on the couch with Mrs. Basso now.

"I guess so," her mother said, "unless you have another boyfriend somewhere."

"He's not my boyfriend." Would Reed have given her such a thing? She didn't know what to think about that.

Miyoko hummed doubtfully. "It was delivered when you were in the shower and Alec was changing his clothes. Nice delivery man. Refused a tip. Handsome, too. He reminded me of that blond actor from *A Beautiful Mind*."

Eve froze with forks in one hand and knives in the other. She felt like her heart should be racing, but it couldn't. Not anymore. "Paul Bettany?"

"Yes. That's the one. Very Scandinavian looking. Had a bit of an accent, too."

The water lily took on new meaning, changing from a lovely gift to a sinister warning. A whiff of something noxious wrinkled her nose and she realized what that meant. Eve's hands shook violently.

The Nix knew where she lived.

As soon as Alec heard the bathroom door lock behind Miyoko, he left the living room and went in search of Eve. He found her in her office seated before her computer.

Her work space was a large room, capable of comfortably holding two large desks—one for her computer and one drafting table for her renderings. It also held a contemporary futon in a soft camel color, a coffee table, and three bookcases.

"Your neighbor is . . . interesting," he said.

She laughed. "She thought you needed some dating pointers."

"I knew you were laughing at me." His hands settled on her shoulders. As he kneaded, his gaze came to rest on the monitor. She was Googling Nixes.

"What do you want to know?" he asked softly. "I can tell you more than Google can."

"Can I kill it with a bullet?"

A grim smile curved his mouth. Eve didn't think she was cut out to be a Mark, but he had no doubts. That didn't alter the fact that he was going to find a way to return her life to her.

"You can, if you blow his head off when he's in full mortal form," he said. "It won't work when he is in liquid form. Decapitation will kill everything except a hydra. You can also dehydrate Nixes by separating them from water. Unlike humans, a Nix will shrivel up within a couple of hours. But it's not as easy as it sounds. Any source of water can recharge them—tap water, puddles, tears, humid air. Unless you drop them off in the middle of a desert, the kill isn't guaranteed."

"That's it?"

"Fire is good. Flame-covered swords work, I've been told."

"And where exactly do I get one of those?" Eve blew out her breath and turned her chair around, forcing him to release her and back up.

"You'll be trained in how to request one."

"Eventually. Someday. If he doesn't kill me first."

His fingertips brushed along her jaw line. "You know I'd show you, if I knew how. I've never figured it out myself and since I've managed to survive this long without one, learning hasn't been a priority."

Her dark eyes were troubled. "What do you think of his gift?"

Alec crossed his arms. "I think he means to kill you."

The knowledge gutted him. He remembered eating at a sushi restaurant once where they'd served the fish still breathing. Slit down the belly, mouth gasping. He felt like that fish.

"Can he?" she asked quietly. "Is he allowed?"

"One of two things is happening here: either he's a rogue who hopes he can justify the kill after the fact, or he's sanctioned."

"Which is worse?"

"They're both fucking bad."

"I get that."

"Why did you have to leave the house, Eve?"

"This is my fault?" She stood. "You really want to blame me for this?"

Alec scrubbed a hand over his face. "No. Damn it, I don't blame you."

Her chin lifted. Despite her slender five-foot-four frame dressed in Betty Boop flannel pajama pants and matching tank, she looked formidable. She *was* formidable. Eve could knock him on his ass with a scowl.

"I left the house," she said, "because I needed a Bible for research. That's how I met the tengu. I hit the beach because I needed air after the tengu incident. That's how I met the Nix."

He blew out his breath. "Shit."

"Nothing is coincidence, you said."

"Right."

"So what is going on?"

"I wish I knew." The possibilities were many; none of them were good. "Did you find a Bible?"

"Yes."

"Are you scared?"

"Terrified."

"Good. You'll keep your guard up, then." He held his arms out to her. Eve hesitated, then stepped into his embrace.

The safest thing to do would be to get far away from her, to allow his scent to fade from her skin so that she couldn't be used against him. But there wasn't a soul he trusted to keep her as safe as he would. If she had to be out in the field, he had to be there with her. It was the only way he'd keep his sanity.

"What do we do?" she asked.

"If the Nix is rogue, killing him will end this. If he's sanctioned, we'll get one of two possible results—either the hunt was labeled personal, which would end with his death, or it was considered an affront to his whole unit and someone else will step in to finish what he couldn't."

"Yikes." She looked up at him. "How can I help?"

"You never leave my side. We'll watch your back. I'll make inquiries and see what turns up."

"We hunt him."

"*I* hunt him."

"I can't go into this blind."

"Angel—"

Her mouth took on a mulish cast. "I need to know what I'm up against, Alec, and I need to be more than a pain in your ass."

"You are *not* asking me to let you handle this as my partner."

"Of course not." She smiled and his breathing faltered. In that moment she was very much like the girl she'd been when they'd first met. "I'm just telling you that I *need* information, as well as your willingness to use me if you need me. Just promise me that you won't be stubborn enough to keep me in the dark."

Alec's instinctive response was to shelter Eve as much as possible. But he knew that would only alienate her and make her more stubborn, although it wouldn't make her foolish. Her quest for a Bible told him she still researched everything to a fault, a proclivity he'd noted the first time he made love to her. She had recited the pros and cons of several over-the-counter birth control methods before he managed to stop laughing and occupied her thoughts with something else instead.

"It's my job to lead, angel. *I* need to know that you'll follow, even if following means staying out of the way.

And, for now, I don't want you leaving the condo without me."

She pondered that a moment. "What are we to each other?"

His brow arched, even as his hands slid down her back and cupped her buttocks.

"Behave," she admonished.

"You like me when I'm naughty," he purred, nuzzling his lips against her ear. He felt her shiver, even as she pushed against him. It was a bad idea to get more deeply involved with her when their parting was certain, but he couldn't resist.

When he let her go, she couldn't come back to him even if she wanted to. Yet if he kept her, if he tried to work off their penance in unison in the hope that one day he could be what she needed, he would lose her.

Evangeline Hollis had *family* written all over her. Husband, two and a half kids, a dog, and a white picket fence. Her sister was married with children. Her parents had passed their silver anniversary. The fact that she rarely dated wasn't so much a fear of commitment as it was a fear of wasting time with Mr. Wrong.

Alec couldn't give her the life she craved, and if he was honest, he would admit that he might never be capable of giving it to her. He was a killer, a murderer. Everyone had a talent, and ending lives was his. He'd never be the nine-to-five family man Eve wanted and deserved.

"I have enough on my plate at the moment," she said hoarsely. "I don't know when you're leaving, what I'm doing, where this mark is taking me, or how the hell I'm going to get my life back."

Alec smiled, the hunter in him relishing the chase.

She wriggled away from him. "I don't need any more complications. Now answer the question: what are you to me?"

"Every field-assigned Mark has a mentor. The training is thorough, but nothing can replace hands-on experience. Mentors guide new Marks in the transition from the classroom to the streets."

"Sounds organized. Training. Mentoring."

"It is. Very much so."

Eve nodded. "Okay. So now I know how to kill a Nix. How can I expect him to try and kill me? The normal ways? Does he have special gifts I should be concerned about?"

"They can kill with a kiss. Their lips seal to yours and they flood your lungs with water, drowning you. They can leech moisture from you, dehydrating you to death. But that takes time. You'd have to be immobilized. And they kill the old-fashioned ways, too."

"So my best option is the commonsense one—keep my distance."

"Definitely. With any luck, your body will acclimate quickly to the mark and you'll soon be able to smell him coming."

"I caught a whiff of him earlier." Her nose wrinkled. "A bit of residual odor on the outside of the vase."

Alec scrubbed a hand over his face. "Usually Marks start out smelling everything, then they learn to control their senses enough to focus on the little things. You're working in reverse. How the hell can you smell something so minor so quickly?"

Eve yawned. "Like I know. That's one too many questions for me today. I'm hitting the sack. I'm beat."

"Want some company?"

The corner of her mouth tilted up and his blood heated. "Not tonight, I have a mother in the house."

"Good point. Tomorrow we'll head out and find your little stone friend."

"Yipee" she said dryly. "Can't wait."

She walked away with a saucy wave.

CHAPTER 10

T his is a bit out of the way for you, isn't it?" Alec
asked, as Eve pulled into the parking lot of St.
Mary's church.

"I drive when I need to think." Her gaze drifted over
the roof of the building before she turned her attention
to finding a spot.

"Busy congregation," he noted.

It seemed odd to Eve to have Alec in the car with
her. For years, she'd pictured him on his motorcycle.
He seemed at home astride it, a part of it, a virile man
and his steel horse. But when he'd offered to drive
she'd swiftly declined. She needed a clear head to absorb the surfeit of information he was imparting to her.
There was no way she'd be able to think with his hips
between her thighs and her arms wrapped around him.

"I guess so," she replied in response to his observa-
tion.

Eve put her car in park, pulled the key from the ignition, and undid her seat belt. Unsure of how their "hunt"

would progress, she'd dressed in well-worn jeans, Vans, and a button-up, short-sleeved top. "Ready?"

He looked at her with a soft gleam in his eye. "Why didn't you just ask me what you wanted to know?"

"You were asleep."

Alec snorted. "That's a cop-out."

"What's the matter with wanting to read it with my own eyes?"

"It's hearsay. A lot of it is more fable than literal truth."

"And you're going to give me an unbiased play-by-play?"

In answer, he smiled and opened the passenger door. She remained seated as he alighted, her gaze riveted to his ass and long legs. He, too, wore jeans. His feet were encased in steel-toed Doc Martens and his torso was covered in a dark blue T-shirt. She was astonished by how normal he looked, when he was anything but.

She got out of the car before he could get the door for her. "Now what?"

"We case the church." Alec slipped on his sunglasses. "Then we spread out slowly on foot until we find where he lives."

"I thought churches were sacred."

"Stick with me, kid," he drawled. "You'll learn something new every day."

"Nothing I want to know," she muttered, slamming the door shut and pocketing her keys.

They weaved through the rows of cars with Alec in the lead. "Where did you see him?"

"Up there." She pointed at the arch. "There were other people around, but no one else seemed to notice him."

"They're not marked."

"Lucky them."

The wry glance he tossed over his shoulder brought a smile to her face.

"Ms. Hollis."

The husky, rumbling voice of Father Riesgo was unmistakable. She paused midstride and turned around, her smile widening at the sight of the approaching priest. She sensed Alec taking up a position behind her.

"Father," she greeted, finding him no less incongruent in the collar today than she had the day before.

She introduced the two men and was startled when Alec reached out his hand and spoke in a foreign language. Father Riesgo replied in the same tongue, his returning handshake firm and his green eyes sparkling.

Riesgo looked at Eve. "This must be the man who prompted you to study the church."

"Uh . . ."

"I am," Alec said, grinning wickedly.

"Excellent. Your relationship must be growing more serious." The priest glanced at Eve. "We have some wonderful couples' meetings you might enjoy."

Alec tossed an arm across her shoulders. "Eve is a bit stubborn."

"The more stubborn they are," Riesgo said easily, "the more devoted they can become. Are you here for morning mass?"

Eve shook her head. "I'm here for a different kind of research. I'm an interior designer. I was told there was a Gothic-style building around this area. Do you know of it?"

"You came to church for that?" He arched a brow. "Why not drive around and look for it?"

She glanced at Alec. His dark gaze was wickedly amused behind his shades. Eve scowled when she realized that he had no intention of helping her.

"It was his idea," she blamed, jerking a thumb toward him.

He responded by wrapping his arms around her. "It got you to church two days in a row, didn't it? I told you miracles happen."

Eve elbowed him in the gut, an act that only hurt her arm and made him laugh.

Father Riesgo smiled. "Mass begins in an hour. Hopefully you'll both be able to attend."

Waving lamely, she managed to urge Alec away.

"See?" he asked, as they left the parking lot. "No one believes you're a lost cause."

She kept walking.

"Are you giving me the silent treatment, angel?"

"I'm looking for my *friend*."

He hummed a doubtful sound and reached for her hand, linking their fingers.

As they rounded a corner and left the quieter side street for the main thoroughfare, the noise picked up appreciably, exacerbating the feeling that she was leaving safety behind and entering an unknown, dangerous new world. Cars traversed Beach Boulevard at the customary Southern California pace, a unique speed somewhere between distracted leisure and impatience. The vehicles that could have their tops down did. The rest had their windows down, allowing a steady stream of music to pour into the air in an eclectic mix of country and rap, alternative and pop.

The sky was powder blue, cloud free, and sunny. Just the right blend of warm sunlight and cool breeze . . .

A breeze that blew a noxious odor straight into Eve's face.

The stench made her nose wrinkle in protest. She couldn't describe the scent even to herself, having no point of reference for something that smelled so horrendous.

Instantly, Alec changed. His grip tightened and his casual stride, shortened to match hers, altered to a predatory deliberateness. Eve noted the change in him and felt the corresponding change in her body. Everything closed in. Narrowed. The background noises faded away, her vision sharpened, her muscles thickened. Adrenaline flowed hot and heavy through her veins. The sudden pulse of power was brutal. And arousing. Not entirely in the sexual sense.

"I smell them," she murmured, shivering. She felt as if she could run like the wind and tear a phone book apart with her bare hands.

Euphoria. That's what it was. And it was caused by aggression. How the hell did the two blend?

"Yeah." He glanced around, then gestured to a business suit–clad gentleman climbing into a Range Rover a few feet away. "There's one."

"Where's his detail?"

"Hidden beneath his clothes or hair. He's a lesser demon, hence the reason he stays in mortal guise for a full-time job."

Eve tugged on his hand, her mouth dry. He glanced at her in a distracted manner, then did a double take.

"I feel weird," she managed.

Alec gave a rumbling purr. "You look awesome. The mark is hot on you, angel."

It felt hot, too, in a wholly primitive way.

She breathed deeply, picking up a barrage of odors—exhaust fumes, heated asphalt, someone's fresh coffee, a rotting soul . . .

"German shepherd," she blurted, startled by the surety she felt in identifying the dog she smelled.

"Good job. The guy across the street with the Starbucks cup. What flavor?"

She sniffed, sifting through perfumes and fabric softeners. "None. It's black."

"Excellent." Alec jerked his chin down the street. "Can you read the headline of the newspaper in that stand?"

"No. It's lying down, smart ass." She narrowed her gaze. "But I can see that brick building about a mile away with a tiny gargoyle on the corner of the fourth floor."

He smiled. His expectation was tangible, thrumming across the space between them.

"You enjoy this," she accused, trying to ignore how infectious his excitement was.

"I'm good at it," he corrected. "Don't you enjoy being good at something, regardless of what that something happens to be?"

Eve released his hand, caught his elbow, and tugged him across the street. Two things astonished her by the time they reached the other side—one, that she'd been strong enough to veer him off course, and two, that they crossed the street before the pedestrian crossing countdown timer had ticked off more than two seconds.

No one could walk that fast. It wasn't humanly possible.

She paused, her brain trying to catch up with her body. "Whoa."

"Your Change is coming along," Alec said with his hand on her back and his gaze trained down the road. "But you'll have to learn how to keep a lid on your skills in public. We can move too fast to be seen, but it's still risky. If we aren't careful, it won't be long before we have widespread panic. Infernals feed off negativity, and they don't need any more fuel."

"It wasn't intentional."

"I know. Just sayin'."

Straightening, Eve blew out her breath. "Okay, I'm ready."

They continued at a more leisurely pace, but there was nothing else casual about them. The closer they drew to the building, the edgier she became and the more focused Alec appeared to be. Sounds and smells washed over her like lapping waves, sometimes intensely, at other times muted. The effect was disorienting and by the time they reached their destination, Eve wanted to lie down.

"It's still under construction," she said, noting that some of the upper windows still had the manufacturer's stickers on them.

"And I don't smell anything. This can't be the building."

"Alec, gargoyles aren't exactly a dime a dozen around here and the ones on this building are identical to the one I saw."

"If there was a tengu here the whole place would reek. Just like you can smell fish blocks away from a wharf."

She crossed her arms. "Okay, fine."

"Fine." He reached for the door, rattling it. "It's locked."

Eve peered through the window. The basic setup for a welcome/security desk and an occupant directory were in place but unfinished. There was a sign of some sort lying facedown inside the window. She suspected it was the property management company's contact information.

She cocked her head. "Hear that?"

"What?"

"Sounds like an air compressor." She stepped back to the very edge of the sidewalk. Leaning against a parking meter, she looked up.

"We'll need to get on the roof."

"Right, but how do we get up there?" Eve looked at him. "With a bionic leap or something?"

Alec glanced over his shoulder with a wry curve to his mouth. "No."

"Good." A sigh of relief escaped her. "I'm afraid of heights."

"We're climbing up the outside."

"Four stories?" She hugged the meter. "That's fifty-three feet above the ground. Are you insane?"

"No, I'm kidding." He winked and held out his hand. "Let's head around back and see if we can get in that way."

Growling under her breath, Eve walked past him and searched for a walkthrough that would lead them to the alley at the rear of the building. She found one just beyond the athletic shoe store, a few doors down.

After they made it to the other side, they discovered

a chain-link fence protecting a makeshift construction site at the soon-to-be entrance of a subterranean parking garage. A dozen men in tool belts and hard hats littered the area. The sign on the fence said they worked for D&L Construction.

"Looks like they have a guard at the gate," she pointed out, referencing the man with a clipboard who was checking off who entered and left.

"Is that usual for a construction site?"

"Sometimes. Depends on how hazardous the site is and the expense of the decor. You want to limit your liability against injury and prevent theft of certain decorative items." She took stock of the building again. "With this type of retro design, it makes sense that the interior would follow suit with some costly period details."

"Excuse me," Alec called out, as they approached the sentry, a rent-a-cop with a massive physique. He looked as if he might eat steroids like breath mints. "What type of building is this going to be?"

"Office space. Really nice."

"Any chance we can take a look around? I'm looking to relocate my offices."

The guard shook his head and reached into his pocket. "Sorry. You have to make an appointment with the property management company." Gray brows drew together in a frown. "I ran out of the gal's business cards. The building is attracting a lot of attention so I'm giving out a dozen or more a day. I'm betting the space will be full long before it opens."

"When is the planned opening?" Alec asked.

"I'm not sure anymore. The contractor is behind

schedule. Plumbing and electrical are still in the works."
The guard shrugged. "Hang on a minute, and I'll grab
some more cards."

The man was about to turn away when a large group
of construction workers rounded the corner in a rowdy
bunch. The fast-food cups in their hands suggested they
were returning from break.

"Sorry," he said with a grimace. "I have to check
these guys in first. We're having trouble with the time
clock, so I have to keep track of their shifts as backup."
His voice lowered. "They get pissy if their hours aren't
right, and since the foreman just left for lunch, there's
no one around to keep them in line."

Alec smiled. "I have an appointment in an hour and
I'll have to change clothes between now and then. Do
you mind if I just go grab a card myself? I'll bring you
back a stack."

Eve tried not to look too surprised. What was the
rush?

The guard's eyes glazed over. He gestured lamely
toward a nearby mobile trailer. "They're in a holder on
the foreman's desk."

"Thanks." Alec caught her arm and dragged her
through the gate.

"How the hell did you get him to let you in so easily?"

"The mark makes us . . . persuasive."

She thought of how she'd felt compelled to be with
Reed and her breath caught. "The Jedi mind trick is
cool, but what's the point in this case? We need to come
back with the Realtor."

"Not everything is a dead end. Always look for a detour."

"A business card is a detour?" She waited while Alec ascended the metal ramp and knocked on the trailer door. No one answered.

"The foreman just left for lunch, remember?" He smiled and turned the knob. "An unoccupied office filled with paperwork is a detour. Come on."

With a last, quick glance around, Eve grabbed the railing and vaulted up the ramp. She was quick, but Alec was quicker. By the time she shut the door, he was already sifting through the papers littering a large desk.

The long rectangular office space was devoid of any dividers. On the right-hand side was a small grouping of lockers and a beat-up sofa. On the left sat the desk and several metal file cabinets that were six drawers high. The walls were decorated with various blueprints of the building, and the linoleum floor was bare and badly scuffed.

"What the hell are you doing?" she demanded.

"These gargoyles look like your tengu, right?" He glanced up at her. With his sunglasses hanging on the back of his neck, he looked too relaxed to be a snoop. "Most likely they were made in the same location. Who manufactured them?"

She glanced nervously at the door. "I guess I'm the lookout?"

"No way, angel. You need to come over here and tell me where to look. All this construction/architectural stuff is familiar to you, but it's Greek to me."

Eve snorted. "Whatever. I bet you're fluent in Greek, too."

"You betcha. Now bring your hot little ass over here and help me out." He perused every inch of the room in a slow sweeping glance. "From what the guard said, it sounds as if this project has been plagued with problems—setbacks, unruly employees, malfunctioning equipment."

"It's not unusual. Some jobs are just more difficult than others."

"True. And some locations are just plagued with tengu."

"I thought you didn't believe me."

He looked at her. "Do you want to prove me wrong or not?"

"You're humoring me."

"Do you care?"

She sighed. "Who's going to be the lookout?"

Rounding the desk, she bumped him out of the way with her hip and settled into the dusty, duct-taped chair. She shook the computer mouse to wake up the system, then began to dig around the files.

"We don't have the time to waste," he said grimly. "We both need to be working. Just listen carefully. We'll hear them coming."

"Uh . . ." She frowned at the screen, her brain focused on finding what they needed as quickly as possible. "Listen?"

"Yeah." Alec moved to the filing cabinet. A moment later he asked in an amused voice, "Angel? Are you listening?"

"Huh?"

"That's what I thought. You don't multitask well."

"What?" She glanced at him. "Hush. I can't concentrate when you're talking."

He laughed.

Eve worked silently, assisted by her newly efficient body. Before being marked she would have been sweating, her heart racing, her fingers shaking. Now the only effect of their illegal activities was a powerful sense of excitement.

"I have the manufacturer's name here," she said, glancing aside at Alec. "Gehenna Masonry."

He pushed the drawer shut. "Then let's go."

There was something in his voice that disturbed her.

"What's wrong?" She closed the windows she'd opened on the computer and put it back to sleep, then she pushed back from the desk.

"That masonry. Ever heard of them?"

"Sure." Eve searched for the property management's business cards in one of three holders on the desk. They weren't there. Opening a drawer she found the box the cards came in, but it was empty aside from a "time to order more" reminder. "They're out of the biz cards."

"We got what we need." He opened the door. "I don't think the name of the masonry is a coincidence."

"Oh?" She stepped outside and breathed a sigh of relief when no one seemed to pay them any mind.

"In the Bible, Gehenna was a location near Jerusalem where forbidden religious activities were practiced. It was condemned, and became a place of punishment for sinners."

"Oh." Pausing at the end of the ramp, she looked up at the two gargoyles barely visible from her vantage point. She concentrated hard, willing her enhanced sight to kick in. Like an adjusting magnifying glass, the stone creatures came into view. They crouched, frozen, their faces carved with broad grins. And they were identical to the one that peed on her.

She sniffed the air.

Alec caught her arm and laughingly pulled her toward the gate. "You look silly."

"I'm trying to use my superpowers."

"We're done here."

They reached the gate and Eve explained to the guard that they were out of business cards. Then she and Alec started walking back toward the church.

"Be careful what you wish for," she said softly.

He looked at her. "What?"

"I'd been thinking about some kind of change in my life. Maybe a new employer, a shorter haircut, or a redesign of my condo."

"You're an adventurous woman." He shoved his hands in his pockets. "The way we got together proves that."

"I've never really thought of myself that way."

"Do you want a family?"

There was something in his tone, a kind of tense anticipation.

Her lips pursed. "This is the twenty-first century, Alec. A woman can have a successful career *and* a family."

"Don't get defensive, I'm just asking."

"I have to go into the office tomorrow," she said instead, "and hope Mr. Weisenberg hasn't fired me."

They paused at a streetlight and waited to cross.

"You want to go back to work?" Alec's brows rose above his shades. "Knowing all that you know, you're just going to go about your business? What if your boss is a Nix? Or your coworker is a succubus? You're just going to ignore that?"

"That's not funny."

"It's not meant to be." He leaned his shoulder into the lamppost and watched her. "They can smell you. They'll know what you are."

"What am I supposed to do? I have to work. I have bills to pay." Eve shoved her hands into her pockets. "Until I get called to class, I can't do anything else, right? There's no one I can talk to about getting out of this mark thing until then?"

"You can help me check out Gehenna Masonry."

"Why? You don't need me."

Alec straightened. "It's not about that. It's about right and wrong, and something is *wrong* here."

He caught her elbow and led her across the street. A group of tourists passed them, heading in the opposite direction. The women in the group stared at Alec, their heads turning to follow him with appreciative eyes.

"If I'm right about the tengu being in that building, will identifying him bring him up in the queue?" she queried. "Is taking a leak on a Mark worthy of getting your number called?"

"His number isn't up."

"Reed said there's a queue. No vigilantism."

"That's true. Now, if the tengu had tried to kill you, all bets would be off. Self-defense trumps the queue."

"So what are you doing?" she pressed.

"I'm investigating." He shrugged in a sinuous ripple of powerful muscles. "That's all."

Eve kept her eyes forward, but her thoughts were turned inward. There was a part of her that found the thought of hands-on, pounding-the-pavement research very appealing. The thrill of discovery and the sudden flash of understanding was a rush she craved. It was one of the aspects of her job that she most enjoyed—the pursuit of solutions to problems.

"You're quiet," he said, as they rounded the corner and the church came into view.

"Based on the name," she said, "what are your thoughts?"

"It's possible that when the masonry delivered the gargoyles to the construction site, they had the tengu on the truck. The one that came after you. Maybe he took a potty break while they were unloading. He might've caught wind of you, thought he'd play a bit without risk of repercussions, then rode off into the sunset."

"That's why there's no smell around here?"

"It makes the most sense. And if my theory is correct, we need to find out its final destination. Buildings with tengu have higher suicide rates than those that don't. Higher rates of business failures. Extortion. Evictions. Embezzlement. Adultery. Visit any dead mall in this country and you'll find evidence of tengu infestation. This particular tengu is bolder than most, so it's going to be more troublesome than most."

"Well, your theory also leads to speculation about how widespread this distribution might be," she added. "If you're right about the masonry being involved, it might not be a one-time thing."

"Exactly." He smiled with approval.

Eve hit the remote for her car alarm when they were several feet away, noting that many of the parking spaces were now filled. From the church, faint sounds of voices raised in song could be heard. Sprinklers sprayed the nearby lawn, casting rainbows in the mist.

One of the corner sprinkler heads was broken, creating a stream of water that snaked across the asphalt. It caught Eve's attention only because of the smoothness of the pavement, a rarity in California.

She had traveled extensively over the course of her life—family road trips when she was younger and job site visits when she was older. Nowhere else in the United States had she ever seen such bleached and cracked roads as there were in California. Repairs were made with topical applications of tar, creating a haphazard web of black over gray that was often more prominent than the painted safety lines. But not here at St. Mary's. It was another sign of the health of the church's congregation.

More than that, however, the asphalt made Eve think of her life. Over the years it, too, had lost its color. As cracks had appeared, she'd slapped a Band-Aid on them and kept on driving. Her dissatisfaction almost felt like a midlife crisis, and at twenty-eight years old it was far too soon for that.

"I'll help you," Eve blurted, meeting Alec's gaze over the roof of her car. "But only to the extent that it doesn't interfere with my work."

"Deal." The curve of his lips drew her eyes to his mouth.

Shaking her head at her preoccupation with sex, Eve pulled on the handle and stepped out of the way of the swinging car door. Her gaze dropped to the driver's seat to facilitate sliding into it and the stench of a sewer made her recoil violently. Looking for the pile of shit she must have stepped in, she found herself staring into eyes of malevolent, crystalline blue. A face. In the puddle at her feet. She screeched, kicking instinctively, causing the visage of the Nix to explode in a shower of water droplets.

As her leg came back down, the spray regrouped in a rush, forming a rope of water that wrapped around her ankle. It yanked hard. Eve fell, the ground rushing up to meet her, the Nix's face leering with such gleeful anticipation it struck terror in her soul.

CHAPTER 11

As Eve's knees buckled, she reached blindly for the car door, crying out as her forearms slammed into the thin metal lip that rimmed the top. She caught the edge with her fingertips, her body nearly dangling as water snaked around her calves and pulled at her.

Then Alec was there, catching her around the waist and chanting in a language she didn't recognize. What she did understand, however, was how furious he was. His large frame vibrated with it and his voice hummed with unmistakable menace. She kicked furiously at the puddle, her shins hitting the bottom of the door in her frenzy. The displaced water began to converge, evaporating with unnatural swiftness until it was no longer there.

"Shh," Alec murmured with his lips to her ear. "He's gone. It's okay. Calm down."

"Calm down?"

"I can't believe he came after you while I was here,"

he bit out. "He knew he didn't have the time to hurt you with me nearby. He's just terrorizing you."

She hiccuped, which brought to her attention the fact that she was crying. "*Just?* Damn it that's enough!"

"No. It's too much." He set her down and urged her toward the passenger side. "I'm driving. You're shaken up."

"I'm pissed." And she was. She was scared, yes, but she was mad as hell, too. Her forearms and shins hurt, and aggression flowed across the surface of her skin like a hot breeze.

"We need to add the Nix to our to-do list."

"You're goddamn right we— Ow! Crap!" She hissed as her mark sizzled.

"Watch it."

Alec opened the door for her, then rounded the trunk and slid behind the wheel. He moved the seat back to accommodate his longer legs, then turned the engine over and slid the transmission into reverse. "You okay?"

"No. I'm not okay."

He squeezed her knee, then tossed his arm onto her headrest. He glanced out the rear window as the car backed out of the space.

The drive to her condo was made in silence. Eve wiped her tears, examined her already healing arms, and inhaled resolve deep into her lungs. When Alec pulled into her assigned spot next to his Harley, he sat for a moment with both hands on the wheel. He stared straight ahead at the cement block wall that framed the parking garage. Eve got out.

As she passed through the archway that led to the lobby, she paused at the mailboxes and waited for Alec to catch up. He dropped her keys into her outstretched palm and she opened her box. Mail poured out and littered the marble floor. Eve cursed and pried out the rest with effort. Some of the envelopes were torn, junk mail was crushed, and there were three receipts to pick up packages that wouldn't fit in the box.

Alec whistled, his brows arching. He handed her the mail he had retrieved from the floor. "Popular gal."

"It's been over a week since I checked my box," she reminded, stepping over to the nearby trash receptacle and beginning a cursory sift through the mass. She tossed the sales flyers, coupons, and catalogs. There was a letter from her sister and she set it on top, her fingertips lingering on the paper a heartbeat longer than necessary. She saved a Del Taco flyer with a sudden appreciation of her present hunger, then she paused, unblinking.

"What?" Alec looked over her shoulder. He stilled, too. Reaching around her, he plucked the postcard from her nerveless fingers and flipped it over. "It's stamped, not bulk mail."

"Yeah." A chill swept through her, like the old saying about a ghost walking over her grave. "The date of the cancel says it was mailed the day before I was marked."

Eve took the postcard back and read the text on the reverse. It was an invitation to view the Gothic-style building infested by the tengu. Olivet Place it was called. Only the date preprinted on the card was still a few months away and the collage of photos on the front included blank sections with notes like "insert lobby photo here." It was a mock-up and should not have been mailed.

"Someone wanted me to go to that building," she said, frowning.

"Looks like."

"Why?"

"That's the question." Alec mantled her with his body and rested his chin on her shoulder. "This isn't good."

"Ya think?" She exhaled in a rush, her gaze riveted to the suddenly threatening piece of paper in her hands. "What are the chances that I would be lured to a demonic building at the same time I was marked?"

"Slim to none, I'd say." His voice was grim, his touch possessive.

"Is there any possibility that the bad guys knew ahead of time? The two events have to be connected, right? Seems like too much of a coincidence."

"There is no such thing as coincidence."

She didn't say it, but she was glad Alec was with her. Yes, he'd gotten her into this mess to begin with, but at least he was around to help her deal with the aftermath. "So what do we do?"

"Ms. Hollis?"

Eve jumped at the sound of her name. Alec turned fluidly, pushing her behind him as he faced the man who addressed her. The visitor was dressed flawlessly in a three-piece suit of dark gray, his tall and slender frame motionless with his hands clasped behind his back. His hair and eyes were as gray as his garments, and his thin lips were curved in the vaguest glimpse of a smile that did not touch the rest of his face. Behind him waited a black limousine.

"Yes?" She stepped around Alec despite his protesting murmur.

"Mr. Gadara would like to meet with you now," the man said in a voice without inflection.

"Now?"

"Yes."

"How did you get in here?" The parking garage had a gate that required a remote or a resident code to enter.

One gray brow arched. "Gadara Enterprises is the trustee of this property for your homeowners' association."

Eve glanced at Alec, whose jaw and frame were tense. "I'll need a few moments to change," she said.

"I am afraid there is no time for that," the man in gray replied, pivoting to gesture at the open rear door of the limo. "Mr. Gadara has a flight at four."

"I'm wearing wet jeans," she pointed out. She had no makeup on, her hair was in a messy ponytail, and she probably had a shiny forehead and nose. Beyond that, however, Gadara had stood her up for their last interview, so she wasn't feeling too accommodating. "I also need my portfolio."

"Mr. Gadara is familiar with your work."

"He can't expect me like this."

Gray Man said nothing, simply waited patiently.

"Okay, fine," she conceded.

"I'm coming with you." Alec's gaze never left their guest.

"That is not advised," Gray Man interjected.

Eve's gaze narrowed. "He comes if I say he comes."

"Mr. Gadara will not appreciate the request, Ms. Hollis," Gray Man drawled.

"Well, I don't appreciate the last-minute notice to go see him," she retorted.

"As you wish." Gray Man moved to reenter the limo. "I will advise him of your sentiments."

Eve made a split-second decision. She could keep protesting the crap being shoveled her way, or she could do something about it. She looked at Alec. "I have a jacket in my trunk; could you get it for me, please?"

Alec looked startled, then none too pleased with the request. "You're not going alone."

"That's fine. I knew you wouldn't like being left behind."

She glanced at Gray Man, who had paused. He didn't seem to catch her hint, but Alec's pursed lips told her he hadn't missed it. "You could toss all the mail in there, too," she suggested with a wide innocent smile. She secured her mailbox and handed him the keys.

Alec headed toward her car, glaring over his shoulder. While he was occupied with finding the right button on the remote to open the trunk, Eve slipped into the backseat of the limo. "Let's go."

Without hesitation, Gray Man climbed in and they set off. Alec shouted something after them and Eve winced inwardly. She knew he was pissed at her, but she thought it best to dance to Gadara's tune for a bit and see what "shook out," as Alec said. She'd been marked in Gadara's building, after he stood her up. Since Alec insisted that there were no coincidences, Eve thought it was necessary to go back to the beginning. If the only way to do that was to go alone, so be it. She wasn't helpless; not with her new super skills. Clueless about being marked, maybe, but not helpless. And Alec would be only a step or two behind her.

Fear didn't enter into the equation. Or maybe she

was scared to death and her brain was too scrambled by shock to notice. Without the accompanying physical reactions it was impossible to tell. She was grateful for that, since the lack of emotion kept her mind clear.

Reaching up, Eve removed the elastic restraining her hair and ran her fingers through the mass. Luckily, she had inherited her mother's thick locks, which seldom tangled too greatly.

"How did you know I wasn't at work?" she asked, taking a lame stab a conversation.

Gray Man's face split with his grimace-smile that made him look more constipated than pleasant. He said nothing.

"Is Mr. Gadara going on vacation?" she prodded. "Or is he leaving for a business trip?"

Again, nothing.

Eve refastened her hair and looked out the window at the passing scenery. Despite the uncomfortable silence, the trip to Gadara Tower passed swiftly. That was no doubt due to the traffic lights on Beach Boulevard, which stayed green for them 100 percent of the time. She had barely gathered her thoughts when the limousine drew to a halt outside the revolving front doors. Foot traffic was steady as usual.

As Eve followed Gray Man out of the car, she lamented her lack of heels and suit. She would have felt armored then. In jeans and a T-shirt—and reeking like a demon—she felt worse than naked.

They crossed the packed foyer on their way to the glass tube elevators. Unlike the last time she was here, she found the sickly sweet fragrance of the atrium flowers almost nauseating. She concentrated hard on turning off her Spider-Man sense of smell but it didn't work. And then something else drew her attention.

The door to the stairwell where she had been marked.

Memories hit her in a rapid-fire series of heated images. She could smell Reed's scent in her nostrils and feel his rough touch on her skin. The recollections were both disturbing and a turn-on.

She growled low in her throat. Her libido was now officially a royal pain in the ass.

"This way, Ms. Hollis," Gray Man said, gesturing to an elevator that was separated from the others.

Looking away from the past and ahead to the future, Eve began to notice the number of stares directed her way. They were prolific. She tugged surreptitiously at the hem of her shirt and lifted her chin. When the elevator doors closed behind her, she breathed a sigh of relief.

Gray Man inserted a key into a lock in the panel and the car shot to the top without pause. She looked down at the atrium below, watching normal-size people shrink into teeny ants. So industrious. So inconsequential. Is that what she looked like to God? Is that why he didn't care that he had set her life spinning like a top?

The elevator dinged, and the doors opened. Eve turned and found herself looking directly into a massive, well-appointed office. An intricately carved mahogany desk was angled in the far corner, facing the bank of windows on the opposite side. Two brown leather chairs faced the desk, a fire crackled in the fireplace, and a portrait of the Last Supper decorated the space above the mantel.

"Ms. Hollis. So glad you could come on such short notice."

Her head turned to find Gadara. He faced away from her, his attention on a file he read directly from a filing cabinet built into the wall. He returned the file to its place, then closed it. The drawer front settled into a clever wooden facade that looked like a wooden chest of drawers.

"Mr. Gadara."

"Please, call me Raguel." He faced her and smiled.

She had seen photos of him, but they didn't do him justice. Dressed casually in a guayabera and linen slacks, Gadara was no less imposing than he would have been in suit and tie. He was African American, his skin espresso dark, his salt-and-pepper hair cropped short, his cheekbones dotted with sunspots. His eyes were dark and ancient.

He assessed her from head to toe, then gave a nod that seemed approving. "I apologize for missing our last appointment."

Her mouth curved slightly. He couldn't sound less apologetic if he tried.

Gadara's eyes narrowed when she did not reply. "Do you still want the job?"

"The position as described would be a dream come true. I'm sure you know that."

He gestured toward one of the chairs set before his desk. When she was seated, he rounded the corner and settled opposite her. His pose was deceptively relaxed, as if this was a social visit. He had one ankle crossed over the opposite knee and his forearms rested lightly on the armrests. But his gaze was as sharp as a hawk's and when he picked up a remote control from his desktop, she grew wary.

"I am not certain breaking into my construction site

today was advisable then," he drawled, pushing a button that lowered a screen over the windows, blocking out the light and providing the canvas for a projection.

As images of her accessing the computer at the tengu site flashed in guilty testimony, Eve froze.

Gadara smiled. "I could have you arrested."

She pulled herself together. "If you wanted to do that, you would have done so already."

"True."

"So what do you want?"

His voice came with a sharp edge. "I want you to do your job the way you are supposed to."

Eve's erratic emotions kicked in with gusto. Her mouth spit out words before her brain fully caught on. "I don't work for you—*yet*—Mr. Gadara."

"You have been working for me for eight days now, a circumstance I am beginning to regret."

"Eight days?" She stood, unable to contain her sudden restlessness. She wasn't anxious so much as antagonized, and she was quickly learning that her new disposition didn't take well to antagonism.

"You are a loose cannon, Ms. Hollis, and that is the last thing I need in my firm."

"Your *firm*?"

Eve remembered her conversation with Reed at the beach. *Think of it as a bail bond agency. An archangel becomes responsible for bringing them in—like a bail bondsman.*

Was Gadara the archangel? She suddenly felt dizzy.

The phone on Gadara's desk beeped a subdued tone. He picked up the receiver. "Yes?" Satisfaction lit his dark eyes. "Send him in."

Glancing at the door, Eve fully expected Alec to

enter, yet she was still oddly surprised when he did. Over six feet of aggravated, windblown male.

"Raguel," he barked, tossing a dark glare at Eve. "I don't appreciate you sending for my Mark without me."

"I wanted to see if she would defy you, Cain, and if you would be able to stop her if she did. Regrettably, you both failed to follow orders."

The screen retracted into the ceiling and the dimmed lights brightened. But not before Alec caught a glimpse of the matinee.

"You better find a tactic beyond intimidation," Alec warned. "That might work on other novices, but not this one."

She glanced back and forth between the two, feeling like she was myopic and unable to see the picture everyone else was looking at. However, one thing was painfully clear—Alec and Gadara knew each other quite well. Which couldn't be good.

"What's going on?" she queried.

"You violated one of the most basic tenets of initiation," Gadara said to Alec. "Taking a Mark out in the field prior to training—"

"We weren't in the field."

Gadara stood, thrusting both hands down on the table. The sudden break in his nonchalance was frightening. "Bullshit. She stinks like demon. Whether the assignment was sanctioned or not is moot."

"I can't leave her alone; Infernals are all over her. She's too vulnerable."

"You should have asked her handler for help."

"I would have, if I'd known who it is."

"I thought that was obvious. Abel will manage her."

"Are you shitting me? After the way he marked her?"

"Perhaps you would like to watch the tape?" Gadara asked silkily. "The marking was not as one-sided as you might choose to believe."

"There's a tape?" Eve croaked, knowing she'd be blushing to the roots of her hair if her physical reactions worked the way they used to.

Alec growled, his fists clenching. "I'll take you down, Raguel. I'm not one of your pawns."

"No." Gadara smiled. "But *she* is."

Alec tensed.

Eve stepped up. "I want that tape."

"He's got your life in his hands," Alec bit out, "and you want a sex tape?"

"Yeah." She scowled at Gadara. "If you don't want me around, let me go. I won't complain."

"He's not going to do that." Alec's tone was too subdued.

"How do you know?"

"Because you and I are a package deal, and having God's personal enforcer on his team is a coup he wouldn't give up for anything."

"Damn it!" she groused. "You are more trouble than you're worth, you know that?"

"I come with benefits, if you get around to using them. Besides, the best he can do is transfer you to another firm. Only God can free you completely."

Eve pinned Gadara with a sharp glare. "I hate being in the dark. Explain the firm to me."

Gadara gestured toward her vacated seat. "Sit down, Ms. Hollis, and I will explain—" he looked at Alec "—since your mentor has yet to."

"Save your breath," Alec said dryly. "You can't put a wedge between us." He tugged the second chair closer to hers and sank into it. He caught her hand and held it.

Gadara stared at the display of affection and settled back in his seat as if they had all the time in the world. "Just as Hell has various kings—"

"—Heaven has kingpins," Alec finished.

"I resent that term," Gadara complained.

"If the shoe fits . . ."

"It does not."

"Uh-huh . . ."

Eve squeezed Alec's hand in warning. "Keep going."

Gadara's brow arched at her tone. "The mark system is vast. It needs to be organized and self-sufficient. In order to accomplish that, capitalist ventures were launched that generated the income required to support a large number of Marks and their various activities within existing mortal society. Some ventures were more successful than others. In the end, seven of us rose to prominence. We are loosely divided by the seven continents, but we coordinate often, and those with larger areas share their burdens with those with smaller areas. For example, the African and Antarctica firms work in tandem." He smiled, his teeth brilliantly white against the darkness of his skin. "I am responsible for the North American Marks. All twenty thousand of them."

"Oh my God— Ouch!" She winced as her mark burned.

"Watch it," the two men said in unison.

"So every one of those people in the atrium are Marks?" she muttered, setting her hand over her arm.

"That's why it reeks like the floor was washed in perfume?"

"Some of the people out there are mortals we do business with."

"What about you?"

"I am an archangel, Ms. Hollis."

She considered that a moment, then thought it best to question Alec about Gadara and not Gadara himself. "So I was assigned to your firm because I'm from North America?"

"No." Gadara's voice had a soothing, hypnotic quality. The more he spoke, the dreamier she felt. "Usually Marks are transplanted to make the transition easier. It is less traumatic to start a new life when you are not hampered by the old."

"Why wasn't that done with me?"

"Because of him." The archangel motioned toward Alec with an elegant flick of his wrist. "He tried to get you released. When his request was denied, he asked that you be kept close to your family. I suspect he extorted someone somewhere to get what he wanted."

Eve's gaze turned to Alec, who looked straight ahead with his jaw visibly clenched. Her eyes stung.

"Quite a sacrifice," Gadara purred. "Banished all these years and forced to roam. He could have uprooted you to his homeland. I am certain he misses it."

"Shut up," Alec rumbled. "You don't know what you're talking about."

Her grip tightened on his hand in silent gratitude. "What happens now?"

"You work for me. Your resignation at The Weisenberg Group was effective yesterday after a week's notice. Occasionally, your secular talents will be put to good use, but for the most part, your job is to train to the best of your ability and listen to your mentor, your handler, and me."

"I listen to my gut," she said. She wasn't a believer and thought she should put that out there right away.

"I will not tolerate insubordination," he retorted.

"Fine." Eve shrugged. "Just so we're clear."

Gadara's mouth curved in blatant challenge. The predatory expression didn't suit him. He was far too refined, his voice too cultured, and his words too precise. "What were you looking for this afternoon?"

"A tengu."

Gadara's eyes widened. Alec explained. By the time he finished, Gadara was visibly upset.

"I thought you cared more about your novice," the archangel chastised. "It was not your place to risk her so foolishly."

"What risk?" Alec snorted. "She's already been pissed on and threatened twice. There was more risk in doing nothing at all. And I told you, I can't leave her alone. The Nix knows where she lives."

"You are her mentor. If you wish to allow your feud with your brother to jeopardize your novice, far be it from me to intercede." Gadara's eyes took on an icy glint. "Proceed with your investigation, then. See it to its conclusion, including eradicating the threat."

Eve frowned.

Alec exhaled harshly. "You want to assign her before she's trained? No way."

"It is your choice, Cain. Allow your brother to do his job or you will have to do it for him."

"This isn't your call. Abel is the only one who can assign her to a mission."

Gadara laughed, a deep rolling sound. It was oddly pleasant, considering it wasn't meant to be. "He is a company man, something you would do well to emulate."

"You're both violating protocol." Alec's tone was almost a snarl. "I expect that of you, but Abel? He's never broken a rule in his life. You accuse me of putting her in danger, while Abel is ready to hang her out to dry?"

"It is perfectly acceptable to continue a deviation once it has been set in motion, if proceeding is the only reasonable course."

"Eve and I didn't deviate."

"That is debatable, is it not? I doubt either of us wants to take this upstairs, where we could both face penalties. Better to deal with this on our own, agreed?"

Pushing to his feet, Alec towered over the desk. Although Gadara seemed unaffected, Eve noted the deepening grooves around his mouth and eyes.

Gadara feared Alec. She tucked that information away for future use.

"How is sending an untrained Mark on a hunt the 'reasonable course?' " Alec asked with intemperate frustration.

"If the Infernals think she is hiding or that we are protecting her, they will go after her with a vengeance. With you as her mentor, she needs to be tougher than the average Mark. We cannot afford for her to look weak or frightened. We need to start as we mean to go on."

"No."

Eve stood. "I can handle it."

Alec's dark head swiveled toward her. "Angel—"

"I've got this." She looked at Gadara. It wasn't just the Infernals that needed to know she was tough.

"Good girl," Gadara murmured approvingly.

"Don't talk down to me," she warned. "Anything else I should know? Or can I go? It's been a long week."

Gadara reached into a drawer and withdrew a set of keys. He tossed them to her. "Those will give you access to this building and to your office. All of your belongings from your old employer were moved here. You will be paid by direct deposit and an expense account has been created for you."

"What are my hours?"

"They are 24/7. The office is a front; you will need it as part of your cover, but the field is where you will do the majority of your work. Your household expenses— mortgage, automobile, utilities, and so on—will be managed by the firm. You have also been tasked with the renovation of one of my casinos in Las Vegas. But we have several months before we get to that."

Eve was so stunned it took her a moment to reply. "And here I thought only the devil traded dreams for souls."

"Who do you think taught him everything he knows?" He lifted the lid of a wooden box on his desktop and withdrew a cigar. "All that you will need has been placed in your condominium."

"You had someone in my house?" Her foot tapped rapidly on the carpet. "I don't suppose your affiliation with my homeowners' association is a coincidence?"

"There is no such thing as coincidence, Ms. Hollis."

Alec caught her elbow. "We're done here, then."

"Not so fast," she muttered. "I want that tape."

"And I want world peace," Gadara replied. "I would also like to smoke this cigar, but my body is a temple. We do not always get what we want."

"We'll see about that." Eve smiled grimly and headed toward the elevator.

"Cain."

A shiver moved through her at the sound of Alec's name spoken in that cultured voice. The infamous Cain. Everyone knew his story. But having met both brothers, she knew there was far more to the tale than the few brief paragraphs mentioned in the canonized bible.

Alec paused. "Yes?"

"I have been authorized to credit you for every vanquishing, in consideration of your added responsibility as Ms. Hollis's mentor. Double the indulgences should cut your service in half, if you play your cards right."

The terrible stillness that gripped Alec alarmed Eve. She set her hand lightly on his hip. He caught and held it tightly.

"This isn't a game," he bit out.

"A turn of phrase," Gadara said. "Nothing more."

"Alec?" Eve murmured when he continued to stare, unmoving.

He shook his head as if in disgust, then continued to the elevator, pulling her with him.

When the doors closed behind them, Eve linked her fingers with his. She opened her mouth to speak, then her gaze lifted to the camera in the corner. She held her tongue until they exited the building.

The moment they breathed smog instead of Mark emanations, Eve blurted, "Double the indulgences."

166 S. J. DAY

She fought an inconvenient urge to laugh hysterically. "He's bribing you."

"It's not going to work."

"It has to be tempting."

"Angel." His tone was as sharp as the look he gave her. "It's not going to work. Period."

"You called him a kingpin. Like the mafia?"

"You heard him and saw how he works. They're all like that. We always get a choice, but that doesn't mean the options are equal or favorable."

"So the picture he presented of seven head honchos working harmoniously together was crap?"

"I'd say they work together about as well as Democrats and Republicans." He unfastened the passenger helmet from the back of his bike, then freed her hair of its ponytail. "And they're just as politically minded."

"Lovely."

After settling the helmet on her head, Alec adjusted the strap beneath her chin. He kissed the tip of her nose. "Those in favor get bigger perks."

"Whatever he has against you is personal." She wasn't asking a question. "Because of me, you've played right into his hands."

Alec mounted the bike. Eve hopped on behind him and wrapped her arms around his waist. "The only person who's got their hands on me is you," he said over the rumbling of the engine.

"You'll have to come up with a better explanation than that," she shouted.

"I know." He rolled the hog back, his powerful thighs flexing against hers. "But not here."

They roared out of the parking lot.

CHAPTER 12

As Reed stepped onto the roof of Gadara Tower, he slipped his shades over his eyes and took in the majestic view. A helicopter waited on the nearby heliport, its blades still and shining in the late afternoon sun. A sliver of ocean was visible from this vantage point and the reflection of sunlight on nearby building windows made the sunny day even brighter. A breeze ruffled his hair, caressed his nape, and filled his nostrils with air untainted by the stench of Infernals.

"Abel."

His head turned to find Raguel exiting the stairwell to the rooftop. The man was dressed for the tropics with a straw hat on his head and leather sandals on his feet. An unlit cigar hung between his lips and his stride was elegantly unhurried.

"Raguel." Reed extended his hand and it was clasped in a firm, warm hold.

The archangel pulled the cigar free and said, "You were right. Cain had yet to explain to Ms. Hollis."

Pushing his hands into his trouser pockets, Reed smiled. Eve had been brought up to speed, which meant life was about to get a lot more interesting. "Excellent. When does the next training rotation start?"

"*When* she begins training depends on your brother. He has begun an investigation into a tengu infestation at one of my developing properties. It is a concern to me, so I have asked him to see the investigation through."

"What does that have to do with Eve?"

"Since he refuses to rely on you for Ms. Hollis's care while he proceeds, we will have to wait for them to finish."

"*Them?* You expect Eve to help him in the field?"

"Cain refused to have it any other way."

"That isn't Cain's decision to make."

"No. It was mine."

Reed paused midstep. Raguel continued a few steps before he realized he was alone. He turned around.

"You *assigned* Eve?" Reed was startled more by the roiling emotions he felt than by the blatant deviation from protocol. "Without consulting me?"

Eve was a member of Raguel's firm, yes, but assigning her to a mission was a prerogative that fell squarely and solely within Reed's purview. He liked rules. Perhaps even relished them. It was easier to exceed expectations when one knew what those expectations were. And with Eve, his position as her handler was his sole stanchion in a dynamic of two. He was wedging his way in as the third wheel and he wasn't going to give up his grip without a fight.

Raguel shrugged. "A bit presumptuous, perhaps, but I knew you would agree."

"I don't."

"Oh?" Raguel's brows rose. "What better way to teach your brother to work within the system?"

"What about Eve?"

"What about her?"

"Don't be dense," Reed bit out. "With Cain's scent all over her, she needs to be at the top of her game, not dangling from the bottom rung."

Rocking back on his heels, Raguel grinned. "You say that with such venom, as if the thought of your brother with Ms. Hollis is offensive to you."

"Ridiculous," Reed scoffed. "This has nothing to do with Cain and everything to do with my responsibility as Eve's handler. I don't like to lose Marks."

"This has everything to do with Cain and nothing to do with Ms. Hollis," Raguel countered, gesturing to the helicopter pilot with an impatient wave of his hand. "She is a means to an end. Her purpose is to act as a stick to prod your brother into line."

Reed's fists clenched within his pockets. "Did that come from above? Or from you?"

"It came from common sense." The helicopter's engine whined into motion, its blades whistling through the air in a rapidly increasing tempo. "Cain is a hazard if he does not learn to toe the line."

"He's incorrigible. You think you can succeed where Jehovah hasn't? Your head's getting too big."

"Not at all." Raguel smiled. "You are simply underestimating Ms. Hollis and her effect on your brother."

"You're thinking of her as a woman, not as a Mark."

"So are you."

Reed ignored the jibe. "I'm pulling her off the mission. She needs to be properly trained."

"You do that, and I will transfer Ms. Hollis to another firm and handler."

"Bullshit. You wouldn't pass Cain over for something so insignificant."

"Are you willing to gamble on that?" Raguel yelled, his voice carrying on the wind created by the revolving blades. "He might be less trouble screwing up another firm."

"Screwing up? He has a 100 percent success rate."

"Not for much longer if he disregards you as handler and manages Ms. Hollis by himself. One of them will be killed. As high profile as he is, the loss of him or his Mark under my watch would ruin centuries of prestige. I will not allow it."

Reed's jaw tightened. "You can't expect me to follow the rules if you don't."

"The three of you will be the death of either me or yourselves." Raguel stepped closer until only an inch or two separated them. "Whatever interest you have in Ms. Hollis, I suggest you keep it strictly professional. You have been given an unassailable position of power over your brother through Ms. Hollis. Keeping them together should be your priority. Now, I have to get to the airport to catch my flight. If you still have reservations when I return, we can discuss it further at that time."

"She might be dead by then."

"If that is God's will." Clutching his hat to his head, Raguel ran the distance to the chopper and climbed in.

God's will. Reed spit the bile out of his mouth. God's hand was far from this, separated from the mechanics by layers of seraphim, hashmallim, and angels. For some time now, Reed had begun to wonder if there was a lesson to be learned in the distance between Jehovah and the world. Perhaps it was to remind them that they couldn't hack it on their own. He tried to tell himself that the purpose was edifying—the harder they worked, the more they would appreciate the fruit of their labors. But truly, machinations like this always tested his faith.

"Damn you, Cain."

Once again his brother was disrupting the order of things, and Reed was expected to bend and adjust to make it work.

As the helicopter lifted into the air, Reed's mind sifted through the moves available to him with the same fury with which the wind whipped through his hair. He wanted another round with Eve, but making that move could push Cain completely out of the picture and without Cain, Reed would lose his chance to achieve his ambitions.

He couldn't let that happen. This was his best opportunity to further his long-held position that he was ready for advancement to archangel.

Reed knew, without any doubt, that he could manage a firm and manage it well. The world's population had grown exponentially. The existing seven firms were overtaxed, understaffed, and the archangels heading them were overappreciated because of it. They lusted for God's approval and infighting was rampant. Expansion was needed and Reed was determined to step into play when it happened.

Fucking Eve was hot as hell, but the pleasure was fleeting. If he kept his dick away from her, he could enjoy the extended satisfaction of governing something that Cain thought belonged solely to him.

He shouldn't be conflicted at all. There was no contest between the two options—Eve or the realization of all his goals.

"Eve," he growled, running his hands through his hair.

She was as helpless and vulnerable as a field mouse and Infernals were circling her like ravenous hawks. Hell, *he* was circling her.

Beware of the apples.

He should have foreseen how this would turn out when she gave him that scorching look in the lobby that first day.

Shit.

Reed spun on his heel and left the roof.

Alec pulled to a stop at a red light and balanced his bike with one leg on the ground. Because of Raguel's thirst for God's approval, Alec had known it would be risky to keep Eve close to home, but he never thought Raguel would risk her deliberately. If he'd even suspected that as a possibility, he would have requested a different firm. Antarctica, perhaps. Or Australia.

His knuckles whitened on the handlebars. He was being leashed by the one thing that he gave a damn about, which left him cornered, trapped between a disapproving God, an antagonistic brother, and an overly ambitious archangel who would do anything to achieve his aims. And Eve. Sassy, sexy Eve was the glue holding it all together.

Raguel assumed Alec wanted to shed the mark and

return to a normal life. That was his biggest miscalculation. He thought the lure of double indulgences and the freedom they implied would be irresistible. He didn't understand that Alec had one skill, one talent—killing. Alec could no more turn his back on that and live a "normal" life, than he could stop loving Evangeline Hollis. But his ambition to head his own firm was a secret no one knew. He kept it close to his heart, hidden until the day he could present it as more than a pipe dream.

Eve.

Despite the volatility of his thoughts, nothing could fully distract him from the feel of her soft, warm body wrapped around his back. She was so delicate and fragile. He would have to train her himself for now, a solution that was less than perfect. He'd worked alone for so long. He had no idea where to begin, what to focus on, or . . . anything. He was completely clueless.

Eve tapped him on the thigh and shouted to be heard over the rumbling of the engine. "Go home. I want to check on my mom."

Home. With Eve. His mouth quirked with morbid humor. The part of him that wasn't homicidal was deeply enamored with that dream.

He nodded. When the traffic light changed, he altered his direction and headed for Eve's place. This time, he didn't need to wait for a resident to follow into the parking garage. Eve typed in the code and he rolled into the spot adjacent to the one that held her car. His and hers. The act of taking the place reserved for the significant other in her life affected him in an unexpected way—he grew hard. Dismounting from the bike became a difficult task, but he managed.

The knowledge that their time together was temporary . . . the threats against her . . . the fear that he might not be enough to save her . . . the pheromones her mark exuded . . . His body responded with a primitive desire to claim what was his. When she pulled the helmet off her head and shook out her hair, it was like waving a cape before a raging bull. He struggled against the sudden ferocious need to pin her to the wall and ride her to the finish. He backed away, putting distance between them.

She glanced at him and stilled. He watched the heat he felt spread to her, igniting her dark eyes with a sexual hunger that might match his. This wasn't the timid, inexperienced girl he had loved ten years ago. That girl had quivered when he touched her and cried when he kissed her. The woman who eyed him now made *him* quiver.

Eve locked the strap of her helmet to the backrest loop on his bike and muttered, "Catch me."

That was the only warning he got before she launched herself at him. As slight as she was, the mark gave her force and velocity. He stumbled back at the impact, his keys and helmet crashing to the cement floor. Her legs circled his hips, her arms wrapped around his neck. Her mouth met his without finesse, her soft lips slanting across his with a desperation that stole both his breath and his wits.

She tightened her thighs, levering up, forcing his neck back so that she hovered over him. Her position of dominance rocked him so hard there was no way they were going to make it upstairs before he got inside her. The scent of her lust was heady, sweeping through his senses and across his skin. There was no other fragrance in the world like it, the sensual fragrance of cherries, sweet and ripe. The mark intensified the smell, made it more luxurious, like whipped cream on top.

He gripped her ass with one hand and fisted the other into the thick silk of her hair. As Eve writhed over him, he tore his mouth away, gasping. In response, her fingers tangled in his locks and commanded his attention. His gaze was snared by hers. She was as hot for it as he was, but the determined glint in her eyes told him she wasn't yet completely lost to lust.

Alec set his mind to making her that way. He released her hair and cupped her breast, kneading the full weight, groaning in pleasure as her nipple hardened between the clasp of his fingertips.

Eve leaned closer, their harsh breaths mingling, her tresses shielding their faces in an ebony curtain. "Someone's watching us, right?" she whispered. "And listening?"

"What?" He urged her lower, notching the heated juncture between her thighs against his aching cock. He stroked her along his length. She took over, gyrating fluidly against him, making him shudder.

"My condo," she persisted, her eyes feverishly bright. "The common areas. Cameras. Microphones. There is no privacy anywhere, am I right? Gadara is watching and listening."

Reality pierced through the haze of his desire. "Probably." He remembered that Raguel was trustee of the community and growled, "Most likely. Yes."

"We can't talk freely."

"Who wants to talk?"

The clearing of a throat behind them jerked them

both to an awareness of how public their ardor was. Their heads turned in unison to find Mrs. Basso standing by the mailboxes. She was facing away from them, awkwardly struggling with the lock to her box, but it was obvious she'd seen more than any of them wanted her to see.

"Put me down," Eve hissed.

Alec set her on her feet. "If the kiss didn't shock Mrs. Basso, my raging hard-on might do it."

Eve smacked him. "Behave."

"*You* attacked *me,* angel."

She winked. "Made you smile."

He stared at her a moment, lost in a déjà vu moment from a decade before. He laughed softly.

"I'm losing my touch," he drawled, adjusting himself in an unsuccessful bid for comfort. "You were thinking about Gadara while making out with me."

"I heard the camera move."

Alec paused at that. He wasn't too surprised that he hadn't heard anything. Disgruntled, yes, but not surprised. For the first time in his life, he'd been given something he wanted and he was enjoying her to the fullest. It was Eve's precise hearing that made the statement arresting. "You heard the camera move," he repeated.

Her smile was wicked. "I guess we didn't quite reach the brain cell frying point."

"Next time," he promised, bending down to collect his helmet and keys. "You're a smart cookie, angel. Turns me on."

"What if I didn't have a fondness for James Bond and Jason Bourne? I'd be giving Pamela Anderson a run for the money in the sex tape department."

He took the hit. It stung, but it was true. "I've never mentored before. I'm learning as I go."

"Great."

"I'm a quick study." He glanced toward the lobby. Mrs. Basso was gone.

"You better be." Sighing, she moved to the trunk of her car and opened it, retrieving her mail from earlier. "Or else we're a sorry-assed pair."

Alec grinned. There'd be no hysterics or drama from Eve. Bless her.

"Let's go. We have a lot of work to do." She headed toward the elevator with a determined stride. "And I have to think of something to say to my neighbor. How embarrassing is that?"

"Maybe she'll act like nothing happened." He followed, studying the way she moved and cataloging the self-defense techniques she might excel at. She had long, lithe legs and a hint of defined biceps. He thought kick-boxing might be good for a start.

"Ugh. I hate when people do that," she complained. "I'd rather just get it out in the open and clear the air."

Hard-charging, he thought fondly. That was his angel.

A soft mechanical whirring followed them, the sound of surveillance cameras keeping them doggedly in sight.

"Mom?" Eve called out as she pushed the door open.

"She's not here," her mother called back.

Relief filled her. She smiled at Alec, who just shook his head. As he set his helmet and keys on the console by the door, there was a sparkle of amusement in his eyes, but nothing could hide the set of his shoulders. They seemed weighted by the world.

Miyoko appeared from the hallway. Her feet were encased in Hello Kitty house slippers, her hair was in pigtails, and her arms were filled with freshly washed laundry. She looked like a teenager. "Are you hungry?"

Eve's stomach growled its assent. "Lately, I'm always hungry."

"Maybe you're pregnant."

"Mom!" Her protest was weak, her startled gaze moving to Alec. She'd missed taking her birth control pills for a week while she acclimated to the mark, and they'd burned up the sheets for hours . . .

Alec's jaw clenched. He gave a curt shake of his head. But how could he be sure?

It wasn't a question she could ask now.

"Unless you're a nun or sterile," her mother said, "it's possible."

Eve went to the kitchen. Decades of work as a registered nurse had made Miyoko brutally blunt when it came to discussing health matters. Setting her mail on the counter, Eve grabbed a soda from the fridge and wished a shot of rum would be worth the effort of pouring. Then she thought of babies and the effect of alcohol on them. She returned the soda to the fridge and grabbed a single-serving orange juice instead.

"Don't leave those letters there," her mother said, dropping the laundry on the couch before joining Eve in the kitchen.

"It's my house, Mom," Eve retorted, twisting the cap open and drinking deeply.

"Who cleans it?"

"Who asked you to? I keep my house clean, and I'm an adult. Don't act like I can't survive without you."

Miyoko's face turned into a mask. "I know you don't need me. You never have."

Alec walked into the kitchen. "How about I make some sandwiches?" he offered.

"I made *onigiri*," her mother said tightly.

"Wonderful." Alec set his hand on the curve of Eve's waist. His voice was low and even in an attempt to soothe ruffled feathers. "I love *onigiri*."

So did Eve, which is probably why her mother had made the little rice "balls" to begin with. Steamed rice flavored with various sprinkled seasonings called *furikake* were shaped into triangular patties. Eve had grown up on them, and they'd always been a relished treat.

Closing her eyes, Eve exhaled slowly. She hated feeling defensive around her mother. After all these years, she should be able to brush off the occasional pointing out of her shortcomings, but her mother had always been able to trigger volatile responses in her. One moment condescending and critical, the next cheerful and praising. Eve knew their chafing was due partly to culture clash. Her mother had come to the States in her midtwenties and she returned to Japan for annual visits. While she was a naturalized American citizen now, Miyoko was still a Japanese woman at her core.

"I'm sorry, Mom," Eve said, setting her drink down and leaning heavily into the counter. Not for the first time, she made a small wish for a smoother relationship with her own children when she had them. "I'm having a really bad day. I appreciate everything you do."

Her mother stood there for the length of several heartbeats, her small frame tense with indignation and hurt. "Does your crabby mood have something to do with your new job?"

"How did you know about that?" Eve was superstitious—she didn't like to share anything good that wasn't a sure thing.

"I'm your mother. I know things."

Eve groaned inwardly.

"Someone stopped by while we were gone?" Alec asked, reaching into the container on the counter and pulling out a rice cake liberally sprinkled with beef-steak *furikake*. He handed it to Eve, then picked out another wrapped in seasoned *nori*—seaweed—for himself.

"Yes. Two young men. They left a briefcase and a box for you."

Straightening, Eve asked, "Where is it?"

"I put it in your office."

"Did they say anything?"

"They were very nice." Miyoko managed a smile. "I made some coffee, and they talked a little about Mr. Gadara's accomplishments. It sounds like a wonderful opportunity for you."

Eve shivered at the thought of Gadara's men around her mother, charming and impressing her. Winning her over. Snakes in the grass.

"So it that why you're grumpy?" her mother repeated. "Changing jobs is one of the most stressful events a person can go through. You need to take more vitamin B."

"That's part of it." All of it. She glanced at Alec, who eyed her orange juice with odd intensity.

"You didn't tell me you were thinking about quitting." Miyoko's tone was peeved.

"I didn't want to jinx it. Working for Gadara Enterprises is a monster leap, and I wasn't sure I would make it. Besides, I only had an interview."

"And it turned into an offer?" Her mother wiped the spotless counter with a dishtowel. "You shouldn't be so surprised. You're beautiful and smart. Anyone would be lucky to have you."

Eve's irritation fled completely. "Thank you."

Miyoko shrugged. "It's the truth. Is he Jewish? Or Middle Eastern?"

"Gadara? He's African-American. Why?"

"His name. It's in the Bible."

"It is?" She glanced at Alec, who was reaching for another *onigiri*.

"Gadara is the place where Christ turned demons into swine," he explained before taking a bite.

"Did he pick that himself?"

"Who picks their own name?" Miyoko shook her head. "Aside from celebrities. Anyway, I'm going to finish the laundry and go home."

"Is Dad coming back today?"

"Tomorrow, but there are things I have to do."

Eve sighed, feeling terrible for having hurt her mother's feelings. "I wish you would stay."

"You have a guest. You don't need me."

"I don't have to need you to want you around, Mom."

"Not today." Miyoko rounded the island the opposite way and returned to the living room. She sat on the couch and folded laundry.

Alec rubbed between Eve's shoulder blades. "You okay?"

"No. My life sucks."

"I can help you forget about it for a while," he purred softly.

She pivoted and faced him head on. Her mouth opened, then shut again. The kitchen wasn't the place to talk about sex and the inevitable ramifications of it. Her hand fisted in his shirt and she tugged him to her office.

"I'm sterile," he said curtly before she could speak.

She gaped. Alec was the most virile man she'd ever come across. "W-what?"

"I watched you exchange the soda for orange juice. You're not pregnant."

Hurt straightened her spine. He said the words with such finality, his dark gaze cold and remote, his lips thinned.

"God forbid, right?" Her mouth curved in a mocking smile. "You wouldn't want the complication, I'm sure."

"Don't tell me what I want," he snapped. "There is nothing Heaven or Hell can dish out that is as painful as the loss of a child. Still, I might go through it again for you. But there's no chance, Eve."

"Why?"

"I almost lost my mind when the last of my children died. I said things to God that I regret. I couldn't understand why I had to be punished in that way, too. Why I had to live interminably while my children lived mortal lives."

Her throat clenched in sympathy. "Alec . . ."

"God *did* forbid it, angel." His arms crossed. "The mark sterilizes everyone now. Female Marks don't menstruate and the males shoot blanks."

Time froze for a moment, then rushed at Eve in a deluge. Years of dreams and hopes washed over her in a flood of tears that escaped in a hot stream down her face. "Will I get it back?"

"I don't know. Eve—" His entire frame vibrated. If she breathed deep enough, she could smell the turbulence in him. Alec was a man who felt as if every move he made was the wrong one. Another mistake in a lifetime of mistakes. He was passionate, impulsive, and headstrong.

But could she blame him for what was happening to her? He couldn't have foreseen how the decisions he made for himself would impact others. Bad shit happened to people. Rapes, beatings, muggings, abuse . . . and countless other horrifying things. Miscarriages, accidents, starvation. But being a victim was a choice one made, and Eve refused to be a victim.

"Angel?" Alec stepped closer, a move that was jerky instead of his usual graceful prowl.

"Give me a minute." She turned away to wipe her tears and was arrested by the tall, exceptionally dressed figure lounging in the doorway.

"Rough day, babe?" Reed murmured, his gaze examining her closely.

"It keeps getting better." She swiped impatiently at her cheeks.

"How can I help?"

"Get the fuck out," Alec snarled. "You've done enough damage."

"You only wish you could toss me out," Reed retorted.

Eve's circumstances were what they were. Everything happened for a reason. She didn't need to be religious to believe that. And it would take more energy to bitch than it would to do something about it. Instead of feeling crushed, her determination was strengthened. One thing at a time.

Figure out the tengu.

Deal with the Nix.

Lose the mark.

It was all doable.

"I'm going to take a shower," she said, wanting out of her jeans, which were stiffened by the dried water from the Nix. "Then I'm going to do some online sleuthing in regards to Gehenna Masonry. You boys can either kill each other, or help my mom fold laundry."

They stared.

"Or cook dinner, if you know how. I'm starved." She waved over her shoulder on the way out the door.

CHAPTER 13

Eve stared at her computer monitor with focused intensity. She had allowed herself a good, hard cry in the shower—a shower that now had an aluminum cross dangling from the showerhead. She, a lifelong agnostic, now had a cross hanging in her shower and the Mark of Cain on her arm.

Laughter at her situation had come first, then the tears that wouldn't stop. She let it all out, her frustration and anger, her sadness and worry. She was pretty sure she cried more tears than she ever had in her entire life. And then she told herself that was all the self-pity she was going to wallow in. It took too much out of her.

But the aftermath wasn't pretty. She felt wrung out like a dish towel. Both Reed and Alec watched her with guilt and wariness. She'd finally retreated to her office to save them all the discomfort.

Reed had folded laundry with her mom, while Alec made a thick hearty stew for dinner. Miyoko insisted on cutting vegetables and offering spice suggestions, then she left for home with obvious reluctance. Stubborn to the last. Eve fully expected a phone call tomorrow, asking why Reed—her supervisor—would come over for dinner and fold her clothes. She hoped she had a good excuse by then.

Presently, she was using Google in her search for information about Gehenna Masonry. She had been distracted for a time by a brief search of Meggido Industries. It existed. And Alec was listed as the CEO and founder. The name "Meggido" also came up as a location better known as Armageddon. Alec had called himself a headhunter specializing in disaster avoidance. She had to laugh at his twisted sense of humor.

"What's so funny?" Reed asked.

Eve glanced up and discovered him lounging in the doorway as he'd been when he first arrived. It was an insolent pose with his hands in his pockets and his pale blue dress shirt open at the throat. The room was dark, which allowed backlighting from the hallway to turn his silhouette into a dangerously compelling form.

She shrugged in feigned nonchalance. No matter what he did or said, she couldn't dispel the memories of their encounter. "Nothing. What's up?"

"What's up with you?"

"I'm researching the mason who created the tengu." Eve's gaze returned to the monitor.

"How's it coming?"

"Fine. It's hard to know if you've found what you're looking for when you don't know what it is." She watched him enter the room with that delicious stride that was just short of a swagger. The brothers moved so differently, yet they affected her equally. "Where's Alec?"

"Checking the balcony for any water leaks."

"Because of the Nix?"

"Yes."

"Can he get in that way?"

"He can get in anywhere there's a water source." Reed stood beside her, staring down. He watched her with that indecipherable look she was becoming familiar with but didn't understand. She got the "I want to jump your bones" part of it, but the rest—the confusion, regret, and sympathy—she didn't understand those.

Eve turned in her chair and leaned back to look up at him. She kept her exterior cool and unaffected, even though he presented an intimidating sight. With the planes of his face lit only by the glow from the monitor, he looked more devil than angel. "Gehenna is a relatively local company," she said. "They're based in Upland, California."

"That's what? Forty-five minutes from here?"

"Depending on traffic."

He nodded.

"Their web domain name is only a few years old," she continued. "They're obviously a new company, but they became solvent quickly from the looks of it."

The light came on and Alec walked into the room.

"We need to go there." He directed a narrowed glare at his brother. "Take a look around. See what they've got going on."

"Go yourself," Reed argued. "I'll stay with her. No need to endanger her unnecessarily."

"Bullshit." Alec approached the desk. "You should've considered that before you assigned her to this. You can't have it both ways."

"*I* assigned her?" The incredulity in Reed's voice was undeniable.

Eve's gaze darted to him, trying to visually verify the surprise she heard in his voice. She caught him quickly adopting a frozen mien that gave nothing away. But the brief glimpse of astonishment was enough to spark the suspicion that Reed wasn't as in charge of things as he should be.

"Didn't you?" she queried.

"He won't tell you the truth," Alec scoffed.

Reed's arms crossed. "Don't speak for me."

"You're a one-hit loser, bro. Better get that into your head. You're never going to be alone with her again."

Eve stood. "Enough. I find the 'hit' reference offensive."

Alec muttered, "Sorry, angel."

"I make my own choices," she said. "And right now, I'd really like to go back to that building with the gargoyles and take a closer look at them."

"Why?"

"Because we can't go out to Upland tonight; it's already too late. And I feel restless, as if I should be doing something. I don't like that feeling." She looked at both men. "It can't hurt."

"It's not going to be open."

"Is that normally a deterrent to you?" she challenged.

"It'll be guarded," Reed interjected. "But you should have a Gadara Enterprises badge. As one of his employees, any guards should let you in with no problem."

He glanced at Alec with eyes lit with triumph. "You've got a lot to learn, *bro*."

Turning to the black lacquered box that had been left for her earlier, Eve lifted the hinged lid with its inlaid ivory cross and rummaged inside.

"They left a box for you, too, Alec," she said, gesturing to a cardboard packing box waiting on the sofa. "It's in there."

"Fuck that," he snapped. "Raguel only wishes he could file me into his ranks."

Eve's box was the size of a large shoe box and it was filled with a haphazard collection of items ranging from some type of pepper spray to lip balm. She dug out a leather wallet-looking thing and flipped it open. Inside was a picture ID featuring the photo taken of her when she went in for the initial interview. She shivered thinking about how everyone had known she was minutes away from being marked, yet no one said anything or interceded in any way. If it had been the other way around, she would have told the recruit to run like hell and don't stop.

"That's it," Reed acknowledged, looking over her shoulder.

Eve's fingertips traced over the embossed Gadara logo. Reflective watermarks caught the light and prevented easy duplication. The symbols were a combination of familiar images—such as a cross—and others that looked like hieroglyphs. "I thought all of Gadara's employees were Marks. Can't they smell what I am? What's the point of this badge?"

"The employees who work in Gadara Tower are Marks," Reed explained. "They act as an early warning system to keep Raguel safe. It would be impossible for an Infernal to infiltrate the building undetected. But subsidiary companies and satellite buildings have some mortal employees."

"Keep him safe? I thought he was an archangel. Who would mess with him?"

"An Infernal looking for a major promotion."

"Couldn't an archangel kick their ass?"

"If they saw the hit coming. The seven firm leaders live temporal lives, aside from seven weeks a year when they are free to use their powers while training Marks."

"They lose their powers?"

"They have a choice," Alec corrected. "They can use their gifts, but every time they do, there's a consequence. It's up to them to decide whether the transgression is worth it."

She snorted. "Another example of God trying to drive someone crazy."

"How else would they sympathize with mortals, angel? The archangels need empathy and understanding in order to maintain their motivation. They refused to bow to man as God ordered. What better way to see the error of their ways than to walk a mile in mortal shoes?"

"Empathy and understanding?" Eve smiled without humor. "Frankly, I would be tempted to be frustrated and resentful. Why should I have to lose the privilege of using my powers to protect people that don't give a crap about me? Unless the archangels are truly angelic— which Gadara certainly didn't seem to be—the whole power-versus-punishment deal is just stirring the pot."

" 'Angelic' and 'devilish' are mortal constructs," Reed pointed out.

"I caught that earlier. Gadara said demons pull their

tricks from the same bag as angels. They're brethren, right? Fruit of the same tree, borne of the same father? It stands to reason that they'd be prone to the same vices, including getting pissed off that they're denied something through no fault of their own."

Reed scowled. "Why are we talking about this?"

Eve dropped the badge on her desk and stood. "Because it needs to be talked about. When do the archangels regain full use of their powers?"

"After Armageddon." Alec's arms crossed and his stance widened. It was a battle pose, one of readiness.

"So might it be possible that they'd like to hurry that along a bit?" she suggested.

"You're thinking like a mortal," Reed bit out.

"News flash: I *am* a mortal. This mark on my arm isn't going to change that. Tell me you haven't thought about the firm leaders playing outside the rules."

Reed's brows arched. "I haven't."

She rounded on Alec. "I know *you* have. You don't like to wear blinders."

"What are you implying?" Reed snapped.

"Gadara says you're a company man, Reed. You toe the line." Eve shrugged. "You want things to be a certain way and that's the only way you allow yourself to perceive them."

He took a step closer. "Don't try to analyze me! If you want to shrink someone's head, why don't you try the homicidal maniac you're fucking?"

"I touched a nerve," she drawled.

"You're talking smack. Want me to turn it around and see how you like it?"

"Step off," Alec warned. "Keep pushing her, and I'll push you back."

"Shut up." Reed's fists clenched. "If she wants to make wild conspiracy theories, she'll have to manage the aftermath on her own."

Eve studied the violence of Reed's response with a calculating eye. Alec was taking her questions with only minor tension, but Reed was strung tight as a bow. She looked at Alec. "So outside of the Gadara Tower, some of the employees are mortal."

He nodded.

"And if I flash this badge, they let me in, but they'll also record that we came by, right? And the company credit card, listening devices, video cameras . . . it's all cyberstalking in lieu of the divinely powered kind, right?"

"Sure. What are you thinking?"

"Nothing." Eve stepped around her desk. She'd said enough for the benefit of whoever might be listening through the bugs in her house. The rest she would keep to herself until she felt that she could speak freely. "Let me get ready and we'll go."

Reed moved to follow. Alec stepped in his path. "Leave her alone," he warned.

"I'm doing my job." Reed's voice was dangerously soft.

"Relax, Alec," she admonished.

A low, predatory rumble filled the air. She exited the room with a shake of her head. Those two were going to have to figure out on their own how to work together.

Eve was shutting her bedroom door when it was halted midswing and pushed back in. Reed entered, his gaze sweeping around the room and coming to rest on the bed.

"Feng shui," he murmured. "There's at least a little bit of believer in you."

"What does feng shui have to do with anything?" She watched him close the door, secretly impressed with his observational skills.

"You're trying to tap into energies you can't see or prove. Whether you think they come from God or not isn't as important as the fact that you acknowledge forces outside of yourself."

"You're giving me a headache."

He laughed, the velvet-rough sound flowing over her skin. "You can't have headaches anymore."

"That's what you think." She went to her closet and pushed the hanging wooden door along its track. It had taken her a long time to find two matching bleached pine panels of suitable size, but the effort was worth it. When she lay in bed, she studied the grain of the wood as she drifted to sleep.

"Listen." His tone was so grave that it drew her gaze to him again. "When Marks go on the hunt, they change."

"Change?"

"Their senses hone. You'll experience a kind of tunnel vision. You see it in felines when they crouch low and prepare to pounce. They're so absorbed in what they're doing, they don't register anything else."

"I think I caught a bit of that before."

"You might have. All mentors are specially trained to widen their focus to encompass their charges. Much like using bright headlights versus the regular ones."

Eve pulled out her most worn pair of jeans. "And Alec hasn't had this training."

"Right. He's really good at what he does, but I'm afraid he's going to leave you unprotected. You have to be extra vigilant. Somehow, you're going to have to remind yourself to take in everything."

"Are you telling me this to make your brother look bad, or are you serious?"

"I only wish I could make up stuff this good." He leaned back against the door. "You're going to have to trust me, babe. It's my job to keep you alive and working off your penance."

"I wouldn't say that assigning me to kill things prior to being trained is a good way to keep me breathing," she said wryly.

The tightening of his jaw was nearly imperceptible, but Eve was looking for it. Gadara was yanking them all around. She knew what leverage he had on Alec—her. But what was Reed getting out of this? Perhaps Gadara was holding something over him, too? It was in her best interests to find out.

Reed's glance moved back to her beautifully made bed and a smile curved his mouth. "You're not sleeping with Cain."

"How would you know?"

"His scent is fainter in here than in the rest of the condo."

"My mom just washed and made the bed."

"Uh-huh . . ." He looked at her with dark, slumberous eyes. Reed was like a firecracker, hot and explosive. The part of Eve that craved quiet evenings at home was shocked by how attractive she found that quality.

She turned away, determined to get ready for the task ahead and stop thinking about sex. "Don't get cocky and think his absence has anything to do with you."

"It has to do with something. You've been thinking

about him for ten years, but now that he's here, you're keeping him at arm's distance?"

She thought of the make-out session in the parking garage and smiled. "My personal life is none of your business."

"Keep telling yourself that. Eventually you might believe it. But it still won't be true."

"Whatever. Got anything else for me?"

"Oh yeah, I got something for you, babe. Come and get it."

"Eww." Eve tossed an arch glance over her shoulder. "You just crossed the line from arrogant to crass."

His gaze dropped. "Sorry."

She sighed. He was faultlessly elegant on the outside, but on the inside . . . The man had some rough edges. Oddly enough, she didn't want to smooth them away. But she did want to understand them. "Where did that little bit of tastelessness come from?"

Straightening, Reed reached for the doorknob. "Hell if I know," he muttered, stepping out to the hallway.

The door closed behind him with a quiet click of the latch.

"It's cold," Eve muttered, pulling her sweater coat tighter around her.

Alec tossed an arm around her shoulders and bit back the obvious question. It was easily sixty-eight degrees outside, a temperature many individuals would say was balmy. The brisk stride with which they approached their destination would have kept most people warm. Eve's chill came from somewhere inside her, created by either her changing body or her somber mood—a mood Abel had also carried with him when he'd left the house.

Braced for some type of goading, boastful comment from his brother, Alec had been astonished when Abel simply exited Eve's bedroom and shifted away without a word. There one second, gone the next. Shifting was a blessing for all angels, except for Alec. He was the only *mal'akh* to have the gift stripped from him, another example of how he was denied even the basics. He'd been given very few breaks in his life, and now the one thing he cared for was at risk.

Intimacy. He hadn't been prepared for it to happen between Eve and Abel. Sex was sex. It was nothing compared to the nonphysical intimacy Alec sensed developing between them. Jealousy ate at him. He and Abel had used women to irritate each other in the past, but never had they cared equally about one. It was a threat Alec didn't know how to manage. After a lifetime of the same old, same old, he was now confronted with too many unknowns.

"It looks different at night," Eve said softly.

He looked at their destination. Strategically lit with exterior illumination, it appeared stately and established, as if it had existed for decades rather than mere months.

As they neared the front entrance, Alec inhaled deeply. No stench, no infestation. He slowed his pace and gazed up at the gargoyles. From the alley, two were visible and they were both in their positions.

"What's the matter?" Eve asked, reaching into her pocket for her badge.

"It doesn't smell, angel."

Her brow arched. "Not that again."

"I wanted to believe you."

She smiled. "I appreciate that."

Flashing her credentials at the guard, Eve led the way with that kittenish sway to her hips that had once lured him to sin. Who was he kidding? It still lured him to sin.

"Angel." He whistled after her. "Are you feeling frisky?"

She stopped at the bank of elevators and winked. They were met by a second guard in uniform who told them the elevators weren't operational yet. They'd have to take the stairs.

"Race you to the top," Eve challenged, before gripping the handrail and sprinting up.

He could catch her. His legs were longer. But it was far more fun to bring up the rear. They burst onto the roof in a rush of limbs and laughter . . . but the sight that greeted them quickly turned merriment into startled silence.

"Holy shit." Alec slid briefly along the metal roof before gaining purchase.

Eve, still new to her strength, almost skid directly into the bonfire that was the source of his astonishment. Instead, she fell on her ass. "Ouch!"

Feeling as if he were suffering the effects of a hallucinogenic drug, Alec gaped at the tengu who danced around the hellfire with gleeful chortles. None of his mark senses registered the beast in front of him. Aside from the frail mortal vision he'd been born with, there was no other way to detect the demon. Yet it wasn't that his senses had failed him. He saw the pit of hellfire. As a demonic conjuring that cast no illumination and no shadow, it was impossible to see with Unmarked vision.

But if his mark senses were functioning properly, he would also be able to smell the tengu and see his details. With that information, Alec would know which king of Hell he belonged to and how best to eradicate him. As it was, Alec was up shit creek without a paddle. And Eve was along for the ride.

Pivoting, he searched for the other gargoyles but found his view blocked by massive air-conditioning units. Were there more tengu to manage?

"Pretty Mark, Pretty Mark," the tengu sang, his beady eyes on Eve where she still sprawled. He didn't seem to notice Alec at all. "Pretty Mark came to see Joey."

"You piss on me again," she warned, pushing to her feet, "and I'll kick your ass."

"Joey's ass is stone, Pretty Mark. Pretty Mark break foot kicking Joey's ass." The tengu laughed, still hopping in a frenzied jig to some tune only he could hear.

"My foot's bigger," Alec rumbled.

The tengu looked at him and a smile split his face. "Cain, Cain, good to see you again."

"You know him?" Eve asked, stepping closer.

"Hell if I know. Without any details, I can't tell."

"What do we do?"

"Capture him."

She snorted. "How are we supposed to do that?"

"Pretty Mark want to dance?" Joey cried, then he lunged at her.

Alec leaped between them, grunting against the vicious impact of hard, heavy stone to his gut. He hit the deck on his back and rolled with the writhing tengu. A brick safety ledge surrounded the roof's perimeter and they crashed into it with a jolting thud.

The creature was hot to the touch, charged by the evil of the hellfire. As Alec grappled with the wriggling demon, his bare palms sizzled. The stench of burning flesh filled the air and he briefly considered tossing the damn tengu over the edge to shatter into pieces on the ground below. But he needed him intact so they could study him.

What the hell was it?

Aided by weight and his small size, the tengu crawled up Alec's torso. As he rose with both hands fisted together as a mallet and prepared to swing, Eve lashed out with a swift kick. Her boot caught the tengu in the face and sent him flying. Screaming, it crashed into the bonfire.

"We've got to put the flames out." Alec leaped to his feet. "It will keep recharging him, and we'll wear out before he does."

The tengu vaulted from the flames as a red-hot missile, and Eve ducked. He overshot and crashed into a van-sized air conditioner. A pipe feeding into the unit broke, spilling water across the roof.

"Will that work?" she asked.

"Only if it's holy."

"How the fuck are we supposed to get holy water up here?" She kicked droplets at the fire. The tengu disengaged from the massive dent he'd made in the AC unit and came running for Eve, screeching unintelligible words.

"Give me a second to work on that." Alec tackled the crazed demon before he reached her.

Eve stared in horrified fascination. The two combatants were so disparate in size, yet seemed almost evenly matched. Alec definitely had his hands full. She glanced around for anything that could be used as a makeshift weapon.

"*Adjutorium nostrun in nomine—*" Alec shouted. "*—Domini.*"

"What?" She raced around the air conditioner and was thrust backward with stunning strength. With the wind knocked from her, Eve could only gape up at the creature who sat on her. It was another tengu.

"I kill you," the tengu said, in a lilting feminine voice so at odds with her frightening visage.

Alec continued to yell at his opponent in what Eve guessed was Latin. She yanked her head to the side as the tengu swung at her. The sound of the metal roof rending near her ear was deafening and painful, but the pain dissipated as quickly as it came. Using the tengu's forward momentum, Eve tossed the heavy creature over her head and rolled to her belly. She scrambled to her feet, barely managing to gain her footing before the tengu was after her again.

"Alec!" she yelled, kicking the demon and sending her skidding through the growing lake of water. Eve was sick of being wet. Totally sick of it.

The tengu slid into the fire and popped up a moment later, laughing. Alec threw his tengu into the other one, causing a collision that cracked off the leg of one and the arm of the other. The two collected their missing appendages and leaped into the fire.

Standing over the gushing water, Alec made the sign of the cross. "*Commixtio salis et aquæ pariter fiat in nomine Patris, et Filii et Spiritus Sancti.*"

His voice rose in volume, the words rolling off his tongue in a richly nuanced incantation. Eve turned to the broken air conditioner, hoping her superstrength was fully operational. She grabbed the end of the broken water pipe and yanked hard, ripping a piece free. Wielding the section like a bat, she pivoted. "Joey" barreled toward her and she dispatched him with a home run hit that sent him flying over the lip of the roof. The pipe was ruined by the impact. She dropped it with a curse and searched for a replacement.

"Eve!" Alec barked as a tremendous crashing noise was heard from the street below. "We need one of them."

She winced. "Sorry. Don't know my own strength."

The one-legged tengu shrieked and hopped after Eve in retaliation, wielding her broken-off leg like a club. Alec lashed out with a fist, but haste threw off his aim. He struck the beast's rear lower flank, sending her into a tailspin. Her velocity increased, then she struck Eve, knocking Eve to her back.

The tengu landed on her thighs. Stone arms rose to brain Eve with the leg. Eve screamed and recoiled, shielding her head with her forearms. Braced for the beating, she squeezed her eyes shut.

Then a hideous stench roiled over her, turning her stomach and making her choke.

A roar filled the air, like the sound of a mighty waterfall. The ground slithered beneath her back, dragging her several feet. Her eyes flew open and she watched the scene unfold as if in slow motion.

The water surged into a tidal wave. An all-too-recognizable face emerged within the center of the liquid wall. The tengu shrieked and dropped the leg.

"She's mine!" the Nix roared.

In a churning, foaming mass, the Nix swept the tengu over the edge of the roof.

And took Eve with it.

CHAPTER 14

A lec!"
 Eve tumbled inside the wave like a wiped-out surfer. Her back hit the edge of the brick safety surround and she flipped over the top, arms and legs flailing. Her fingers grappled for purchase, one digit breaking in the effort. Then she was falling, weighted down by the tengu that clung to one leg and the Nix that was wrapped around her entire body in a swirling vortex of water.

As the lip of the roof escaped her vision, an arm reached over and clasped her wrist in a viselike hold. She glanced up, watching how her momentum and gravity pulled Alec inexorably until he dangled from the waist. She screamed. Not from the fear of falling, although she was deathly afraid of heights, but for Alec, who appeared ready to tumble over the edge with her.

"You're going to die," she yelled at Alec, kicking madly at the screeching tengu. "Let me go!"

"No way." He clutched at her with both hands.

"Deus, invictæ virtutis auctor, et insuperabilis imperii rex, ac semper magnificus triumphator—"

As Alec continued to speak, Eve flopped from side to side. Her shoulders creaked with the tremendous weight of the beings hanging on to her. Her arms felt on the verge of ripping from their sockets. She was fairly certain that would have happened already if she weren't superhuman.

She looked down, aiming at the tengu's eyes with the heel of her boot and kicking at her with all her might. Alec slid farther over the ledge, his hips the only anchor keeping them from free-falling four stories to the ground.

"Per Dominum nostrum!" Alec roared.

The water exploded outward with teeth-rattling violence, knocking the tengu free and slamming Eve into the brick facade. Alec yanked her up and over the top with such force that they both landed in an ignoble sprawl of tangled limbs. From below, the reverberation of the crashing tengu caused a car alarm to wail.

"What the fuck happened?" she gasped, pushing her soaked hair out of her face.

Alec lay beneath her, laughing. "I asked for a blessing of the water. God made it holy and it kicked the Nix out."

"How can you laugh?" She smacked his shoulder. "This job sucks. And we're empty-handed."

"We're alive. And you were right." He cupped the back of her neck and gave her a quick, hard kiss. She cried out at the unintentional jarring of her broken finger. He set her beside him, then sat up. Catching her hand, he looked it over. "Angel . . ."

She couldn't look. Regardless of whether or not she

was capable of physically vomiting, the thought of seeing her distorted finger made her sick.

"Come here," he murmured. Bending forward, Alec took her mouth, first gently and sweetly, then deeper. So startled was she by the action and the first tendrils of desire that she failed to register his changed grip until he yanked her finger into place.

Eve screamed just as the door to the stairwell burst open and the two security guards rushed out to the roof. Slipping in the water, they skid several feet before falling on their asses.

"My life just keeps getting better," she groused.

As Eve traversed the distance from the elevator in her condominium complex to her front door, she left a trail of droplets in her wake. From behind her, the sloshing of water in Alec's boots was clearly audible. It had taken a direct phone call to Gadara to get them off the hook with security. That had taken longer than she would have liked. She couldn't even think about the fact that he'd lagged on getting to the phone because he was schmoozing in Las Vegas while she waited sopping and sore: it pissed her off too much.

She was cold. She couldn't shiver and her teeth didn't rattle, but she was a Popsicle nevertheless. Her attire didn't help matters. When wet, her sweater coat had weighed a ton. She'd been forced to take it, and her shirt, off. Unfortunately, the only garment she'd had in the car was a black leather trench coat. Paired with her black lace bra and low-rise jeans, she looked like a prostitute, which wasn't conducive to improving her mood.

Alec had tried to cheer her up, but finally realized that silence was wiser.

Eve looked at her once-broken finger. It was fully healed now, with no bruising or swelling to bear witness to the injury. If only her psyche could be set right so easily. There were some things a person shouldn't have to experience. Tidal waves on roofs, attacks by ghoulish creatures, and being suspended fifty-three feet above the ground were some of them.

"Got your keys?" Alec asked.

"Yep."

As they passed Mrs. Basso's door, it opened. She took in their appearances with one wide, sweeping glance. "You look like drowned rats."

"I feel like one," Eve muttered, though she managed a tight smile.

"What the hell were you doing if you don't mind my asking?"

"Uh . . . surfing?"

"With those clothes on?"

"It was spontaneous."

Mrs. Basso looked at Alec, who shrugged. She shook her head. "Young people these days. I get worn out just thinking about your courtship rituals. Whatever happened to drugstore chocolate shakes and drive-in movies?"

Eve laughed softly. Mrs. Basso reminded her that life was normal for some people. She wanted to feel that way again, if only for a short time. "I'm worn out, too, so you're not alone. I'll see you tomorrow."

"Mr. Cain," Mrs. Basso said. "Could I talk to you a moment?"

Alec's brows rose, but he nodded. "Sure. Let me get out of these clothes."

"Of course."

"Want to come over in about five minutes?"

Mrs. Basso glanced at Eve, who got the impression that she shouldn't be around when Mrs. Basso talked to Alec.

"I'm going to take a long, hot bath," Eve said, moving to her condo. It was ironic that she would want to sit in water after days of being soaked with it, but she couldn't imagine a faster way to warm up.

Once she was inside the sanctity and comfort of her home, she began to strip her way down the hall. She opened the louvered doors that hid the laundry alcove and shoved her wet clothes into the washing machine. A low whistle turned her head. Alec stood at the end of the hallway where it emptied into the living room. If the heat of his gaze had been less than tangible, she might have been embarrassed at her blatant display of nakedness. She was certain Mrs. Basso's likening of her appearance to a drowned rat was apt.

His voice came low and husky. "Your place has a great view."

"You got a thing for wet rodents?"

"I've got a thing for you. Hot, wet, and naked."

"Charmer." Her voice was come-hither husky. "No way you can start and finish anything in less than five minutes."

A slow, lazy smile curved his mouth. "I can make your bathwater safe."

She sighed. "That's not as sexy as what I was thinking."

"Hold that thought." He approached with the sultry stride she'd always drooled over. Catching her elbow, he led her through her bedroom to the bathroom, which was separated from the sleeping area by her closets. There, her sunken whirlpool tub waited to froth her worries away.

If only it could be so easy.

Alec plugged the drain, turned the taps, and blessed the water. Eve found herself swaying to the lulling cadence of his words.

"You better hop in," he drawled when the tub was full and he was done, "before you fall asleep standing up."

"Shouldn't the mark cure exhaustion?"

"Sleep reminds us that we're not invincible."

"Whatever."

He kissed the tip of her nose and cupped her bare breast. "You need to move out to the boonies," he whispered, the pad of his thumb brushing over her taut nipple. "No meddling neighbors."

"I'll get right on that. But she's not a meddler. She just worries."

Smiling, he left her and she sank into the steaming water with a sigh of relief. The sight of the cross hanging off the adjacent showerhead made her grumpy so she closed her eyes. A few moments later she heard a knock at the front door, a sound that would have been impossible to detect before having her super hearing.

The vague whisper of subdued voices reached her ears. She concentrated hard, trying to hone in on the individual syllables. The Change was like putting a stethoscope to her ears.

"Mr. Basso saw it on TV one night a year or so ago,"

Mrs. Basso was saying, "and he started a monthly sub-scription. Now that he's gone, I have no use for them."

"I don't understand," Alec murmured.

"Take the box." Eve heard something rattle as it ex-changed hands. "You're a fit young man, but swimming with your clothes on at night . . . and that business in the carport . . ."

Mrs. Basso cleared her throat. "Oh, this is terrible. I should learn to leave well enough alone."

Again the rattle came, like beans in a jar, and Eve frowned.

"Male enhancement?" Alec croaked.

Eve sat up so fast, water sloshed over the rim of the tub.

"The walls are thin," Mrs. Basso muttered. "A cou-ple nights ago . . . No man can keep that pace indefi-nitely."

The silence from Alec was deafening. Eve bit her lip. He was speechless, and she was going to burst.

"You can't be any more embarrassed than I am," Mrs. Basso said. "Hear me out and I promise never to interfere again. Women with drive make the best wives, my late husband used to say. I know it can be exhaust-ing, though, and intimidating. Just don't give her up without a fight. Don't give up, period. You'll never find another girl like Evangeline."

"I know." Despite how low Alec's voice was, Eve heard it clear as day. Her throat tightened and her eyes stung.

She grabbed her terry-cloth-covered inflatable head-rest and leaned back with her eyes closed. Fact was, life wasn't bad when you had good friends, which brought her best friend, Janice, to mind.

Eve hoped her trip to Europe was fulfilling its purpose. They had both spent a year bitching about feeling stagnant. First, they'd blamed it on a lack of good men. Then, they'd realized that was just a tried-and-true excuse for the real problem—themselves. Janice had decided a complete change of scene would give her a new perspective and as a bartender, she could easily take her livelihood with her. Eve had said her job prevented her from going, but that wasn't entirely true. She just hadn't known how to break the news to her parents, and the idea of backpacking seemed so far out of line with her desire to put down roots.

"Hey." Alec's voice penetrated her thoughts at the same moment she registered the shutting off of the spa jets.

She blinked sleepily up at him. "Hmm?"

"You have to get out, angel." He reached for her. "You've been in here so long, your skin is pruning. Considering you're a Mark, that's saying something."

"What?"

"You fell asleep." He plucked her out of the deep tub as if she was a child, heedless of how her wet body soaked his boxers. He was naked otherwise, and mouthwatering. She knew she had to be half dead with exhaustion, because her super libido could only manage a slight twitch of interest.

"Figures," she muttered.

He set her down on the rug and scrubbed her down with a towel.

"You're good at this baby-sitting stuff," she said. "Do this often?"

The question was only partly teasing. She did won-

der if he'd cared for another woman with such tender-
ness before.

"Only for tasty Asian babes." He tossed the towel in
the hamper.

She stepped back and eyed him. Long muscular
legs, taut abdomen, beautifully delineated biceps, and
a thick, weighty bulge in his drawers. She licked her
lips. "Where's that male-enhancement stuff?"

His arms crossed. "Excuse me?"

"Think it'll work on me?"

Alec smiled. "You don't have the necessary parts."

"Oh yeah? Why don't you ask your parts if they think
my parts are necessary or not? They might disagree."

"You're barely standing."

"I can lie down."

He tossed her over his shoulder. She almost protested,
then pushed his boxers down instead and admired his
flexing buttocks. He swatted her ass. "Behave."

"You like me naughty," she said, tossing his earlier
words back at him.

"I like you awake, too."

Eve sighed. "Technicalities."

Alec tossed her on the bed and she bounced lightly.
Catching the edge of the blankets, he covered her and
kissed the tip of her nose. "Good night, angel."

"Where are you going?" She yawned.

"To bed."

"I've got one of those."

He tugged up his boxers. "You won't get any sleep
if I join you and you need the rest. We have a confer-
ence call with Raguel tomorrow."

She snorted and curled into her pillow. "I'm taking
tomorrow off."

"No such thing."

"Watch me."

As he closed the door, she heard him chuckling.

"Smells awesome."

As he fried bacon, Alec smiled at the sound of Eve's voice. He glanced back her, finding her dressed in her red kimono robe and wearing a towel on her head. "There's coffee in the pot."

"Will I get a buzz off it?"

"Nope."

"Good thing I like the taste of it, then."

She padded barefoot to the coffeemaker, poured herself a cup, and moved over to one of the stools on the opposite side of the island. He'd set the newspaper there and she immediately spread it out and began reading.

"After breakfast," he said, "we need to call Raguel."

"I told you, I'm taking the day off."

"Don't be stubborn." He set down the fork he was using to flip the bacon. "This is bigger than you and me now, angel."

"Because we couldn't smell them?"

"Or see their details. If there's a new faction somewhere operating completely outside the rest of the system, every firm needs to know."

Her lips pursed. "You can handle the talk with Gadara without me."

"Talk to me."

Eve looked up from the paper. She looked faultless, refreshed, and alert, but the lack of shadows under her eyes didn't hide the fact that she was weary. "I need a break, Alec. Just for a few hours, at least."

She let the paper rest on the counter. "I need some time to be normal. For my own sanity. Think about the last two weeks of my life, okay?"

"I understand."

"Do you?" Her slender fingers drummed atop the newsprint-covered granite. "Then handle Gadara by yourself. There's nothing I can add to what you're going to tell him."

"Fine." He turned back to the bacon and tried to hide his volatile response to her withdrawal. All morning long, he'd been whistling with contentment. The concern over the tengu and the possible rippling effect their existence would have over every facet of the mark system gave him a feeling of anticipation. Surely a new firm would be needed, and he had the only known hands-on experience with this new threat.

But Eve was unhappy and possibly scared. She had a right to feel both of those emotions. And he was an asshole for thinking only of himself.

"You're angry," she said.

"Not with you."

Silence followed. He continued browning the bacon and set to work on frying eggs. In another pan, he made pancakes. Behind him, he heard the rustle of flipping newspaper pages. It was a quiet domestic scene, but the intimacy he craved was lacking and sorely missed.

"There's a story in the paper about a series of animal mutilations," she murmured. "There's speculation that they're ritualistic."

"Then they probably are."

"I figured. And the fact that the latest animal—a Great Dane—was found in the back of a Gehenna Masonry pickup truck can't be coincidence, because there's no so such thing as coincidence, right?"

Alec turned off the gas burners and moved to the island. He read the story over her shoulder. The *Orange County Register* was covering the latest ultimate fight at the Upland Sports Arena. Lower down the page was the mention of a recent spate of dog mutilations and killings in the area. Two animal carcasses had been found in the arena parking lot just a week before—one of them had been found in the back of a Gehenna truck left in the lot overnight due to some construction the company was doing.

"I smell a rat," he said.

"I smell breakfast," she retorted, "and I'm hungry."

He pressed his lips to the crown of her head. "Yes, Your Highness."

Returning to the stove, Alec finished up the cooking, filled two plates, and brought them back to the island.

Eve looked at her overflowing plate. "You're going to make me fat."

He smiled. "Don't eat what you don't want."

"I want all of it."

"I'll help you work it off."

"How generous of you."

"I'm here to serve."

And that was the true crux of the matter, he realized as he stabbed at the yolk of one over-medium egg. He couldn't serve God's needs, his needs, and Eve's needs at the same time. Something had to give.

He found himself wishing that she would learn to like the mark, so he could have it all. Then he thought of the night before and remembered the terror he had felt as he watched her being swept over the side of the roof. If he'd been capable of having a heart attack, he would have had one.

"I think I'm going to take Mrs. Basso to the movies today," Eve pronounced before munching on a piece of crunchy bacon, "while you're talking to Gadara. The theater is away from water and far from the tengu building. I need a price on my head before anyone else can take a crack at me, right? So it should be nice and uneventful."

He swallowed hard. The thought of her going out alone scared the shit out of him. "I wish you wouldn't."

"I know." She set her elbows on the counter and rested her chin on her hands. "If you think it's really unsafe, I won't leave. I'm not an idiot. But if you're just worried, please let me go. I would really like to spend a couple of hours watching other people live average lives. I need the fantasy, if only for a little while."

Alec looked out the window. It was a crystal-clear day. No rain, no mist. If she went straight to the movies and came right back, she should be fine. "Don't use the john."

"Okay. Now let's talk about why I can't go to the bathroom. That Nix is stalking me. I can't figure out what his deal is. I swear I didn't do anything to him. He flicked his snake's tongue at me and I freaked. I said something offhand by complete mistake and it wounded him. He had to see that I was clueless and no threat to him. Why is he acting like I ran over his dog?"

"I don't know." Alec tapped the tines of his fork against his plate. "This is completely outside the norm. I'm going to talk to Raguel about it and see what he says. We can't sit here waiting for the Nix to strike again. We have to find and vanquish him."

"Sounds good to me." Eve pushed back from the island. She pulled the towel off her head and draped it over the back of her stool. "I'm going to run next door and see if Mrs. Basso is up for a movie. She wanted to see the new Hugh Jackman flick, and there's a matinee in an hour."

Alec nodded and continued to eat his now tasteless food, his thoughts occupied by the Nix. He listened to the multiple locks disengage, then the door opening. Perhaps talking to Raguel alone was the best way to go. Separating himself from Eve might help to alter the image of them as an indivisible team. Their paths would eventually diverge; they had to for her sake. Then he would need to continue on his present course alone. That would be difficult if it was perceived that he was useful only in regards to his association with her.

Of course, part of him wondered how useful he could possibly be without her.

As Eve exited to the hallway, she left her front door open. Her gaze returned to Alec against her will, her stride faltering just past the threshold. The sight of him in her kitchen—completely at ease and half dressed in only T-shirt and boxers—was as bizarre as being attacked by the tengu. The incongruity of his presence in her life after a ten-year absence brought home a possibility she hadn't considered before—perhaps his return and the marking weren't the detours in her life. Perhaps the last ten years were.

It was a crazy thought, but how else could she explain why she wasn't a shell-shocked wreck at this point? Or why this new skin she wore felt so much more comfortable than the one she'd been born with?

And her sexual advances toward Alec . . . she could say that was an expected aftereffect of a near-death experience or blame her super libido. But she'd be lying to herself, and as screwed up as the rest of her life was, she needed her head on straight more than ever.

Eve stopped before Mrs. Basso's door and knocked. As she waited, she tightened the belt on her robe. She looked up and down the hallway, admiring the sunshine coming in through the window on the other side of her door. She spread her arms out and stretched, briefly wondering if she should have dressed before stepping out of her house. Luckily it was a workday and most of the residents weren't home.

She rang the doorbell, knowing that a knock was sometimes difficult to hear from the rear bedrooms. Her mark began to tingle, then burn, as it did when she took the Lord's name in vain. Frowning, she rubbed at it. Why the hell would the damn thing start bothering her now?

"Mrs. Basso?" she called out, just in case her neighbor wasn't answering in avoidance of solicitors. Salespeople weren't supposed to come into the building. Anyone caught putting up solicitations was quickly booted out, but often the easiest way to get rid of them was simply to ignore them.

Her mark throbbed something fierce. Aggravated energy pumped hard and fast through her veins, spreading outward from her arm until it inundated her body with restless anticipation. Eve's nostrils flared, scents intensifying with startling immediacy. Her eyesight sharpened, magnifying minute details such as the scrapes left by keys around the dead-bolt lock.

Before she fully comprehended what she was doing, Eve crashed into Mrs. Basso's door shoulder first. The door locks shattered through the jamb, spraying splinters through the air and filling the hallway with an echoing boom.

"Mrs. Basso!" Eve searched the living room with a sweeping glance.

The mark continued to pulse, pushing a steady stream of adrenaline through her body. Her super senses were functioning in high gear. The doors and windows were closed, but she heard the crashing of waves against the shore and the screams of seagulls as if they were directly in front of her.

"Eve."

Alec. She pivoted. Met his gaze. He stood on the threshold, barefoot but sporting hastily donned jeans.

"The mark," she explained. "It's freaking me out."

He entered. "Mrs. Basso?" he called out, his voice strong and steady.

"Maybe she's at the restaurant?"

The sheer lack of emotion on his face said more than words could.

Mrs. Basso's floor plan was the mirror image of Eve's, but the decor made the homes entirely dissimilar. While Eve's pad had a modern, minimalist style, the Basso residence was traditional Italian elegance. Faux painted walls and heavy leather furniture invited guests to linger in warmth and comfort. Yet Eve was chilled by the silence, broken only by the ticking of the beautiful clock on the living room wall.

She stared at its oversized numbers and wrought-iron scrollwork, marveling at the steadiness of her breathing and the rhythmic beating of her heat. Mentally she was panicking, but physically she could be visiting for espresso and tiramisu for all the stress her body felt. There was a brutal primitiveness to the combination of physical calm, coursing adrenaline, and super sensitivity. It was entirely inelegant . . . and seductive.

"Eve."

Eve froze at the sound of her name, spoken softer than a whisper but heard louder than a gunshot.

"Mrs. Basso?" She moved down the hall, first tentatively, then faster.

"Eve."

"Mrs. Basso!"

Bursting into the master bedroom at a run, Eve gasped in relief to find Mrs. Basso standing by the bed. Dressed in white slacks and a pale pink shirt, she looked lovely and ready for the day. Turning with a smile, Mrs. Basso eyed her from head to toe. "Cute pajamas."

Eve gave a breathy laugh, feeling silly for her overreaction. Her mark enhancements were obviously still whacky. "You scared me when you didn't answer."

"It's been an . . . *odd* morning."

Wincing, Eve recalled her abrupt entry. "About your door . . ."

"Is that what the ruckus was?" Mrs. Basso smiled. "You have so much energy."

Eve frowned. "I wanted to see if you'd like to catch that movie you mentioned."

"I would love to, but I'm afraid I can't."

Alec's hand touched Eve's back. She looked at him. His lips were thin and tight.

Mrs. Basso smiled at Alec. "Take good care of her, Cain."

"I will."

"I can take a rain check," Eve offered. "I won't go without you."

"You might think about keeping him, Evie," Mrs. Basso said, gesturing to Alec with a gentle jerk of her chin. "Especially if he masters that recipe I gave him."

Mrs. Basso turned back to the bed, affording Eve a view of the nightstand. A clear glass bowl waited there. It was half filled with water and showcased a lovely white water lily.

Eve's wide eyes shot back to her neighbor, who was leaning over the mattress. She was tucking in the frail figure lying peacefully amid the pillows—a figure easily seen through the gradually increasing translucence of Mrs. Basso.

Two of them. One ghostly, one . . . dead.

A sob escaped Eve, shattering the quiet. She covered her mouth.

The silver hair that fanned out on the pillow was wet, as was Mrs. Basso's skin, yet she appeared to be sleeping.

She looked so peaceful, so serene.

So lifeless.

CHAPTER 15

E ve accepted the sweater Alec handed to her and shrugged into it. She was frozen to the bone, her blood icy with grief, fury, and fear. They stood just outside her front door, staying out of the way of the paramedics and police detectives who swarmed around the Basso apartment.

"Now, let's run through this again," the detective said in a tone of voice that told her he didn't believe a word she said. Detective Jones, he'd said his name was. He was a nondescript man in a cheap suit dyed a shade of shit brown Eve was certain had been discontinued in the seventies. His partner was Detective Ingram. He had better taste in clothes, but was taller, fatter, and boasted a handlebar mustache.

For some reason, the two men offended Eve. They were so drab and worn, their voices monotonous and their eyes flat. Beaten down by the dregs of society and completely unaware of what they were really dealing with every day.

"What condition was the Basso door in when you found it?" Jones asked.

"It was locked," she said, wondering why she had to go over this so many times. She'd already told the story to two other detectives.

"Who broke in?"

"I did."

"Through two dead bolts?" Ingram was clearly disbelieving.

"Yes."

"Can you demonstrate how," Jones asked, "using your door?"

Eve exhaled harshly and turned around. She closed her door, then grabbed the knob with one hand and bumped the portal with her shoulder. "I used a little more force, of course."

"Of course." He wrote something in his notepad.

"You don't have to believe me," she said. "Just look at the security tapes."

"We will." His smile was tight. "Did you move the body?"

"I didn't move anything."

"The medical examiner says the body is wet," Ingram informed, "but the bed isn't. Someone moved the deceased to the bed. Then they tucked her in."

"I wouldn't know."

"Did Mrs. Basso have any family nearby? Or close friends?"

"Not that I'm aware of."

"Any children?"

She shook her head.

"The act of moving her and arranging her so nicely suggests that the person felt close to her. Do you know anyone who might fit that bill?"

Eve's lower lip quivered and tears welled. "No."

Thoughts of what the last minutes of Mrs. Basso's life must have been like made her sick. Eve swiped at the tears that coursed down her cheeks.

Alec altered his stance, moving from beside her to slightly in front of her. It was a protective pose and she was grateful for it. His hand reached back for her and she clasped it. "Ms. Hollis has been through enough today," he said. "I'm going to have to ask you to leave her alone for now."

Both detectives narrowed their eyes, then nodded in near unison. Ingram reached into his pocket and withdrew a business card, which he held out to Eve. "If you think of anything that might help, please give us a call in addition to the other detectives you spoke with earlier."

Eve frowned as she read the information imprinted on the card. "Anaheim Police Department? A bit out of your jurisdiction, aren't you?"

Then something more disturbing caught her eye. "*Homicide?*"

Alec's fingers tightened on hers. "You think this is a murder?"

"That's all we need for now," Jones said. "Thank you for your cooperation."

"Why do you think this is a murder, Detective?" Alec repeated, this time with an oddly resonant tone to his voice.

Persuasive. Eve watched the two detectives in silent fascination, wondering if the Jedi mind trick would work on them.

Ingram and Jones stood silently for a long moment, then Jones said, "Water lilies."

Eve's mark tingled and she released Alec's hand to rub at it. He glanced at her, then asked, "What's significant about water lilies?"

"It's an unusual flower to keep inside the house," the detective said.

"Explain."

"The lily is a calling card."

"How many have you found?" Alec prodded.

"A dozen in the last six months."

Eve leaned heavily into the door. "All in Anaheim?"

"Until today."

The Nix was a serial killer. In Anaheim. Where her parents lived.

"Detectives!" A young woman in a blue windbreaker jacket leaned out of the Basso apartment. "The M.E. is asking for you."

"Excuse us," Ingram said.

"God be with you," Alec murmured.

Jones smiled grimly. "Thanks."

Eve was inside her apartment in a flash, racing toward the console where she kept her purse and keys. She heard the door shut.

"What are you doing?" Alec asked.

"My parents live in Anaheim."

"So?" He stood with arms akimbo before the door, blocking the exit. "You go there now, you might lead him right to your family."

"It's not hard to find them, Alec. We have the same last name. Shit, he could have followed my mom home when she left here."

"Let the mark system do what it's supposed to."

"Which is what exactly? Fuck up everyone's lives?"

Alec came to her and pulled her close. Unfamiliar with relying on a man for emotional support, she resisted at first; then she sank into his strength, too weary to resist. He was so warm and hard. There was no external softness to him, no hint of weakness. Solid as a rock. But he wasn't truly. Nothing was solid when it was impermanent.

"Let's go to Gadara Tower," he suggested. "There we can access the resources needed to keep your family safe."

"I need to be with them. They can't fight him off."

"He's after *you,* angel. We can make them safer without you around. Grab what you need and let's go. If I don't ease your mind and you still want to be with them, I'll go with you."

Eve dug into her purse and withdrew her cell phone. She speed dialed her parent's number. It rang four times and with every ring, she grew more agitated. Then, finally, it picked up.

"Hi, you've reached Darrel and Miyoko Hollis . . ."

The answering machine. A terrible fear gripped her. Then the line connected. "Hello?"

"Dad?" Eve collapsed into Alec. "Are you all right?"

"I was in the garden with your mother. What's up?"

It took her a moment to reply. "Nothing. Just wanted to hear your voice."

"You don't sound good. What's the matter?" Her dad was using the low concerned tone that always made her want to spill her guts. She'd learned to hold her tongue over the years. He was a great listener but a poor doer. It was Miyoko who argued with teachers and principals on her children's behalf. She was also the one who never let her kids live down mistakes, rehashing them whenever she deemed the time was right.

"My neighbor died this morning." Eve was croaking like a frog, but she couldn't help it—her throat was tight as a fist. Alec's hands stroked up and down her back, which just made it worse.

"Oh, I'm sorry, honey," her dad said. "I know how much you liked her."

"I did. Very much."

"Hang on. Your mother wants the phone." Her dad couldn't hide his relief. Dealing with emotions wasn't his forte.

Eve gave a shaky sigh.

"What happened?" Miyoko demanded in the clipped tone of a seasoned nurse. When a crisis hit, she always became no-nonsense and precise.

"Mrs. Basso died this morning."

"Heart attack?"

"I don't think so," Eve said.

"What did the paramedics say?"

"They haven't said anything to me."

"Hmph. Go ask."

"I can't."

"Why not?"

Eve grimaced. "Because I can't, Mom. And does it really matter *how* she died? She's gone, and I'm devastated."

The doorbell rang. Alec pressed his lips to her forehead, then moved to answer the summons.

"I have to go," Eve said. "I'll call you back in a bit."

"Okay. Call back soon."

She snapped her phone shut and shoved it back into its dedicated pocket in her Coach bag. She wasn't a designer junkie by any means, but she had to have purses that didn't fall apart. Period.

"Sorry to trouble you again," Detective Ingram said. Alec kept him out in the hall.

Eve rubbed at the space between her brows. She didn't have an actual headache, but she definitely felt stressed. Making sure her parents were safe was vital, and she wanted it done *now*.

"I'm sorry, but I am in a hurry, Detective," she said impatiently.

"I just need to know if you touched anything next door." He had one hand at his waist while the other stroked the end of his handlebar mustache. "The forensic team will do their job, of course, but it's always nice to know what you're going to find."

"The phone in the living room," she said. "To call 911."

He nodded, his gaze moving past her to sweep across her living room. "Nice place. My partner says you're an interior designer."

"Yes." She adjusted her purse strap on her shoulder. "If you will excuse me."

Ingram stilled, his gaze narrowing on something beyond her shoulder. Eve turned to see what had caught his eye.

The bowl that had once held the water lily rested empty on the coffee table. Alec had moved it there after she'd ground up the flower in the disposer. Eve cringed inwardly.

"Can I help you with something?" Alec asked, stepping into the detective's line of sight.

Ingram attempted to peer around Alec's tall frame. "Where did you get that bowl on your table?"

"I bought it," she replied tightly.

"Do you have the cups?"

"What?"

He looked at her. His eyes weren't dull anymore—they were sharp as knives. "The cups that go with that punch bowl."

"I don't know what you're talking about."

"That is a three-gallon punch bowl from Crate and Barrel. It comes as a set with ten matching cups and a plastic ladle. If you bought the bowl, you must have the cups, too."

"I didn't get it at Crate and Barrel."

"Where did you get it?"

"I don't know. Salvation Army, maybe?" Eve shrugged. "It was a long time ago. Listen, I really have to get going."

"Ah, that explains the missing cups." Ingram tugged on his mustache. "Do you want to know why I know so much about punch bowls, Ms. Hollis?"

"Not really. I—"

"I've seen a few of those particular bowls lately," he continued. "Too many of them. Saw one this morning, actually. Right next door. Did your bowl come with a flower in it?"

"No." Her mark burned something fierce and her jaw clenched. Like a damned electric dog collar, the mark was acting like a behavior modifier. "Are we done now?"

Ingram's attention turned to Alec. "What about you,

Mr. Cain? Do you have to run out, too? I might have a few questions for you."

"I can't add any more to what Ms. Hollis has already told you," Alec said. "And yes, I'm going with her."

Eve admired Alec's poise. He looked calm and relaxed, while she felt strung-out and edgy.

"Mind if I take that bowl?" the detective asked.

"Actually," Alec answered before she could. "We need that."

She looked at him with raised brows. She didn't want it in her house. Part of her also hoped the Nix had left something identifiable behind, like fingerprints.

"You promised to bring a punch bowl to the employee party," he said.

The sudden tension weighed heavily. It had never occurred to her that the mark system might need the item. Now the detective was even more suspicious. She could smell it on him.

She winced apologetically. "He's right, Detective. I'm sorry about that. You can have it when we're done with it."

"If it doesn't break or go missing first." Ingram's hands went to his hips in what she suspected was a customary pose for him. It spread the lapels of his suit wide and accentuated his portly midsection. "I'm trying to catch a serial killer, Ms. Hollis, and you know more than you're telling me. If this guy has contacted you, I need to know. If he's threatened you, I can help."

Eve held her pose for the length of a heartbeat, then all the rigidity left her. This man wasn't the enemy. He was a good guy, fighting the good fight. "If I had anything helpful, I would share it. I swear."

The mark didn't burn, because she was telling the

truth. Nothing she could say would help the police. But it didn't make the situation any more comfortable.

Detective Ingram pointed a frustrated finger at her. "Don't travel far without letting me know where you're going."

She suspected she could argue the legality of that order, but didn't see the point. She wasn't going anywhere while that Nix was out there. "Okay."

Ingram left. Alec retrieved the punch bowl and they exited her home, locking the door securely behind them. She grimaced as she turned the key in the multiple locks. Once she'd thought such barriers would be a deterrent that would keep her safe.

No one was safe.

As they moved down the hall, a gurney rolled out of the Basso home. Eve halted in her tracks, devastated by the sight. Two paramedics stood at either side. She recognized one immediately, even without seeing the name *Woodbridge* embroidered on his shirt. He paused.

"Hey," Woodbridge said. "I thought I remembered seeing this address recently. How are you?"

Eve's chin lifted. "She was my friend."

"I'm sorry." Concern filled his blue eyes.

"Thank you. I appreciate that."

Alec took up a position beside her, his hand coming to rest at the small of her back. It was a proprietary gesture and it added to her stress. Her life was complicated enough as it was.

She watched as Mrs. Basso was taken away and the full force of her loss hit her. She thought of all the movies and meals they'd never share. No more unexpected visits that cheered her day. No one else to shop for when she went to the store.

Eve suddenly felt very much alone.

"We should go," Alec murmured, squeezing her hip gently.

Nodding, she skirted the people milling around the hall and waited for the elevator to return. She stepped inside and released the breath she hadn't known she was holding. As the doors closed, shutting out the view of the chaos on the floor, Eve absorbed the fact that her world had irrevocably changed.

Whether she shed the mark or not, her life as she knew it was over.

Stepping into a firm was always a heady rush for Alec, no matter which one he visited or where it was located. His entire body hummed with energy and his heart rate lurched into an elevated rhythm, as if the other Marks shared their energy with him. He breathed deeply, inhaling the scent of hundreds of Marks confined in one space.

Beside him, Eve made a choked noise. Her nose wrinkled, making him wonder what sensory input she received. She appeared to find the smell disturbing rather than pleasant. Then he pushed the thought aside. Of course everything would be disturbing to her. It was all new and unwelcome, and she'd received a terrible shock today. One thing at a time. Making sure her parents were safe was first on his agenda. He knew Eve wouldn't be able to function properly until that was ensured.

"This way," he said, directing her toward a set of elevators tucked away from general public use. Unlike the private elevators that went directly to Raguel's office, these cars only went down to the bowels of the building. There, nestled deep into the earth, existed a small complex complete with morgue and various specialized departments.

Eve didn't appear to notice where they were going. As the elevator descended, her gaze remained on the floor, unfocused. Alec adjusted his grip on the punch bowl and reached out to her, stroking her bare arm. She was so far away mentally she didn't register his attempt to connect. He withdrew and leaned against the metal handrail. He had no idea how to get inside her beyond the physical and it left him feeling . . . impotent, which in turn was driving him insane.

A heavy, impenetrable silence filled the car, despite the instrumental Barry Manilow elevator music that whispered around them. He listened to her breathing, then sharpened his hearing to listen to her heart beating. It was so impossibly steady, like a machine. He used to listen to his own heartbeat, and he'd curse the mark that stole its ability to race or skip. Was a person's humanity contingent upon that organ? And if so, was the removal of its frailties the catalyst that led to the removal of a Mark's soul?

In the past, it was only when he was in a firm that he felt truly vital. He had come to crave the feeling of renewal. Until he'd met Eve, he hadn't known of any other way to feel so alive. It scared him that the last time he had entered this building—in his pursuit of Eve—he hadn't felt anything at all until he found her.

The elevator slowed, then stopped with a ding. The doors opened and Manilow's "Mandy" was drowned out by pandemonium.

A screaming banshee's wail rent the air, as well as any nearby eardrums. Two writhing bodies, locked in combat, rolled past the elevator. One was covered in coarse animal hair, the other boasted flowing inky tresses. A werewolf and a lili. Around them, a crowd made up mostly of Infernals had gathered to feed off the negative energy.

In the corner on the left, a receptionist's desk was staffed by another wolf, this one in human form. She stood, dressed in a white blouse and black skirt, watching the melee with a wide smile. To the right, chairs lined the walls, filled with both Marks and Infernals waiting for processing. The untrained eye might see the crowd and think it was Halloween. The mixture of oddly dressed and naked Infernals wouldn't make sense on any other day of the year. Straight ahead was the hallway that led to the various offices. That's where Alec was headed, if everyone would get out of the way.

Alec stepped out of the elevator and held the door for Eve. She stared at the ruckus with wide eyes. Her fingers pinched her nostrils closed and she yelled, "What is this place?"

"Hell on Earth."

He didn't raise his voice, but the din around them quieted as if he'd shouted.

"Cain," the receptionist breathed, blinking momentarily before dropping into her seat. The standing crowd also sank into their chairs. The couple on the floor gaped at him; the wolf with his terrible maw and the lili with her perfect pouting lips. Locked together in a mock embrace, they seemed to forget that they had been tearing each other apart mere seconds ago.

"Are you done?" Alec asked them with a raised brow.

"It stinks down 'ere," Eve mumbled through her plugged nose.

"He insulted me," the lili said, disentangling herself and pushing to her feet.

"She has a nice rack," the werewolf rumbled, straightening.

Alec looked at the lili. "You couldn't take that as a compliment?"

"I could die today," she muttered. "I want to go out with some respect."

"We could all die today," Eve drawled, dropping her hand. The wolf shifted into his naked human form and she whistled.

Alec gritted his teeth. "It's not polite to stare."

"I have a better chance of dying than most," the lili retorted, glaring at Eve. She turned her demonic green gaze to Alec. "You suck. I thought older brothers were supposed to be protective."

"If I'm older than you," he countered, "I'm not your brother."

Eve's mouth fell open.

"You could act on the principle of it," the lili argued.

"She's a lilin," he explained to Eve, grabbing her elbow with his free hand and tugging her away from the blatantly interested wolf. "One hundred of them die daily. They never know when their number is going to be up."

"Brother?"

"She wishes," he scoffed. "My dad hasn't talked to Lilith in ages. And that lili is too impetuous to be older than me."

"I'm confused. Who's Lilith?"

Alec looked at the receptionist just as she was lifting the phone receiver from its cradle. "Cain's here," she said to whoever had answered. She beamed at Alec, then winked. Wrapped around that flirtatious eye was the detail that labeled her a werewolf, formerly under the rule of Mammon, the demon god of avarice.

"Lilith was my dad's first wife." Alec hefted the punch bowl and directed Eve down the hall. The sound of their booted footfalls on the polished concrete echoed ahead of them. Behind them, furious whispers followed.

Eve's sloe eyes widened. "First wife? I thought Adam had Eve, and that was it."

He shook his head. "Don't worry about it."

"No, seriously. Why didn't I know that? No one's ever told me that."

"Angel." Alec opened a glass inset door that said Forensic Wiccanology in gold sticker lettering. "One thing at a time."

Inside the room, the overhead lights were out. Pendant lamps hung over various island stations, spotlighting specific work areas.

"Cain!" The coarseness of the voice was reminiscent of Larry King and it originated from the distant right corner. "It's been far too long since you came to see me."

Alec's head turned to find the robe-clad crone who approached with a shuffling stride. As she moved from the shadows into the light, she changed from a hunchback into a lovely, willowy redhead. Her robe altered from an all-encompassing shroud to a tightly fit and strategically cut gown.

"Hello, Hank," Alec greeted. He held out the punch bowl. "I need you to find the Nix who touched this."

Hank's full lips curved in a winsome smile. "I'll do my best." She looked at Eve, her head tilting. She shifted form again, taking on the appearance of a firmly muscled, carrot-topped male. The gown changed into a black dress shirt and matching slacks. "Nice to meet you."

Eve blinked rapidly. "Hi."

Alec touched her elbow. "Evangeline, meet Hank. Hank, this is Eve."

"Hi, Eve." Hank licked his lips.

Eve waved lamely.

"We'll check in later," Alec said, pulling Eve toward the door.

"Bring her with you when you come back." As Hank moved away, his form returned to that of a stooped crone.

Once they were in the hall, Eve took a deep breath and wondered if the stench of Infernals was affecting her brain. She looked at Alec. "I feel like one of my teenage acid trips has come back to haunt me."

"Not possible."

"What is Hank?"

"An occultist. A demon who specializes in the magical arts and tapping into the power that threads through all of nature."

"No, I meant is it male or female?"

Alec shrugged. "I'm not sure."

"Great. What is this place?" She tried breathing through her mouth to avoid smelling anything, but it was pointless. The odor was steeped into the walls. "Unless my nose is completely wrong, I'd say most of these beings are demonic."

"Your nose isn't wrong." He pointed down the hall. "It's an amalgamation of things. Various Infernal entities are kept here because they're useful in some way."

"Kept?" Eve took in her surroundings with an examining eye. The lower level of Gadara Tower reminded her of a fifties film noir with its muted lighting, inlaid glass doors, and smoky air.

"Some are held against their will," Alec clarified, "others come by choice, because they want protection. There's no such thing as honor among the damned. If you piss off the wrong guy, they'll hunt you down."

"You don't have to tell *me* that," she muttered, noting the occasional alcoves that boasted widows featuring a nighttime view of a metropolis. It was amazingly believable, but it was still daylight up above. "Is that real?"

"No. Most Infernals go nuts if they feel confined in any way. They prefer night to day, so that's what Raguel went with." Alec paused before a new door labeled Orange County Power and Water Management. Eve frowned, knowing that there was no such entity. He knocked and they waited. "The illusion of being topside keeps them functioning properly."

The door swung open, revealing a young, lanky man standing behind a desk situated directly before the door. He wore gray overalls with his last name—Wilson—embroidered on the breast and military-grade "birth control" glasses; nicknamed for their ability to make anyone look like shit. Beyond him, a partition blocked the view of the rest of the interior. Filing cabinets flanked his left and a large potted palm tree flanked his right. The air escaping the room smelled like cotton candy, which told Eve the man was a Mark and not an Infernal.

"Cain," Wilson said, smiling. "What can I do for you?"

Eve snorted softly. Alec entered a room and everyone started kowtowing. With every day that passed, the image she'd long held of an evil, reviled Cain wore away.

She was bringing up the rear when a group of three Marks rounded the corner—two females and one male. The girls were sporting an odd sort of look consisting of jungle boots, black parachute pants, and strategically ripped tanks in bright colors. The man wore jeans and a baby blue polo shirt. In unison, their gazes raked her from head to toe.

"She's not all that," one gal said to the other with a wrinkle of her nose.

"Cain gets all the pussy," the male said. "I hear Asian chicks are hot in bed."

"Excuse me?" Eve said.

"There's no excuse for sleeping your way to the top," hissed the second girl as they passed.

Eve turned to watch them go, feeling an odd mixture of anger and nausea. "There's no excuse for those clothes you're wearing either," she called after them. "News flash: the eighties ended a couple decades ago."

"Angel?" Alec's voice drew her gaze. He held a clipboard in his hands. "What are you doing?"

"Lagging." She left the hallway and the door clicked shut behind her.

"Come on." Alec held the paperwork out to her. "Fill out your parents' information. And yours."

She looked at the form, noting that it asked for name, address, and phone number for up to three individuals. "Okay."

He smiled. His expression was warm and pleased, telling her how much he appreciated her obedience. That surprised her, considering how easily he accepted the same from everyone else. He seemed more comfortable in command than Gadara did. Gadara manipulated to get what he wanted; Alec simply expected that his orders would be followed.

Alec looked at Wilson. "We have a Nix problem."

"We'll take care of it."

Eve looked up at him. "How?"

"As with any possible infestation," Wilson said, "we prevent the pest from gaining access in the first place. In the case of Nixes, we insert a deterrent into the main water pipe to the residence."

"After you do that, can I take down the crosses I have hanging in my showers?"

"You could." Wilson smiled. "It would only be a benefit to you, though, to keep them up."

She looked at Alec. "Since I'm living in a Gadara-managed building, why didn't I have something like that in place to begin with? It would have saved Mrs. Basso's life."

"We don't work like that." He pushed his hands into his jeans pockets. "Imagine if Infernals set up a barrier in the town of Baker, California. It would effectively prevent Marks from traveling between Nevada and California. We have to work case by case, Infernal by Infernal. Otherwise, we'd end up battling for territory, which would put mortals in the crossfire. We—Marks and Infernals both—need mortals to survive. Since we have a mutual need, we make certain concessions."

Her pen tapped against the clipboard.

He rocked back on his heels. "When, in the last two days, did we have a chance to come in here? Besides, you were safe with me. I never thought he'd hit your neighbor."

The phone rang on Wilson's desk and he answered it. Eve returned her attention to filling out the paperwork.

"They're right here," Wilson said into the receiver. "Yes, of course. I'll tell them." He hung up. "Raguel will be calling in ten minutes. He wants you to take the call in his office."

Alec nodded. Eve passed over the clipboard.

Wilson's gaze was sympathetic behind his glasses. "I'll send someone out immediately."

"Send two people simultaneously," she suggested, "so there's no one to follow from my house to my parents and vice versa." She set the pen on his desk. "Will whatever you're doing keep my parents safe?"

"The Nix doesn't know where they live," Alec reminded. "If he did, he would have gone after them instead of Mrs. Basso. Can he find another way in? Yes. If he finds them and he has the time, he can work it out. But this will slow him down. Hopefully long enough for Hank to find him."

She nodded. As far as feeling better went, it wasn't much, but what else did she have?

"One thing at a time," Alec repeated in a murmur. "We're dealing with the Nix. Now, we'll go upstairs and deal with Raguel. We'll get it all done. Trust me."

Her mouth curved ruefully. "You're good at this, you know. It's a shame you're stuck with someone clueless like me. You should be managing bigger fish."

Alec's face closed, although his pleasant mien did not change. It was more of a feeling she had of a sudden withdrawal, as if she'd struck a deep chord.

The sensation set her mind spinning. By the time they returned to the elevator, she'd thought of something she hadn't before: if nothing was a coincidence, how was it that she lived in a building for which Gadara was the trustee?

Had he been lying in wait for her? If so, what was the event or purpose that set her marking in motion?

And what would it take to be free of it?

CHAPTER 16

"Hello, Cain. Ms. Hollis."

As the elevator emptied Eve and Alec into the antechamber of Gadara's office, the archangel's secretary greeted them with a wide smile. He was an elderly man, one who appeared a wee bit past the retirement age. He smelled like a Mark, though, which made Eve wonder what he could have done to get into trouble so late in life. "Can I get you both something to drink?" he offered. "Coffee, perhaps? Or a soda?"

Eve declined. Alec simply shook his head.

The secretary led them into Gadara's office and gestured for them to occupy the two chairs before Gadara's desk. He used a keypad to lower the projection screen and dim the lights. Eve was once again taken aback by the size of the room. It was cavernous and richly appointed. As an interior designer, she was well aware that a person's preference in room size and shape said a great deal about him. Gadara obviously felt a need to astonish and impress. How much of that was directed toward the mortals he did business with? And how much of it was for the benefit of the Marks under his command?

"A penny for your thoughts," Alec said, once the secretary had left.

"I'm not sure they're worth that." Her tone was as dry as her palms. After all she had been through the last several days, she should be a nervous wreck.

"Are you okay?"

Eve looked at him, noting that even in poor lighting Alec was drop-dead gorgeous. The planes of his face were strong and bold, but softened slightly by his overly long hair. She could get used to seeing his face every day. If she let herself. "I don't think everything has sunk in yet. Ask me again, once we've had a chance to settle down."

A soft beeping noise filled the air, then the screen flickered to life. Gadara's face appeared. His dark skin and eyes held a wealth of majesty and a touch of divine refinement that was enchanting. Eve was once again arrested by the sheer force of his charisma, evident even across the digital signal that broadcast him. Behind him was a window, and beyond that was a view she recognized immediately—the Las Vegas strip. He was dressed in a suit and tie today, and the more formal look suited him. It complemented his air of power and affluence.

"We've got a problem," Alec began.

"Yes, you do," Gadara drawled. "Where is Abel?"

Eve's brows rose.

"He doesn't know anything."

"Exactly." The archangel leaned back in his chair

and ran a rough hand through his coarse gray hair. "He is her handler, Cain. He needs to be kept in the loop."

"If that's his job," Alec retorted, "he shouldn't need help doing it."

"The two of you are going to get her killed."

"If you don't manage to do that first."

"I'm not going to die," Eve interjected quietly.

The sound of clapping turned her head. Reed exited the elevator in an expertly tailored three-piece suit of graphite gray. The sheer perfection of his appearance— the faultless cut of his garments, the perfect combing of his inky hair, the sensual curve of his welcoming smile—took her breath away. "That's my girl," he drawled. "Don't let them push you around."

Alec pushed to his feet. "Eve was right. The tengu had no details and no scent."

Silence gripped the room so completely Eve could have heard a pin drop.

"What do you mean, 'Eve was right'?" Gadara bit out.

"When the tengu first attacked me a few days ago," she explained, "I noted that he didn't have any details. Alec and Reed both said my super senses hadn't fully developed and that's why I couldn't see them."

"'Super senses'?" Gadara laughed.

"But obviously, they were wrong," she continued. "Alec didn't see anything last night either. You can't tell me he hasn't come into his gifts yet."

Reed moved to the desk and leaned against it. "It's never happened before. All of these centuries, millions of Infernals . . . It's never been possible for an Infernal to hide its details. There has to be an explanation."

"Such as?" Eve asked.

"Perhaps his details are a similar color to the stone from which he's made."

"Okay. Why didn't he stink?" she countered.

Gadara made an odd noise, drawing all eyes to him. "Tell me everything that happened, Cain."

Alec went over the events of the night before, finishing with the death of Mrs. Basso.

Reed moved from the desk to Eve and set his hand on her shoulder. "Were you close to her?" he asked quietly.

"Yes. I loved her."

"I'm sorry for your loss."

"The police came," Alec said. "They say the Nix has been killing for some time. If that's true, why hasn't he been vanquished?"

"The order did not come down, until today," Gadara replied.

"That's sick," Eve said.

"It is the way we work, Ms. Hollis." Gadara's gaze was hard. "We are not vigilantes."

"He's killed at least a dozen people! We're not talking about vigilantism. We're talking about justice and protecting the innocent."

"Do not lecture me," Gadara said coldly. "You want to shed the mark and go back to your careless life. You do not give a damn about protecting the innocent."

A slap in the face could not have affected Eve more. "Don't make me feel guilty for wanting my life back."

"It is one thing to be ignorant; it is quite another to deliberately bury your head in the sand."

Reed moved to a spot a foot or so in front of her. "Don't attack her for our own shortcomings."

"We need to decide what to do about this," Alec interjected, his stance widening and his arms crossing. The pose made him imposing, depicting him as immovable, stalwart.

"What do you suggest?" the archangel asked.

"Both of the tengu on the roof lacked details and smelled normal. The first question I have is whether or not Gehenna Masonry has something to do with it. Did they create both? If so, we know the source."

"I pray we're lucky enough to have this restricted to tengu," Reed said.

Eve looked around at the grim faces of the three men. "Explain the possible ramifications of this to me."

"We do not have enough Marks." Gadara's voice was weary. "We supplement with mortal labor, like the guards you met at the building last night. We also do business with mortals. If Infernals hid in that guise, there is no limit to the places they could go and the information they could obtain."

"Infernals would have a tremendous advantage," Alec said. "They'd smell us coming a mile away, but they could be completely under the radar. If they've created a mask of some sort, we need to eradicate it."

Eve stood. "So we have to find out how they did it. We have to go to Upland, where Gehenna Masonry is."

All three men looked at her.

"Not with the Nix after you," Alec argued.

"And the tengu," Reed added.

"Yes." Gadara smiled like a proud parent. "You should go. The tengu seem to like you, Ms. Hollis, and the Nix has been assigned to a Mark, as of this morning. Right, Abel?"

"Right," Reed said tightly.

"Bullshit." Alec's voice was a low growl. "This is too important to use as a novice training assignment. Eve is in over her head. You need to send someone more experienced."

"Ah, but there is no one more experienced than you," the archangel pointed out.

"Then I'll go alone."

"I have to concur," Reed said.

"With who?" Alec snapped.

"You."

Eve might have laughed at Alec's blatant surprise, if the circumstances had been less somber.

"See, Ms. Hollis?" Gadara drawled. "Miracles do happen."

She looked at Alec. "I can't go home; I can't face it now. And I can't go to my parents' house. If you leave for Upland, what will I do?"

"You can wait for Hank's results."

A dry laugh escaped her. "I'm not going back down there. The Infernals creep me out and some of the Marks are hostile. After I'm trained and can hold my own, no problem. Until then, no thanks."

Alec frowned. "Hostile? What are you talking about?"

Reed drew abreast of her. "There is some jealousy in the ranks."

"She *must* go," Gadara said. "Once a mentor is paired with a Mark, they stay together until the Mark is self-sufficient."

"Don't start playing by the rules now," Alec snapped.

"And do not presume to dictate to me, Cain. If you separate from Ms. Hollis, I will make that separation permanent and pair her with a mentor who will keep her close at hand."

Eve's hands settled on her hips. "No one's buying your 'following the rules' line, you know. Why don't you just tell us the truth?"

Gadara's face split with a smile. "I want you to get your feet wet."

"Whatever," she scoffed. "I've gotten wet plenty of times in the last week."

Alec cleared his throat. Reed grinned.

"You know what I mean," she mumbled.

"Okay," Gadara conceded with laughter in his deep voice, "Whether you believe me or not, I would like you to get your hands dirty. I want you to see firsthand what we do and why we do it, and I trust that Cain will keep you safe under his watch."

I want you to get your hands dirty. Eve considered that statement carefully. Since Gadara didn't strike her as being overly altruistic when his own needs were involved, his statement made her contemplate whether or not her acceptance of the mark was important in some way. And if that was the case, what could her rejection of it mean?

"That settles it, then," she stated, determined to play the hand dealt to her until the end of the game. If Gadara insisted she go, she had to know the real reason why. And frankly, she *wanted* to go. There was a thrumming anticipation in her blood that was becoming all too familiar, a darkness like black velvet—soft, warm, and sensuous. She'd started the morning wanting a few hours of normalcy. Now she wanted to beat the shit out of something not human. Something that would give her a good fight, but wouldn't leave any guilt behind.

"It's not settled with me," Alec retorted.

Reed exhaled audibly. "Just be careful, Eve."

"What?" Fists clenching, Alec glared at his brother. "You're going to agree with this? You pansy-assed motherfucker!"

"Screw you," Reed bit out. "It's what she wants."

"I don't give a shit. She doesn't know better. She hasn't been trained and she's pissed off."

"Um, excuse me." Eve waved. "I'm right here. Don't talk about me like I'm not."

"Sorry." Coming up to her, Alec pulled her into a bear hug.

Eve rested her hand against his abdomen and tilted her head back to look up at him. "We didn't do so bad last night. We're both still kicking."

"You were almost splattered across the street like roadkill." His tone was exasperated . . . and resigned. "How much worse could it have been?"

"This is not open to debate," Gadara said. "Her handler and I are agreed."

Alec's head turned. He shot a killer glance at the screen. "You had better pray that nothing happens to her."

"I pray every day, Cain. Can you say the same?"

Eve tugged Alec toward the door before the situation grew any more explosive.

"This isn't a game, Eve," he warned darkly as the elevator doors shut out the view of a somber-faced Reed. With his hands propped on the handrail, Alec leaned back and glowered.

"It is to Gadara." Her mouth curved grimly. "But damned if I'll play the part of the pawn without making some moves of my own."

* * *

Reed watched Eve disappear behind the closing elevator doors, then he faced Raguel. "This is too serious for just one team to handle."

"I am inclined to believe it is their synergy that is causing the problem, not a mask." Raguel adjusted his tie. "I have a meeting with Steve Wynn in a half hour. I wish I looked as good in my suit as you do in yours."

"Are you kidding me? You're going to completely disregard what Cain and Eve told you?"

Raguel relaxed into his chair with a sigh. "You heard his story. He was as focused on Ms. Hollis as he was on the hunt."

"So? He was doing his job."

"Was he? Or is his heart ruling his head? There is a tremendous difference between happenstance and calculation. Cain hasn't been trained."

Reed felt a chill move through him. He knew deliberate obtuseness when he saw it. "You're gambling with something so potentially damaging that I'm at a loss for words. I don't understand why you're not erring on the side of caution."

"You want my job?" Raguel's voice was dangerously soft. "Be my guest. Manage the situation as you see fit."

"With what resources?"

Pristine white teeth flashed within the frame of coffee-dark skin. "With the ones you have at your disposal. I must function within my station. So, too, must you."

"Your station is greater than mine."

"Exactly," the archangel hissed. "Do not forget that."

The screen went black, leaving Reed in turmoil. He had twenty-one charges in total, including Eve. At any given moment, at least one of them was locked in combat that would lead to death—either the Mark's or his or her prey. From the heavens, orders streamed down into Reed's consciousness like water, forcing him to shift through the various threads. He assigned Marks to various hunts based on their experience, location, and a multitude of other factors, not the least of which was the needs of the firm to which he was assigned.

To his knowledge, no handler had ever thinned his charges by setting them on a task of his own design while relying on the others to pick up the slack. Doing so would weaken all of them. Some Marks were better able to handle specific Infernals than others. Assigning a less-talented Mark to the hunt because his more experienced team member was occupied by an unsanctioned task was so dangerous Reed couldn't believe he was even thinking of it.

But what options did he have?

He could use an Infernal, either one presently working within the firm or one scheduled for vanquishing. He could offer a bargain—cooperation or death. Infernals were survivors; they would do whatever was necessary to keep their lives. But it was not his place to decide which Infernals were worthy of saving and which were destined to burn in Hell. As with his previous option—using Marks—Reed had no idea what the ramifications would be for reaching so far beyond his assigned duties, but he knew they would be dire. He needed someone farther up the food chain than he was. Someone to take the heat, if necessary.

He needed an archangel to assist him.

It wasn't completely improbable. As long as he offered a perceived benefit, he could solicit help. Cain made devil's bargains all the time.

Reed avoided the elevator and moved to the reception area instead. He paused before the desk of the elderly Mark who answered Raguel's phones. "Do we have any visiting firms in the area or one scheduled to arrive shortly?"

The firms always kept each other appraised of visits. Putting two archangels into close proximity required greater security, plus they felt it was their due to be shown deference by whoever was visiting.

"The European firm sent seven Marks yesterday," the secretary replied. "Sarakiel is scheduled to visit next week."

Reed nodded grimly. "Thank you."

Of course it would have to be Sara. God forbid his task should be easy for him.

As he prepared to shift from his present location to her office, Reed steeled himself for the task ahead. She'd want his blood.

It was true. Hell hath no fury like a woman scorned.

It was a thirty-minute drive to Upland from Anaheim on a good day. To say the freeway traffic in Southern California was horrendous would be an understatement. Stop-and-go speeds added hours to most trips, and accidents often turned highways into parking lots.

Today wasn't too bad because it was still early afternoon, not yet the time when most residents began their commutes home. Alec stared out the passenger window, the fingers of his left hand brushing back and forth over the denim that covered his knee. He was quiet, contemplative.

He and Eve had left Gadara Tower through the

subterranean parking complex using a Jeep Liberty that belonged to Gadara Enterprises. He hoped that move would throw anyone following Eve's car off the trail, which still sat in the street level parking lot. With suspicious cops and an overzealous Nix, they couldn't be too careful.

Eve drove to a strip mall and parked. Exiting through the rear door of a nail salon, they walked up the road to a Hertz rental car agency and picked up new wheels. Alec paid with cash rather than a traceable credit card. Now they were settled in a Ford Focus whose satellite transponder wasn't monitored by Raguel—at least not at present. The archangel would catch on eventually and when he did he would tap into Hertz's tracking system. For now, however, they were off the radar.

Not a word passed between them during the exchange; there was nothing to say. Eve didn't trust Raguel and Alec couldn't defend him. The entire situation was fucked six ways to Sunday.

"He who is a hired hand," he murmured, "and not a shepherd, who is not the owner of the sheep, sees the wolf coming, and leaves the sheep and flees, and the wolf snatches them and scatters them."

"What?" Eve asked.

Alec glanced at her. "John 10:12."

"You're calling Gadara the hired hand? You think he's tossed us to the wolves, too?"

"I don't know what to think, angel." He leaned his head back against the headrest. "I'm having a hard time understanding how he can be so cavalier about something so important."

"He doesn't believe us," she said flatly. "It's either that, or he believes it and wants the shit to hit the fan.

Any idea what reasoning he would have to allow that to happen?"

"No."

Alec had never liked the archangels. Similar to children, they curried the favor of their father. They competed with their siblings in the hopes of outshining them. Marks and their mentors and handlers were simply a means to that end. That was why Alec had come to appreciate his autonomy; it kept him far beyond their machinations.

"And that whole 'get your hands dirty' excuse is crap," Eve said crossly. "I'm not buying it."

"I'm not either."

"So what's the point?" She looked at him. "What could he possibly gain beyond pissing you off?"

"Are you asking me, or just talking out loud?"

"Of course I'm asking you." Her eyes went back to the road. They were traveling a respectable seventy-five miles per hour on Route 60. The windows were up so they didn't have to shout, but the air conditioner was on. The chilled air ruffled through Eve's hair, blowing loose tendrils from her ponytail across her cheek. She swiped at them impatiently. "You know what's going on better than I do."

"Not really," he said dryly. "That's the problem. I've never had a handler or worked within a firm. My orders come directly from Jehovah. I have no idea how to function within a framework. You and I are completely in the dark with this."

"Okay, then. How would you handle this if you were on your own?"

Alec didn't hesitate to answer, because he'd been thinking of his options ever since the night before. "I would set up camp in Upland. Infernals can smell me coming, so I would stake out the masonry and break in during off hours. Then I'd dig around."

"Let's go back to the smell thing." Her fingers flexed on the steering wheel. "If I was omnipotent and I created a legion of warriors to fight on my behalf, I wouldn't advertise them with a unique scent. I'd want to keep them hidden."

"Deer smell the wolves coming. This hunt isn't any different from what you see in the animal kingdom."

"It's like he's giving them a chance to get away with whatever they're doing."

"The Lord has a strong sense of fair play."

"Or a sick sense of humor."

"Angel—"

"So let's follow your plan," she said quickly. "We'll grab a hotel room, then stake out the masonry."

His eyes closed. He reached out blindly to set his hand on her thigh. "We don't have a choice. I'm sorry."

Her hand settled over his much larger one. Eve was slender and delicate, far too precious to risk so pointlessly. "One step at a time."

"You sound good," he murmured. "Focused."

"I know what we saw, or more aptly what we *didn't* see." Her voice flowed over his skin like sun-warmed honey. "I've never had aspirations of saving the world, but obviously I am not going to turn my back and pretend nothing is happening."

Alec opened one eye and turned his head. "Don't let what Raguel said get to you."

"That's easier said than done." The corners of her mouth took on a downward curve. "He's right. It's one thing to be ignorant by accident; it is completely different to be ignorant by choice. I wanted to go to the damn movies, Alec, when all Hell has broken loose— literally. What is the matter with me?"

"I understand why you wanted some time alone today. I can't tell you how many times I've wished I could be normal for even an hour. That doesn't make you a coward and it doesn't make you wrong."

"Doesn't make me right either."

Eve looked at him. The sadness in her eyes combined with the determined set of her jaw hit his gut like a blow. He was struck with the knowledge that more than one woman had died today. The young girl he had known and loved was gone, never to return. She had been ripped from her safe, orderly life and thrust into a world where demons hunted her and dear friends paid the price.

Scrubbing a hand over his face, Alec tried to hide his disquiet from Eve. As he mourned the loss of his first love, fury and frustration ate at him. In only a matter of days it had become too late to save her.

Yet it wasn't too late to save the woman sitting beside him now, the woman holding his hand and suggesting she stand with him as he tackled an assignment unlike any he had ever faced before.

"This isn't your fault, Alec."

A dry laugh rasped from his throat. "Are you trying to comfort me? After what you've been through?"

"This hasn't been easy on you either. You've given up a lot for me."

He stood to gain a lot more. But she didn't know that.

Beauty is in the eye of the beholder. One man's goddess was another man's nightmare. Sara Kiel, however, was beautiful to all who saw her. Tall, willowy, yet fully curved, Sara was physically perfect in a way that plastic surgeons would sell their souls to replicate. There had been a time when the mere sight of her could make Reed's blood heat dangerously. Now, he watched her with an indifferent eye, admiring her with only a vague interest.

"I find it nearly impossible to believe that Raguel has not acted on this information," she said, pacing gracefully. She reminded him of a tigress—golden, lithe, predatory. "Perhaps he knows something that you do not."

"Or perhaps he wants to keep the information as contained as possible," Reed countered.

Sipping from a glass of icy water, he lounged on the golden velvet chaise in Sara's Parisian office with one arm slung over the back. The head of the European firm of Marks was often assumed by theologians to be a male. They couldn't be more wrong. Sarakiel was a woman in every sense of the word.

Today she wore a pinstriped pantsuit and tie, an ensemble that might have made some women look masculine. On Sara, it only emphasized her divinely enhanced femininity. Her pale blonde hair was pulled into a classic chignon and her face was devoid of the makeup that funded her firm. Sara Kiel Cosmetics was a worldwide phenomenon, with sales inspired by the unequaled face of its owner.

There had been a time when Reed thought they were exceptionally suited to one another, but that was long ago. He had become jaded enough to admit that an outward sense of style and a mutual fondness for rough sex was not enough of a foundation for any sort of lasting relationship.

"Raguel knows," Reed continued, "that Cain is too much of a loner to approach anyone else for help and Evangeline is too green to do anything on her own."

"Ah, the notorious Evangeline," Sara cooed. "I plan to visit Raguel soon. I am dying of curiosity about Cain's woman. In fact, I sent a team to California yesterday to prepare for my arrival."

Notorious. Reed's jaw tightened. "She's just like any other woman."

"Is she? She is the only thing besides blood that you have shared with your brother." Sara's smile turned brittle. "Tell me, *mon chéri*, what is it like fucking a woman who bears your mother's name?"

"Who says I fucked her?"

"There is no way you could resist. And certainly she would not be able to refuse you."

He shrugged.

Sara returned to the topic at hand. "I am certain Raguel expected you to keep the news quiet, because doing so places your brother in jeopardy."

"Who knows what he thinks?" Reed dismissed.

"I am more concerned with what you are thinking. I admit to being surprised that you are here. Moreso than I am that he is not."

"This goes far beyond the North American firm. The development of an Infernal mask places everyone in jeopardy."

"So what do you want me to do?" Her fingers stroked sensuously along the length of her tie.

Behind Sara, Reed could see the Eiffel Tower glittering with lights in the darkness. Odd that the backdrop would be so similar to the one he'd seen behind Raguel just a short time past. Two archangels, two continents, same view. They had more in common than that; they were both ambitious and frighteningly competitive.

"I want you to lend me the team of Marks you sent to California," he said.

Sara laughed. "You do not ask for much, do you?"

"Nothing you can't afford."

"The question is: can you afford it?" The glint in her eye confirmed his earlier suspicions about what she'd want from him.

"You ask that as if it were a hardship," he drawled. He deliberately focused on not betraying his growing tension. "Don't forget how much you stand to gain beyond the immediate. To have your team outwit Raguel's would be quite a coup for you."

"I know how this benefits me, but what does it do for you?" Her blue eyes narrowed. "In addition to incurring Raguel's wrath, you are also foregoing the possibility of humiliation for your brother."

Reed stared through his drinking glass to the cubes of ice within. He rattled them absently before casting Sara a sidelong glance. "Forego Cain's humiliation? Darling, you wound me. What could be more perfect than being the instrument of his deliverance and the tool by which he is rescued?"

He didn't say that Jehovah might find his initiative pleasing, especially considering the possible consequences of failing to act. Pleasing God would only increase his chances of gaining a firm of his own.

But Sara was aware of some omission, as evidenced by the doubtful humming noise she made.

Setting his glass on the gilded coffee table, Reed stood. It was time to move in for the kill.

She held up one hand. "Did I not say that you would come back to me . . . on your knees?"

A smile curved his mouth. "But it's so much more fun for both of us when you are on yours."

Her lips parted and she backed up a step.

Reed moved toward her with deliberate leisure, his fingers on the buttons of his waistcoat. If he didn't see to his own undressing, Sara would tear his garments from him. She took such pleasure in ripping into his outer shell, as if that would somehow expose the man he was within.

He could see the anticipation race over her skin and knew her nipples would be tight and hard, her sex hot and slick. Two weeks had passed since he'd indulged in Eve. Two weeks of celibacy that should have left him hungry for the hard screwing Sara relished. He hadn't gone this long without a woman in centuries.

Shrugging out of his coat and waistcoat, Reed tossed them over the back of one of the chairs facing Sara's desk. He tugged off his tie and belt, adding them to the pile. With every article of clothing he shed, Sara's excitement grew. He could smell her lust, see it in the brightness of her eyes and the nervous licking of her lips. She reached into his pocket, withdrew his cell phone, and turned it off. Then she tossed it over to the chaise.

Reed reached for his fly. Her gaze dropped. He thought of stairwells and cameras and thickly lashed slanted eyes. His cock finally cooperated with his intentions, hardening from the heated memory.

"Before we get distracted," he murmured, "I want you to tell your team in California to get ready for a mission."

"I need them," she retorted. "I'll send another."

His hands dropped to his sides. "They may not get there in time. That isn't a chance I'm willing to take."

Sara's jaw tightened when she realized he'd leave if he didn't get what he wanted. "You drive a hard bargain, *mon chéri*."

"Isn't that why you like me so much?"

CHAPTER 17

E ve pulled into the parking lot of a Motel 6 just off the highway in Upland. There was a convenience store adjacent and a grocer's up the street. Turning off the ignition, she glanced at Alec before opening the door. He hadn't said a word over the last few minutes, retreating into himself and hoarding his thoughts. She knew this was as difficult for him as it was for her. If she'd ever consider praying to a higher power for anything, it would be for the ability to help him instead of hinder him.

She pushed the door open and exited. Resting her forearm on the roof of the car, she looked around. Upland was inland from Orange County, which made the temperature hotter and the air drier. She missed the ocean breeze already, but Eve suspected that was part of a general homesickness for anything familiar. She was separated from her family and her best friend, she'd lost her job, and Mrs. Basso was gone. A hotel stay in a strange town only added to her feeling of being a fish out of water.

Water.

Thinking of the Nix, Eve pushed away from the car and shut the door. Alec appeared on the opposite side. Tall, dark, handsome, and brooding. He slipped shades over his eyes, hiding his thoughts from her visual probe. There was a huge gulf between them at the moment. Like the tide against the shore, they crashed together and drew apart.

"After we get a room," she said, "I need to hit the convenience store for a soda and a prepaid cell phone."

He smiled. "You'd make a good spy, I think."

"I have a fondness for action flicks."

Alec came around the trunk and offered his hand. She accepted, but the closeness was only superficial. Emotionally, he was miles away, which was why she took a room with two double beds.

"You two got any pets?" the desk clerk asked. He was a young man in his midtwenties, Eve guessed. Overweight by about sixty pounds and a mouth breather.

She shook her head. "Just us. Please don't put us in a room that has had pets before. I'm allergic to cats."

"No problem." He leaned over the counter and lowered his voice. "Someone in the area has been stealing pets and hacking them up. It's in all the local papers. Just wanted to warn you."

"Hacking them up?" she repeated, remembering the article she'd read earlier that morning.

"Nasty stuff. Disemboweling, removing the eyeballs . . . that sort of thing." His tone was more gossipmonger thrilled than it was disgusted or disturbed. "I read once that most serial killers start out mutilating animals, then they progress to people."

"So this area isn't safe?"

"It is for humans." He shrugged, straightening. "Not so much for pets."

While she signed the paperwork, Alec paid the balance in cash. He stared at her from behind his shades, but didn't say a word until they went outside.

"Something you want to say to me?" he asked as they skirted the front office and crossed over to the 7-Eleven parking lot.

"About what?"

"About the two beds?"

"No pressure."

"Hmm."

An electronic beeping announced their entrance into the convenience store. Out front, three cars were filling their gas tanks at the pumps. Inside, an elderly woman with big white hair manned the counter and two teens stood by the coolers against the rear wall, looking at the soda.

Eve grabbed a hand basket by the door and moved to the prepaid phones hanging on an end cap.

Alec gestured to the soda fountain. "Want something to drink?"

"Diet Dr Pepper, if they have it. Otherwise, I'll get it in a bottle."

"Okay."

Alec walked away and she rounded the aisle, grabbing beef jerky, nuts, and Chex Mix. She had a vision of lying across her motel bed with junk food, soda, and a movie on the television. The mere idea of a few hours of decompression was heaven on earth. They wouldn't head out to the masonry until night, so she had time to vegetate and make sense of life as she now knew it. With that in mind, she grabbed chocolate, too—Twix, Kit Kats, and Reese's Peanut Butter Cups.

Eve was making her way around the next aisle when the Infernal stench hit her. She sought out the source of the putrid smell and settled on the teenagers by the rear cooler. One wore a hooded sweatshirt with the hood up. The other wore a Hurley T-shirt and unkempt hair. On his nape, a tattoo of a diamond animated. It rotated, displaying the glimmer of its various facets.

She gaped, unmoving. As if he felt the weight of her stare, the hooded boy turned his head toward her. Eve's gaze dropped, her obscenely steady hands absently pulling unknown items from the shelf into her basket. She continued down the aisle, witless with fear.

Look harmless and busy, she told herself.

"Angel."

Jumping a good foot into the air, Eve spun to face Alec, who approached with a rapid stride. He caught her elbow and drew her farther down the aisle, away from the Infernals.

They were everywhere. How could she have forgotten that for even a moment? The weight of the knowledge was crushing.

As they feigned a preoccupation with shopping, Eve and Alec furtively watched the two young men withdraw energy drinks from the cooler and head up to the register. The clerk greeted them cheerfully and rang up their purchases. Her eyes were rimmed with gobs of mascara à la Tammy Faye Bakker and her lips were rimmed with the wrinkles of a lifetime cigarette smoker, but her smile was genuinely warm and her manner sweet.

The woman had no idea what she was dealing with.

"You okay?" Alec murmured as the young men left the store.

Eve nodded and released her pent-up breath. "They just took me off guard."

He rubbed her lower back.

"You know," she said. "I appreciate being able to smell them. I think I'd always be terrified if I was second-guessing everyone I met."

Alec nodded grimly.

"I guess my nose still isn't working right, though," Eve noted. "You smelled them from across the store. I had to get within a yard of them."

"I didn't smell them."

"Then how did you know?"

He glanced at her. "One of those boys just got his number called."

It took a heartbeat's length of time before she understood. "You?"

"Yeah. Me." He urged her to the register. "Our stay in Upland just got a lot more complicated."

Reed's fingers were sliding between Sara's thighs when he felt the first wave of Eve's terror. Like ripples on water, the distance between them made the feeling faint, but it was unmistakable nevertheless.

Squeezing his eyes shut, he rested his forehead against the window where he'd pinned Sara. There were other sensations to process beyond Eve and the woman in his arms—there were the other twenty Marks under his watch, orders from the seraphim, and the occasional check-in from Raguel's switchboard.

"Tease," Sara whispered, her lips to his ear.

Distracted, he moved by instinct, parting her and stroking through her slickness. She moaned. He knew just how to touch her, how to pleasure her, how to give her exactly what she wanted.

Her teeth nipped his ear and he reacted accordingly. The hand he had pressed against the window for leverage moved to her throat. Reed fought the urge to hurry the business along. He had to keep her busy long enough to make their agreement worth Sara's while. Otherwise, she could withdraw her Marks from his command before they had a chance to be put into play.

Sara's manicured fingertips dug into his waist and her lungs labored, pushing against his chest in an elevated rhythm. Sex was one of the few times when a celestially enhanced body responded without restraint. Orgasm-induced endorphins were the drug of choice for many, including Reed.

As Eve's distress peaked, goose bumps swept across Reed's skin. Sweat dotted his upper lip and pooled in the small of his back. The urge to go to her was so strong he quivered with it. He told himself it was because she was untrained and therefore dangerously vulnerable. It was an occupational reaction, nothing more.

"I love it when you shake for me," Sara purred, her nails raking the length of his back.

Reed kept his eyes closed, imagining that the silky tissues that clutched at his thrusting fingers belonged to another woman.

I-I don't normally . . . do things like . . . this.

Eve's trembling voice whispered through his mind.

She didn't know it—and he wasn't certain he would ever tell her—but their coupling in the stairwell had been raw in more than just the fierceness of the sex. He had compelled her away from the crowd, but once they were alone he'd done nothing to keep her there. He hadn't been able to, because he was too focused on her—the smell of her, the feel of her, the depth of her hunger. It had been as intimate an encounter as he'd ever experienced.

Sara liked rough sex, period. The person administering the roughness was moot. It was the thrill and the acts that she relished, not her partner. Eve, on the other hand, had been completely taken aback by her enjoyment of his handling. It had been *him* she responded to. No other man could have reached her the same way.

"Hurry," Sara hissed, her sex sucking voraciously at his pumping fingers. She released his waist and pushed impatiently at her wide-legged slacks. They fell to the floor in an expensive pool around her Manolos.

He stepped back long enough to shed his own pants. He briefly noted her black garter belt and silk stockings, then he gave a hard tug to her thong and dropped the ruined undergarment to the floor. She couldn't shrug out of her jacket fast enough. Before she could loosen her tie, he'd shoved her back into the window, pinning her to the cool glass.

Her smile lit up the room.

There was a brief moment when Reed thought about bending her over the desk and fucking her from behind. But this way had memories he was relying on to perform over the next several hours.

With his hands behind her thighs, he lifted her. Then

he paused, his gaze locked with hers. "You know what to do."

Sara reached between them and positioned him at her entrance. He stepped forward and dropped her simultaneously, impaling her in one hard thrust. Her cry pierced the air and charged his nerve endings. With his erection clasped in slick, liquid heat, his body took over from his brain. Finally.

Using his arms and thighs, Reed moved her up and down over him, stroking deep and fast. The erotic slapping of their bodies filled the room and spurred his lust. He focused on the feel of her clenching and releasing around his aching cock, the sensation hardening him further, making him throb with the sudden rush of blood to the swollen head of his dick.

She moaned as he filled her, stretched her, the grip of her body becoming fistlike in its intensity. Physically, it was damn good. He worked her up and down his cock with greater fervency, charging forward in his drive to culmination. His balls drew up, his spine tightened, his lungs heaved with his exertions. Sara's orgasm rippled along his length, bathing him in the creamy, fiery wash of release. Her moans only added to his pleasure. For all her angelic beauty, Sara sounded like a porn star during sex. It roused the animal in him, turning him on to a near fevered pitch.

Which was still nowhere near as hot as he'd been in the stairwell.

Emotionally, he and Sara were on different continents. Sara's eyes were closed, her head thrown back, her thoughts her own. Reed's mind was with Eve, his sexual energy focused on her, his soul directed toward soothing the fear he felt in her.

His rhythm faltered when he sensed her reaching back, a chaste touch, like a handhold in the darkness. Her spirit brushed across his as ephemerally as smoke, yet it rocked him to the core. With a roar, he climaxed. Sara shivered into another orgasm with a high-pitched squeal.

Eve brought him to his knees before the glass, with Sara scratching at his back and hours of servicing her left ahead of him. In the aftermath, he gasped for breath and longed for a shower. Left unguarded by the force of his release, he wasn't prepared for the sudden piercing agony that broke his connection to Evangeline.

One of his Marks was dying.

Reed groaned in agony and pushed Sara away. His back arched, thrusting his chest forward and his arms out. Pain and sorrow radiated from him with white-hot heat. His skin glowed with the effort to contain the herald of his charge—an instinctive cry for help from Mark to handler that was occasionally so powerful it was sometimes sensed by mortals. A sixth sense, some called it. The feeling of something being "wrong" or "off," but they didn't know what.

"Takeo," he gasped, calling out the name of his charge. Takeo had waited too long to call for help; Reed could feel the power of the mark draining from him. It was an aching feeling of loss that was amplified through Reed and sent outward to the firm. The death of a Mark was news that was carried through the soul and not through secular lines of communication. As the force of the herald left him, Reed collapsed forward, gulping in air.

"I have to go," he panted.

"You cannot save your Mark." Sara's lovely face

was flushed, her lips red and swollen even though he hadn't kissed her. "And if you leave before we are done, you will not save *her* either."

"Her?" Reed reached for his slacks.

"Evangeline." Her smile didn't reach her eyes. "You think a woman does not know when the man she is fucking is thinking about someone else?"

"Sara . . ." he warned, his fists clenching.

"It is too late to save Takeo and you know it. You just want to alleviate your guilt by consoling him in his final moments." She stabbed a perfectly painted red nail into his pectoral. "I want you to live with that guilt. I want you to remember how you failed your Mark because you were whoring for your brother's lover."

He slapped her, open-handed across the face. "You don't know what you're talking about."

She laughed and rubbed at the red mark left by his palm. Then she spread her legs, revealing the glistening pink folds of her sex. "Get to work, before I decide you are not worth the inconvenience you have caused me."

"How did you get called?" Eve asked, as Alec led her quickly across the parking lot back to the motel.

"The mark tingles," he said, "then burns. Toss me the car keys."

She did as he asked. "Like when you lie?"

He shot her an arch glance. "I don't lie."

"I did. And the mark burned."

Alec gave a wry laugh.

"It also burned when I entered Mrs. Basso's condo," she said. "It gave me the energy to break through the locks."

The line of his mouth thinned. "I know. The burning of your mark is just like getting an FTA—a failure to appear notice for a bail bond skip."

He unlocked her car door, then rounded the vehicle to the driver's side and climbed in.

"You didn't mention the door-breaking thing to Gadara," Eve said, just realizing that omission.

She accepted the bag of merchandise he set in her lap, moving it to the floorboards between her feet. Straightening, Eve was arrested by a sudden rush of warmth moving through her chilled veins. The sensation felt almost as if a warm blanket had been tossed around her shoulders. A blanket that smelled distinctly like Reed.

"I wanted to see if Abel would say anything." Alec turned the key in the ignition and backed out of the parking spot. "He's the one who triggered your mark. That's his job as your handler."

Eve watched him maneuver into traffic, still processing the rapid disbursement of her fear. One moment she was scared out of her mind, the next she felt cocooned and protected.

As if he was guided by radar, Alec quickly found the two boys strolling down a side street and fell into a safe surveillance distance behind them.

"What does that mean?" she queried. "Did he know about Mrs. Basso?"

"Handlers aren't necessarily aware of the particulars of the crime. They usually only know what class of demon the target is and which Mark in their stable is both local *and* qualified."

"Well, you can't get any more local than right next door."

"Or any less qualified that an untrained novice." He exhaled harshly. "Abel's job is to assign the most capable bounty hunter to each individual hunt, even if that means the Mark has to travel like we did today."

Eve's hands fisted in her lap. "Once a Mark is assigned, can another one step in?"

"Another Mark won't get the call, no."

Reed saved him for me.

Warmth blossomed in her chest, which scared her. She was grateful to be given a chance to kill. What did that make her? Besides homicidal?

"Raguel knew nothing about Abel assigning the Nix to you," Alec continued grimly, "which means Abel is acting on his own."

"Do handlers work for multiple firm leaders?"

Alec shook his head. "They work for one firm, that's it. But they are somewhat autonomous. They're *mal'aks*—angels—so they have full use of their gifts. They can route assignments to whomever they wish."

"Perhaps Reed doesn't trust Gadara either."

"Or maybe Raguel deserves the benefit of the doubt and my brother has something crafty up his sleeve," he snapped. "But I guess you don't want to think about that."

"Hey." Eve twisted in her seat, adjusting her seat belt for comfort. "Don't get pissy."

"Raguel is an archangel, Eve. His love for God is absolute."

"I don't buy it, I'm sorry. I haven't seen a drop of compassion in that guy. A lot of self-interest and bullshit, but love and compassion? Not at all."

"And you've seen love and compassion in Abel?" he scoffed. "When exactly was this? When he was banging you into servitude in the stairwell? Or when he blew off your training to assign you to a demon bent on killing you?"

Alec pulled the car over to the curb just before a cul de sac. The street sign named it Falcon Circle. The boys had turned the corner just a minute earlier. Eve hopped out before the vehicle stopped rolling. She continued on foot, anger and frustration riding her hard. On the left side of the road, the streets were open-ended. On the right side—the side she was traversing—all the streets were dead ends that butted up against a short field with a copse of trees beyond it.

The engine shut off and the driver's-side door slammed shut behind her, but Eve kept going. When she reached the corner, she paused and watched the two young men enter a home at the very end of the street. It was a two-story house with a deeply arched roof. The paint was a popular eighties-era scheme of light brown with chocolate trim. In the yard was a tricycle that had seen better days, and a lawn with bare patches and weed-infested flower beds. A covered car sat on one side of the driveway, while the adjacent side was stained with the remnants of an oil leak.

The day was bright and sunny, but a massive overgrown tree shaded the house and kept it in darkness. The residence was depressing, especially amid the other homes that showed signs of owner pride and attention. Alec's prey lived in the neighborhood eyesore, and the air of decay and neglect gave Eve the chills.

"Now what?" she asked when he drew abreast of her.

"Now I wait until the time is right. I know where to find him."

"Can you tell me how we're expected to get anything

done? You're getting called . . . I'm getting called . . .
we're both getting called together. How much shit is
God going to throw at us?"

"He doesn't know what's happening, angel."

She snorted. "The all-seeing, all-knowing creator of
everything is clueless?"

"He listens, He doesn't watch."

Eve opened her mouth to argue that point when she
remembered that God hadn't known Alec had killed
his brother. He'd had to ask to find out. "Maybe you
should tell him to give us a break, then."

"Usually, a mentor's sole job is to teach. As Raguel
said, once a mentor/Mark team is created, they are
inseparable until the Mark is capable of functioning
alone." Alec gestured impatiently back at the car. "In
my case, God wasn't willing to lose me as an individual unit. I told Him I would do both jobs at the same
time. It was the only way to be with you."

Eve's pique drained away in a rush. "Alec—"

"That doesn't explain why Abel is giving you hazardous assignments before you're ready or why Raguel
doesn't know about it."

"You don't trust your brother at all."

"No, I don't. I have yet to see him give a shit about
anything besides himself."

"That isn't how the popular story goes, you know."

The look he shot her was derisive. He opened the
passenger door and waited for her to get in. "I know."

"So tell me what happened. What have you two
been fighting about all these years?" She had to wait
for him to settle into the seat beside her. Though it
only took a minute or so, it seemed like forever.

As he pushed the key into the ignition, Alec kept his gaze straight ahead. "What do all men fight about?"

"Territory, goods, women."

"Right."

"Well, which is it?"

He put the transmission into gear and turned the car around, heading back the way they'd come. "All of the above."

Raguel returned to the penthouse suite of the Mondego Hotel in Las Vegas, Nevada, which he owned. It had been a long day and since it was only six o'clock in the evening, it was nowhere near over. The red tape involved in renovating a resort was daunting and exhausting. There were months of meetings and mountains of permits to file. Soon he would need Ms. Hollis's input to continue. It would give them plenty of time to work together and forge a bond, a bond that would assist him in managing Cain.

Raguel briefly noted the panoramic views afforded by the walls of windows around him, before turning his attention to the desk in the corner.

"Report," he ordered the secretary who waited there. Kathy Bowes wore dark slacks and a white turtleneck sweater, and looked every bit as young as she'd been when marked at the tender age of fourteen. She was kept close to home to keep her alive. There was more than one way to kill a demon, and some Marks were best suited to safer tasks than a physical hunt.

The secretary stood and read from a pad of paper in her hands. "Three Marks lost today. Two Marks acquired. Possible sighting of a new breed of Infernal. Uriel called and would like you to call him back—"

Raguel scowled. "Three Marks? Who were the handlers?"

"Mariel lost a mentor/Mark team to the Infernal she didn't recognize—"

"Is that the possible new breed sighting?"

"Yes."

He loosened his tie. "I want her full report."

"The recording is on your desk."

"Who else?"

"Abel lost one."

Raguel paused, disquieted. "Who did Abel lose?"

"Takeo, a former Yamaguchi-gumi yakuza member. He was very good. Forty-seven kills."

Relief flooded the archangel, and reminded him that he was taking a dangerous gamble. The loss of Evangeline Hollis would create an enemy in Cain that would jeopardize centuries of work. But the possible rewards were worth the risk.

Raguel knew that Ms. Hollis needed to find self-confidence in her abilities *in spite* of Cain rather than *because* of him. Past observations of her had revealed that she was ambitious and determined. Cain's mentoring of her had been a curve Raguel wasn't expecting, but he believed it was still possible for her to achieve an identity separate from her mentor.

The seven archangels were tasked with the training of new Mark recruits. They rotated the duties for the sake of fairness. For seven weeks a year, each archangel was given free rein to use his or her powers in the training process. Raguel had deliberately delayed Ms. Hollis's training so that it would fall into his rotation. He would give her a level of attention he'd never bestowed on any other Mark. A bond would form organically. He fully intended for her to align with him so completely that she related to him more than with her mentor and her handler.

Cain responded to stress with aggression; he always had. By keeping him edgy and off-guard, Raguel would promote tension between him and Ms. Hollis. Abel's obvious infatuation with his brother's lover would assist with that. She couldn't have both of them, and being torn between the two would prevent a deep attachment from forming with either one.

"Is Abel's report on my desk, too?" Raguel asked.

"He hasn't filed one yet. Just the herald has come in."

The archangel frowned. Abel was unfailingly prompt with all his reports, which were voice recordings made on the scene that were later transcribed onto celestial scrolls for future reference. While some handlers required time to absorb the loss of a Mark, Abel found }solace in the act of witnessing the Mark's sacrifice for divine consideration. Some Marks were forgiven their trespasses, regardless of the number of indulgences earned.

Raguel moved to his office. He briefly skimmed the various items that had been left on his desk for perusal and approval. He flipped through several mock-ups of advertisements for his numerous ventures, pausing briefly on two options for invitations to the grand opening of Olivet Place. It was fortunate that the tengu had been vanquished prior to the ribbon cutting. Then he picked up the disk labeled Mariel.

Something niggled at him.

"Ms. Bowes!" he yelled.

"Yes?"

"Confirm Cain and Ms. Hollis's whereabouts."

"Of course, sir. I'll see to it immediately."

Eve never thought she would be happy to hang out in a Motel 6. Her personal preferences were much more upscale. But right now, she was looking forward to the tiny room off Highway 10 as if it was the penthouse suite in the Mondego.

She climbed out of the passenger side of the Focus and stretched. An aftereffect of the mark's release of adrenaline was the lingering sense of physical restlessness. Emotionally, however, she just wanted five minutes to enjoy some chocolate.

Pulling the motel key from his pocket, Alec unlocked their ground-floor room and ushered her inside. The space was small, about the size of Eve's guest bathroom. The two double beds barely fit inside, with the bed farthest from the door pushed up right against the bathroom wall and the nearest bed having scarcely enough room to fit in the window air-conditioning unit. The decor was motel classic—busy-printed coverlets that hid stains, nondescript wallpaper, and a three-paneled painting of the beach above the two headboards. A small fridge sat by the dresser and the sink waited beyond that, conveniently—though unattractively—built outside the shower and toilet area.

Alec set the keys and their purchases next to the television and pushed his shades onto his forehead. He leaned back against the dresser and crossed his arms.

Eve sank onto the edge of the bed nearest the door. "Can you pass me a Kit Kat?"

He reached for the bag. Digging inside, he laughed. "What the hell did you buy?"

She thought back to her time in the store. "I'm not sure. For a while there, I freaked out."

Alec straightened and dumped the contents onto the other bed. Eve stood and surveyed the pile.

"Antibacterial dish soap?" He arched a brow at her. "Floral air freshener. Unscented baby wipes. Two packages of lime-flavored gelatin. Beef jerky. Facial tissue enhanced with lotion."

She picked out the chocolate and the cell phone, arranged the pillows on her bed, and sprawled against the headboard. A moment later she was munching on what she considered to be manna from someone's god. She plugged the AC adapter for the phone into the outlet in the base of the nightstand lamp. Then she dialed her parents' house.

It rang three times before, "Hello?"

Eve breathed a sigh of relief at the sound of her mother's voice. "Hey, Mom."

"Where are you calling from?" Miyoko asked. "The Caller ID says 'unknown caller'."

"Long story. How are you?"

"I'm okay. Your dad isn't. He's mad."

Darrel Hollis's version of mad was a long-suffering look. He never raised his voice, never got physical. Eve suspected his blood pressure was on par with her new Mark stats. "Oh? About what?"

"The city turned off our water and started digging up the yard. They have to fix a leak. I told your dad it was time to resod anyway."

Eve smiled, relieved that the mark system had moved so promptly. "Tell him to look on the bright side," she suggested. "This might save you money on your utilities bill."

"Your dad says I'll spend the savings on the new yard, so he's not getting ahead."

Her mother's love of horticulture and feng shui had led to a desire for a curving stone walkway flanked by lush flower beds. Her dad, on the other hand, thought their straight cement pathway was just fine.

"He'll get over it," her mother dismissed. "Want to come over for dinner?"

"I can't tonight."

"You have a hot date?"

Eve laughed softly. "Not even close. I have to work."

"That's good. A woman should always be self-sufficient—" Eve's father said something in the background. "Your dad says congratulations on the new job."

"Tell him thanks for me. You're not going anywhere today, are you?"

"No. Why?"

"No reason. I've got to go now, Mom. Did this phone number show up on your caller ID?"

"Yes, the number is here. Just no name."

"Okay. Call me if you need me."

"Evie-san . . ." Her mother's voice took on a concerned tone. "Are you okay?"

"Yeah, I'm fine. There's just a lot going on right now."

"Take your vitamins," Miyoko admonished, "or you'll get sick. Stress weakens your immune system."

"I will. Talk to you later." Eve snapped the phone shut and stared at it for a long moment.

"Are they all right?" Alec asked.

She nodded and bit into a Twix bar.

"I want to stake out the masonry," he said. "Are you up for that?"

She was up for anything that gave her something to do besides contemplate how screwed up her life was. "Why did we come back here, then?"

"Bathroom break."

"Gotcha." Eve chewed with gusto.

Alec's arms crossed, causing his T-shirt to strain around his biceps in a way that melted the chocolate in her hand. As she licked her fingertips, he watched her with a guarded expression. "Are we fighting?"

Eve shrugged. "I'm just waiting for you to finish your explanation about your brother."

"I don't want to talk about him."

"Okay, then."

He exhaled in a rush. "I don't want to talk about him *with you*."

"I got it."

She turned her head to look out the window. The sounds of the nearby highway blended with the sound of blood rushing through her veins. She inhaled and smelled the familiar scent of Alec the instant before he climbed over her and caged her to the bed.

"Hey," he murmured, tossing his sunglasses onto the nightstand tucked between the two beds.

"Hmm?" She stared up at him, admiring the fall of dark hair over his brow. Every part of her tingled with awareness. Determined not to act as devastated by his nearness as she felt, Eve stuck the other Twix in her mouth.

Alec lowered his head and bit off the protruding end of the candy bar. A low sound of pleasure rumbled up from his chest. She watched him turn the act of chewing into foreplay, the steady clenching of his jaw a surprisingly erotic sight.

They swallowed in unison. Their lips parted in tandem. Then his tongue was stroking across hers. She shivered beneath him. Sexual tension and chocolate, could anything be more divine? Alec's hand moved to her waist and anchored her, his hips sinking between her thighs as she opened them.

Her arms wrapped around his shoulders, pulling him closer. His body mantled hers, his warmth and strength became hers.

"I'm sorry," he whispered.

Eve didn't know what he was apologizing for. His curtness earlier? Or maybe everything?

She pushed her fingers into his thick, silky hair. It felt so good to be held. A tear slipped down from the corner of her eye, then another. Tears that had been lying in wait since she'd found Mrs. Basso that morning.

Alec rolled to his back, taking her with him. He draped her over his body, whispering soothing words of comfort. In her mind, another soul touched her. She didn't know Reed at all, but that didn't matter. She found solace in the evanescent feel of him.

Together the two brothers gave her the brief respite she needed.

CHAPTER 18

Reed flinched away from the nails that scraped down his back. He stood with his forehead resting against a granite shower stall, one arm hanging at his side, the other pressed against the wall above his head. Steam swirled around him and scorching hot water sluiced down his spine.

"Leave me in peace," he growled, his lower lip throbbing from the sting of Sara's bite.

"The team is ready to go," she said. "They're waiting in Ontario, California."

She was docile now, appeased and somewhat contrite. It didn't matter. He hated her in that moment, hated how she made him feel about himself, hated that she'd seen motives he hadn't wanted to acknowledge. But most of all, he hated that Eve was in pain and he'd had to feel it while buried deep inside another woman.

He shouldn't give a shit about Eve. What did he know about her?

Sadly, the excuse had no validity. Cain didn't know any more about Eve than Reed did, but Cain loved her.

Reed shut off the water and accepted the towel Sara offered him. She wore a short white silk robe and her silver-blonde hair hung loose around her shoulders. She couldn't look more angelic. "You are truly worried about her," she said.

"You should focus less on her and more on the reason why there's cause for concern."

"I *am* focused," she retorted. "That is why I am accompanying you."

"Like hell." He scrubbed his head with the towel.

"You forget your place."

Dropping the towel on the floor, Reed brushed past her and moved into her office. He retrieved his clothes and dressed with deliberation. There was no point in arguing. He was in full control of his gifts. The archangels, however, paid a price for using their powers. Reed could be in California in a blink of an eye. Sara had a long flight ahead of her.

"I want you to fly with me," she said.

He glanced at her and smiled.

Her gaze hardened. "We were good together."

"Occasionally."

"Then why are you so distant?"

"You manipulate me, Sara." He crossed over to the wet bar and used the mirror there to adjust his tie. "I'm just an object to you."

"You used me, too."

"You're right, I did." He had once been foolish enough to hope that she might help him achieve his own firm. They could work together, he'd thought, and thereby be twice as strong. Then he realized that not only would she never allow her "boy toy" to achieve similar stature, she also didn't want to add to her competition. Perhaps more so than her six counterparts, Sara saw the other archangels as impediments in her relationship with God. "We both got something out of it."

"Then, why her and not me?"

His gaze met hers in the mirror's reflection. "You don't love me," he scoffed.

"I am not talking about *my* feelings. I am talking about yours."

A bark of laughter escaped him. He returned to her. "I don't love her."

She studied him with narrowed eyes. "But you want her."

"And you've hit on Cain in the past." His hands gripped her forearms through the silk, his thumbs stroking rhythmically. "Do I hold that against you?"

Her hands went to his waist and he released her, backing up. He pulled on his coat and waistcoat, then slipped on his shoes. "Let's not make this more complicated than it has to be."

"It could be wonderfully simple," Sara said. "We could work together."

Reed paused in the act of buttoning his vest. Why would she offer help now when she wouldn't before? "Doing what?"

"Getting Cain away from Raguel." Her arms crossed. "It would leave the field open for you."

Cain. Of course. Reed's jaw clenched. Raguel would

no longer have such a heavy advantage over Sara without him.

"I'll think about it," he said, then he shifted to Takeo.

Eve splashed water on her face, then leaned into the counter. Her eyes stayed fixed on her own reflection. It was safer than looking through the open bathroom door at Alec in the shower. They'd received a discount on the room because they didn't need a bathtub. She hadn't considered that they might get a glass-enclosed shower stall.

"Angel?"

Her fingers dug into the counter. "Yeah?"

"Can you hand me a washcloth?"

She looked at the towel rack on the wall next her. Pulling a rolled washcloth free, she took a deep breath and entered the bathroom. Alec stood with arms akimbo and feet planted slightly apart. He faced her head-on, his mouth curved in a wicked smile. Surrounded by steam and dripping with water, he was the embodiment of her hottest sexual fantasies. Ripples of lust flowed over her skin, building with every passing second.

"You're rotten," she scolded, tossing the washcloth over the glass.

He caught it with a wink. "Care to join me?"

"I showered this morning." She set one hand on a cocked hip. "Besides, we've yet to have sex that didn't last several hours. We don't have that kind of time."

"A quickie?"

"I'm marked, too, if you've forgotten." Eve pulled open the glass door. She touched him reverently, brushing her fingertips over one dark nipple. His sharp inhalation made her smile. "I could probably ride you for *days* and call it a quickie."

Alec caught her hand and kissed her knuckles. "I'll take a rain check."

Revved up with nowhere to go, Eve returned to the bedroom. She busied herself with cleaning up the second bed, returning their convenience store purchases to the bag. That took about half a minute. Then she sank onto the mattress and gazed about the room.

"A stakeout." She reached for the nightstand drawer. As was to be expected, a Bible waited there. Eve pulled it out with a resigned sigh. Part of her had always believed it was fiction, or at least highly fictionalized. More like fables than absolute truths. But it was hard to deny the whole of it, when part of it was naked in the shower.

Eve reached to close the drawer. She paused at the sight of the postcards inside. They were generic cards for the motel, worn from frequent handling and boasting a photo taken many years back, if the cars in the picture were any indication. But it wasn't the image that arrested her, it was the card itself.

Alec came out of the bathroom whistling. He wore one towel low around his hips and used another to scrub at his hair.

"Hey." She caught his gaze. "We never figured out what was up with that invitation I received for the tengu building."

His arms lowered.

"You didn't tell Gadara about it either," she noted.

"I'm not used to sharing every little detail with someone."

"Are you sure it's not because you don't fully trust him?"

"I'm sure."

Her nose wrinkled. "Okay, so I'm playing devil's advocate here—"

"Sammael doesn't need any help." Alec tossed one towel on the bed, then pushed the one around his waist to the floor.

Eve glanced at the window, wondering if the sheers covering the glass really offered any privacy, or if some lucky gal was getting an eyeful. During the day they were opaque, but it was the other side of dusk now and their lights were on.

"What if Gadara orchestrated the tengu thing?" she suggested.

"Why?" He tugged on a pair of boxer briefs. She took in the view with a smile. David Beckham would be out of an endorsement deal with Armani if the advertising team saw Alec in his skivvies.

"As an excuse to keep me out of training?"

"Why would he deliberately orchestrate things to keep you untrained? There's no benefit to anyone."

"You have a better idea?"

"Maybe a masked Infernal did it."

"Why?" she tossed back at him. "Kind of stupid to draw attention to themselves, don't you think?"

"Unless they wanted you out of the picture before you Changed. Dead men tell no tales."

"Are you telling me that people in Heaven don't spill their guts?"

"You're agnostic, angel. Are you sure that's where you would go?"

Eve blinked at him. "Yikes."

He held both hands up in a defensive gesture. "Just sayin'. An Infernal would think similarly."

"The card was mailed the day before I was marked. That's cutting it close, don't you think? Why use the postal service? Wouldn't it have been safer to slip it under my door or something?"

Alec stepped into his jeans. "Good point."

"Okay, let's run with your idea. I'm harmless, so they weren't after me per se; they wanted to get to you. How did they know I was going to be marked? How did they know God had agreed to allow you to mentor me? No matter what—whether it was a masked Infernal or Gadara—it would have to be an inside job."

"Or a mystery." He straightened. The hair on his chest and abs was still damp. Eve fought the urge to lick him like a Popsicle. "Don't forget: Marks are trying to save their souls."

Eve smiled. "I didn't say a Mark did it. But you're thinking it's a possibility."

"Did I say that?"

"I'm learning to read between the lines with you. Maybe the situation is something like the Infernals working for Gadara? Satan has to have something to offer, right? And Marks are made up of sinners, not the pillars of society."

"I'm following, but where is this leading?" Alec pulled his shirt over his head.

"We're just speculating."

"I'm not a speculative thinker. Give me facts and proof."

"I'm a creative thinker. I like to explore all the possibilities."

"Okay, then." His arms crossed. "How about the

possibility that God sent you to that church for a reason? And maybe that reason was to discover that Infernals were masking themselves. After all, you went there before the invitation ever had a chance to be put into play."

Her nose wrinkled. "What kind of facts are involved in that theory?"

"The spiritual kind."

Alec sat on the bed and reached for his socks. He shifted, pulling the wet towel out from under his ass and tossing it into the corner under the sink.

"Don't you know you're not supposed to put wet towels on the bed?" she asked wryly. Her gaze lowered. "Or the floor?"

"It's a guy thing."

"I don't think so. It's an Alec thing."

His dark eyes sparkled with laughter. "You've never had a boyfriend leave his towels lying around?"

"No."

"Bullshit."

She laughed. "I'm serious."

"You have obviously never lived with a man."

"With parents like mine? Are you kidding?" Eve shook her head. "My dad is the quiet type, but he has old-fashioned values. And my mom is a fan of Dr. Laura. Shacking up before marriage is a big no-no in my family."

Smiling, he stood and held out a hand to help her up. She accepted, then turned to put the Bible in the bag with their purchases. She was taking it with her to pass the time and the last thing she needed was for a motel employee to think she was stealing it.

Alec closed the blackout curtains and went to the door. "Ready?"

"As I'll ever be."

"What do you mean they are *gone*?" Raguel barked, glaring across his desk at Ms. Bowes.

"I'm s-sorry." She shifted her weight from one foot to the other. "I said that incorrectly, sir. They ditched the Jeep at a strip mall. A nearby rental car agency recognized their photos, so we know they aren't on foot."

"Of course they are not on foot! They went to Upland. They just wanted privacy while getting there." Which infuriated Raguel to no end. They could not be allowed to become a self-contained unit. "Abel knows where they are."

"He hasn't checked in since the herald."

Raguel sent an order through the celestial lines of communication that existed between the archangels and the *mal'akhs* beneath them. He was met with silence. "Get him on his cell phone."

"I've tried. It goes directly to voicemail."

Raguel stood and stepped out from behind his desk. The secretary backed up warily.

He told himself the three—Cain, Abel, and Eve— couldn't be working together. There was too much enmity between the two brothers. But what would explain how they all fell off the radar at the same time? What could they be thinking . . . planning? He couldn't afford to lose control of their trinity. He needed them to achieve his aims.

For the space of several heartbeats, Raguel considered

using his gifts to find them. But in the end, he resisted the prod of impatience. He had enough transgressions to pay for and there were other ways to gather the information he needed. Although Abel was presently ignoring him—an aberrance of behavior that increased Raguel's alarm—the other handlers would not.

"I will send Mariel after Abel," he said, running a hand over his short, coarse hair. He had sprinkled it with gray about five years past, to simulate mortal aging.

"Yes, sir."

Ms. Bowes left the room in a rush, and Raguel moved to the window. He took in the view of the Las Vegas Strip below. Sin City. A hotbed of iniquity. And he was trapped here in this world, living a life that wasn't his, working to save the souls of man because God held them in such esteem. They were so small and weak, yet He adored them and considered them His greatest creation. Because of them, He waged a hidden war against the Fallen One, a conflict so deep beneath mortal consciousness that no ripples marred the glassy surface. The Lord would never bring the matter to a head. Devotion was more powerful when it came from faith and not from absolute proof.

So Raguel helped the situation along on his own. Step by step. Carefully planning and maneuvering. The sooner the arrival of Armageddon, the better. He was certain the Lord would appreciate the tapestry, once it was fully threaded. It was, after all, an incredibly clever scheme.

Cain and Abel had set the chain of events in motion by fighting to the death over a woman. It was only fitting that they should bring about the end of days in the same fashion.

* * *

The moon was hidden by the canopy of tree leaves above him, but Reed's enhanced sight had no trouble seeing in the darkness. He moved through the Kentucky forest like a wraith, swift and silent.

His veins still throbbed from the force of Takeo's herald, sent hours ago. Takeo meant "warrior" in Japanese, a fitting moniker. He had been a perfect Mark, his training as a yakuza assassin had stood him in good stead. Reed missed him already and knew he would miss him for years to come. None of the other Marks on his team had been as skilled in killing tommyknockers—malevolent faeries with a fondness for mines. Which was why Reed was so shocked by his death. The assignment he had given Takeo should have been a simple one: vanquish a troublesome tommyknocker.

A twig snapped to his right and Reed paused. The forest was deathly quiet aside from that one noise, a sure sign that nature had been seriously disturbed.

"Abel," a familiar female voice greeted.

"Mariel. What are you doing here?"

The *mal'akh* appeared from behind a nearby tree. Although the night robbed the color from everything, he knew her hair was red and her eyes green. She wore a floral dress, jean jacket, and cowboy boots, as well as an oppressive air of melancholy.

"Raguel sent me after you, most likely as punishment for losing two Marks today."

"I'm sorry."

"As am I." She pivoted and gestured to the right. "This way."

Reed followed her to the edge of a clearing. She

paused there and he drew abreast of her. A chill swept down his spine that had nothing to do with the temperature.

The clearing was not a natural feature. Decades-old trees had been felled and pressed into the ground, deep enough to create a flat surface. The night breeze blew, whistling eerily through the limbs and boughs, fluttering through tissue that clung to stems and errant grass. Tissue bearing the colorful markings of *irezumi*— "hand-poked" Japanese tattoos.

"Dear God," he breathed, recoiling. "Is that skin?"

Blinking, Reed engaged the nictitating membranes that enhanced his night vision. The silver and black of the moonlit vista changed into living color.

Blood red. Everywhere. On every leaf and blade, on every inch of bark, all the way to the sky. As if Takeo had exploded from the inside out, splattering his body from the earth to the heavens.

"What happened h-here?" He cleared his throat. "What did this?"

As if in answer, an owl cooed its sorrow. A wolf howled in torment and was quickly joined by several of its pack. As the forest denizens sobbed their tales of the night's events, a cacophony of grief rose to the heavens. It hammered at Reed from all sides and nearly brought him to his knees.

Mariel's hand reached for his. She squeezed gently. "I don't know."

The din ceased as quickly as it had begun. A weighted sense of expectation replaced the mourning. They wanted to know who would save them from the fate they'd witnessed that night. They listened avidly, unmoving and barely breathing.

"One of my charges and her mentor were killed this way today," she said. "I felt the herald and I went to them immediately. *Immediately.* But it was already past the time when I could have done anything to help them. The mentor was already dead. It was as if they waited too long to call me—"

"Or the Infernal struck too harshly and quickly."

She pivoted to face him. "The same happened to you."

He nodded. Exhaling a shaky breath he surveyed the scene again. There was nothing but gore left of Takeo. "Did you see what did this?"

"Barely." Her green eyes were wide, haunted, and shining with tears. "It was a monstrous beast; easily several feet in height. Flesh, not fur. Massive shoulders and thighs. It crawled inside my Mark . . . disappeared in her. She c-could not c-contain it."

"Mariel—"

"The slaying happened so fast. I barely saw it, didn't even smell it. I was so numb . . ." She gave a shaky exhalation. "I stared Sammael in the eyes once and I wasn't as scared."

No scent.

Reed closed his eyes and reached out to his charges, one by one. They touched him briefly, consecutively, assuring him of their safety. All save one.

Eve, he called.

Like the fluttering of a moth's wings, he felt her. Barely there, too green and untrained, too distant from her own soul to know how to reach out with it. What he felt most keenly was the silence where Takeo used to be. It was deafening.

"I need to make my report," he said softly.

Mariel nodded. "I'll wait for you."

"I have a favor to ask of you instead." Reed leaned closer and lowered his voice. "I need you to go to California . . ."

"Can I get out and stretch?" Eve asked.

Alec looked away from the masonry. He saw the dashboard clock and winced. Almost midnight. As usually happened during a hunt, he'd lost track of time.

Despite the lateness of the hour, the masonry yard was far from quiet. Trucks moved in and out. The perimeter was surrounded by a stonework fence topped with wrought iron. Through the bars, Alec watched bags of what appeared to be cement off-loaded, while various stonework pieces—fountains, statues, and benches—were loaded onto flatbeds and driven away.

Aside from the odd time, there didn't appear to be anything suspicious on the surface. But then again, when it came to Infernals, it was what you didn't see that was the most dangerous. There was also the added difficulty of searching through a facility that was never asleep.

"You must be bored out of your mind," he murmured.

Eve's smile was sheepish. "I'm sorry. I feel like I should be doing something or helping you in some way."

"Just having you here is enough." He reached out to her, catching her hand and lifting it to his lips.

Her fingers tightened on his. "I brought reading material, but I didn't think about the fact that there wouldn't be any light."

"I can help with that."

"Oh?" Her smile widened.

Alec caressed her cheek with his fingertips. "Close your eyes."

She followed his instructions. She waited with an air of expectation that reminded him of their first night together. He'd blindfolded her for a time, teasing her with feather-light touches and whisper-soft kisses until she quivered all over.

As he had back then, Alec drew out the moment, making her wait until she trembled in her seat, allowing the tension to build until it nearly steamed the windows.

"Alec?" she queried breathlessly.

Unable to resist, Alec closed the space between their two seats and pressed his lips to hers. A soft gasp of surprise escaped her and he took the invitation to deepen the contact. Tilting his head, he fitted his mouth to hers. Their breaths became one, mingling.

Eve surged into him with a soft sound of need, her fingers pushing into his hair and holding him close. She gave as good as she got, her lips slanting across his, her tongue stroking deep and rhythmically until his cock ached with the need to pull her over his lap and slip inside her. The mark on his arm began to burn.

Trouble was coming.

He tore his mouth away. "Do your eyelids feel heavy?"

"You have no idea," she husked.

"Roll your eyes behind your lids."

"They're rolled back in my head." She nibbled along his jaw line. "My toes are curled, too."

A laugh escaped him. "Open your eyes slowly."

He pulled back enough to watch her. She blinked, then her head turned back and forth. "Holy strawberries, Batman." Her tone was awed. "I can see in the dark."

"Part of the Change you went through adjusted the nictitating membrane in your eyes. Rather than being useless, they now enable you to hunt with greater precision."

"This is really freaking cool," she said, surveying the world around her.

In the periphery of Alec's vision, a light went out.

"Perfect timing, too," she murmured.

His head turned to Gehenna Masonry and found that the exterior lights had been turned off. He glanced at the clock. Midnight.

"Hey." Eve's voice had lowered. "See that guy padlocking the front gate? Isn't that your assignment? That kid we followed from the 7-Eleven?"

Alec didn't have to confirm the identification visually. The throbbing of his mark and the subsequent pumping of adrenaline through his system told him everything he needed to know. "Yes, that's him."

The young man finished his task, then set off walking down the street with his hands shoved into the pockets of his jacket—a jacket that bore the Gehenna Masonry logo of a gargoyle on the back.

"He works there," Eve noted.

"Yep."

"There is no such thing as coincidence."

"Right."

"So now what? Do you want to go after him?"

"Not yet."

"Why not?"

He stroked the backs of her fingers. "Because he's a wolf. Killing wolves is a messy business. It has to be done in a way that doesn't incite the wrath of his pack. Survival of the fittest is something they understand and respect. A silver-coated bullet to the back of the head isn't."

"You don't have a gun. You're playing it safe because of me."

Alec didn't deny the accusation, because it was true. Eve was going through a trial by fire and he saw no benefit in making it worse. She didn't need any more death today. What she needed was a victory, however small.

"One thing at a time," he said instead. "Let's deal with the masonry first. Once we're certain the yard is cleared, we can hop the fence and take a look around."

"Breaking and entering?"

"Uh-huh."

"Great." Her tone was dry and resigned.

Alec reached over and patted her thigh. "This is just a reconnaissance mission, angel. We get in, look around, and get out. No problem."

"Things haven't worked out that well for me so far."

"The only constant is change," he said, tossing her a reassuring smile. "The tide will turn eventually."

A frown marred the space between her brows and her head cocked to the side as if she was considering something. "The tide, huh?"

She bent over and dug into the bag between her feet. "I wish I'd picked up bottled water instead of some of this other crap I snagged."

"You must be hungry, too."

"Ravenous." Eve straightened with a bag of beef

jerky in one hand and something else that she stuck in the pocket of her pants.

"After this, I'll take you to Denny's."

She winked at him. "You big spender, you."

Alec laughed and exited the car. The masonry was dark and quiet. Rounding the front end of the Focus, he opened the passenger door for Eve and stole a kiss the moment she straightened.

"What was that for?" she asked, eyes bright in the moonlight.

"For being so good about all of this." He didn't explain that he felt the weight of guilt heavily. If he hadn't intervened and requested to mentor her, she might have been assigned a nonfield position. In fact, she most likely would have been, considering she wasn't prone to violent acts. It was his determination to protect her that had put her in danger to begin with.

"Hold that thought." Her nose wrinkled. "I might royally screw things up in a minute."

He shut the door and caught her elbow. "Come on. Let's prove you wrong."

They walked up the road some distance, then crossed the street to the side the masonry was on. The area was industrial and therefore quiet as a cemetery at night. They passed a tow yard guarded by two Dobermans. The canines whimpered softly from a seated position, but made no other noise.

"Some guard dogs," Eve scoffed.

We're very good.

She stumbled. Alec helped her regain her footing. Wide-eyed, she stared at the animals.

"Yes," Alec confirmed. "You heard right."

"They talked."

I *talked*. The bigger dog's head tilted. *My mate is offended by your insult.*

Eve blinked, apparently too stunned to say anything. Then she found her voice, "I'm sorry. I didn't know."

You should train her, Cain.

"I'm trying," Alec replied. "Have you seen anything suspicious going on at the masonry up the road?"

No. They don't come down this way, and we can't see past the auto body shop from here.

"Okay. Thanks."

Alec urged Eve to keep walking.

"Be careful," she said to the dogs, thinking of the motel clerk's gossip.

You, too.

She faced forward, looking more than a little bit stunned. "Okay . . . I'm Dr. Doolittle."

"You're more animal than human now," he explained.

They reached the far edge of the masonry property. Looking through the bars, Alec studied the building and the surrounding displays and empty driveways. "I'll hop over first."

"Go for it."

"See you on the flip side," he said. Then he climbed over.

Eve tried not to be creeped out by the masonry yard, but it was difficult. She had warned Alec that she was a big chicken, but he didn't seem to believe her. Or perhaps he forgot she told him that. Either way, he was progressing through the outside displays with ease and she was jumping out of her skin at every turn.

So many of the marble statues were classical reproductions with their eyes turned heavenward and torment on their alabaster features. Gargoyles with leering maws played hide-and-seek among benches and bubbling fountains. The sound of water chilled her blood and exacerbated her feeling of dread. She was a Pisces and she was now afraid of water. Her hand went into her jeans pocket.

Her eyes never left Alec. Using hand signals, he directed her movements, telling her when to proceed and when to halt, when to crouch and when to stand still. There were cameras stationed at each fence corner and on the corners of the buildings, too. Alec knew just how to avoid them, and Eve found his expertise both impressive and reassuring.

They reached a door to the main building, which housed a showroom. He paused a moment, looking at the security system keypad. Then he signaled for her to keep going. They moved to a larger building in the back, one whose walls were made up of cement blocks. She wanted to ask why they'd skipped the other, but didn't dare make a sound.

Constrained to the shadows, Alec took several long minutes to maneuver the distance from the main showroom building to the workspace in the rear. When they finally reached their destination, Eve noted that there was no security pad on the back building and the doorknob had no slot for a key. Alec opened the door and sniffed the air inside, then he pulled her in.

"Why did we come here?" she asked.

"Gut feeling."

"Is that like a cramp? I've got one of those. I think it's fear."

He squeezed her hand.

Eve took in the gigantic room in a sweeping glance. Even with her super sight, the ceiling vaulted so high above them that it was nestled in shadow. Dominating the space was a massive kiln with rollered tracks leading into and out of it. It was presently cold. A pallet truck waited like a silent sentinel. Alec headed toward it. He moved fluidly, skirting around protruding pipes and hoses from the kiln. Eve attempted to follow suit and hit the floor in a face plant instead.

"You okay?" Alec asked dryly, standing over her with hand extended.

"Bruised my ego, that's all."

She accepted his help to gain her footing, then dusted herself off while looking for whatever had tripped her up. "Who the hell leaves bags of cement on the floor?" she groused.

Alec's head tilted to line up his sight with the lettering on the bag exterior. "The manufacturer's label says it's crushed limestone."

"Whatever. Shouldn't this be somewhere besides underfoot?"

Crouching, Alec scooped up some of the contents that had escaped from the hole she'd created with her boot tip. She sank back down and he held his hand out to her. The limestone hit her nose wrong. It was sickly sweet, but with underlying musky notes.

"It stinks," she said.

"It's bone meal."

"Smells weird."

"That's because it's part canine and part Mark."

Eve froze. *"What?"*

Alec punched through the thick brown paper exterior

of a second bag lying nearby and she gagged from the resulting odor. He looked at her.

"Sorry," she muttered. Her body may not be able to vomit anymore, but that didn't stop her mind from sending the signal to wretch.

His hand came out covered in dark powder. "Blood meal."

"My mom uses that stuff for gardening. I didn't know they had any other uses."

"I don't think they do." He lifted his fingers closer to his nose. "Again, part animal and part Mark."

"How are they getting the blood and bone of Marks?"

"You don't want to know."

She swallowed hard. "Is that how they're masking the Infernals?"

"That's my guess."

"Why is this just lying around? Shouldn't they be guarding this stuff? It's just dumped here like—"

"Like they bailed in a hurry?" He stood and surveyed their surroundings. "If we scared them off, they know we're here."

Frantic scratching broke the silence. Eve leaped a good foot into the air. "Jesus! Oww—" Her hand covered the burning mark on her arm.

They both looked down the length of the massive space. In the far right corner two protruding walls met to create a separate room. From behind the door, the scraping grew more frenzied.

"The animal mutilations," Eve whispered.

"Right."

"We have to get them out of there."

"Yes." Alec dusted off his hands.

They hurried to the door. Grabbing the levered handle, Alec pulled, but the portal didn't budge. Whining could now be heard clearly from inside.

Eve set her hands over his and tugged with him. The door gave way with explosive violence, sending them to their backs on the floor. Nothing ran out in eagerness for freedom.

Alec leaped to his feet, then pulled her to hers, pushing her behind him.

"I've suddenly got a bad feeling about why there's no lock on the door," Eve muttered.

"You should."

Before she fully registered the source of the voice behind her, Eve was lifted and tossed like a rag doll against the kiln. She fell to the floor in an agonized pile. The lights inside the small room blazed to life, revealing a space crawling with tengu.

"Fuck!" Alec said, just before they yanked him inside and slammed the door shut.

Eve gained her hands and knees, lurching forward to help him. She was grabbed by the scruff of her neck and hauled upward. She blinked, finding herself staring into the face of the young wolf.

He didn't smell. He bore no designs. That was all Eve could register before he drew his fist back and knocked her out.

CHAPTER 19

Alec was on the wrong side of an ass kicking.

Backed into a corner, he was barely managing to keep the horde of tengu from overtaking him. There were at least two dozen of them, built of stone and giggling maniacally. Some swung from the shelves, others danced on the fringes, still others hopped from foot to foot and punched with their fists like miniboxers.

With sharp kicks, Alec kept most of them at bay, but the sheer number of them and their crushing weight were beginning to take their toll. It didn't help that he was scared shitless about Eve. He'd heard the force with which she struck the kiln. Even with her ability to heal rapidly, a full-body blow like that was devastating. She was untrained and completely on her own.

A tengu swinging from the ceiling kicked at the space between Alec's shoulders.

"Oomph!" He fell to his knees, groaning.

The tengu laughed and danced with greater frenzy.

"Cain! Cain!" they sang.

Alec glared and pushed to his feet, grabbing the closest tengu and bashing it into one of its brethren. They both shattered. The others recoiled to the walls with a collective gasp.

"Who's next?" he growled.

They hesitated, wavering. Tengu were more mischievous than malicious. They weren't combatants by nature and an implied threat to their lives was enough to send them scurrying for safety. Alec took the opportunity presented to him and lunged toward the door. As if he'd shattered the fear that held them still, they leaped toward him as a single mass, a ton of writhing stone bearing down on him.

They're going to crush me.

Steeling himself for the inevitable, Alec was startled by the sudden burst of power that flowed into him. It originated in his diaphragm, then exploded outward like a supernova, burning through his veins.

He recognized the cause immediately: there was a group of Marks in the area.

Alec hit the door with his shoulder and broke it completely from its hinges. Riding atop the slab, he skid along the cement floor like a body boarder skimming across water. The tengu raced out of the room after him . . .

Then the lights came on.

Alec kept sliding parallel to the lengthy kiln. The marauding tengu paused. The momentum of those bringing up the rear was halted abruptly by those in the front who'd frozen in their tracks. They crashed into each other like a freeway pileup.

A cowboy-booted foot halted Alec's ride with jarring force. He looked up.

"Mariel."

The pretty redhead smiled. "Hello, Cain. Having fun?"

He sat up. Mariel held out a hand to help him to his feet. Behind her stood a team of several black-clad Marks, male and female. They were fully armed with 9 mm pistols strapped to their thighs—the personal guards of an archangel. They took a unified step forward. The tengu tripped over themselves scrambling back into their little room.

"Eve?" he asked, looking around the space.

"She's not with you?"

"No. She was attacked." Dear God. "I was delayed in there." Alec jerked his chin toward the corner where a few of the Marks were restoring the door to its space and securing it by moving the pallet truck in front of it. He breathed deeply, hoping against hope that some trace scent of the Infernal had been left behind for him to follow. But there was nothing.

As the rhythmic beeping of the truck warned any bystanders that it was moving in reverse, Mariel's head turned to watch. "We went to disable the alarms and cameras," she said, "but someone was there before us."

"There's also no way to see which direction they might have taken Eve." He glanced around. "Why are you here and not Abel?"

"Raguel detained him."

"Raguel sent his own guards, but not her handler?"

"They're not Raguel's," she said softly. "They're Sara's."

Alec stilled. His brother had gone behind Raguel's back . . . *for Eve.* Abel never did anything that didn't directly benefit himself in some way and he never broke the rules. Perhaps he expected Eve to be appreciative, or maybe he just wanted to show that Alec wasn't capable of his new and unfamiliar position.

Mariel reached out to him, her hand resting lightly on his biceps. "I saw an Infernal tonight, Cain. One with no scent and no details. Your brother wanted a team available to support you."

Fists clenching, Alec spoke words that cost him dearly. "We need Abel here. He's the only one who can tell us where Eve is."

A consoling smile touched Mariel's lips. "You two will have to work together for once."

He growled low in his throat. "I'm going to take half the team. Can you collect some of the contents of these bags and anything else you find, and get them back to the firm? The sooner we get to working on the mask, the better."

"Of course."

"And fire up that kiln. Burn whatever you can't take with you. Don't leave anything behind." He gestured toward the guards standing nearby.

"Come with me," he ordered, striding past them toward the door. "There's someone who might know where she is."

Reed glanced at his Rolex with clenched jaw. In Las Vegas time, midnight was when the party was just getting started. For him, however, he was achingly conscious of how late it was and how long it had taken to get from point A to point B. Almost twelve hours had passed since he left Gadara Tower. It seemed like twelve years.

Leaning against the railing of the Fontana Bar at the Bellagio, he watched the water show with barely restrained annoyance. How could Raguel go about his business with such insouciance after listening to both Cain's and Mariel's recountal of the day's events? And how could he insist that Reed report in person, knowing he was needed elsewhere?

"Where have you been?"

Reed turned and studied Raguel as he stepped out to the patio dressed in a classically simple tuxedo with a two-carat diamond stud in his right ear. Around him was an entourage of Marks—protection against Infernals. Once, the archangels had made every effort to keep as low a profile as possible. Now it seemed that with every new persona, they strove to outshine each other. They claimed it was necessary in order to create sufficient funding to manage their firms, but whether that was true or not only they would know.

Pride was one of the seven deadly sins. Had they forgotten that?

"Didn't you listen to Mariel's report?" Reed asked.

The archangel's arms crossed. "Of course."

Reed tossed the jump drive that held the final words spoken on Takeo's behalf. He prayed his advocacy would be enough to spare the Mark's soul. "The same thing happened to my Mark."

"Do you agree with Mariel that the Infernal is of a new class of demon?"

"I don't know. I didn't see it or any trace of it; nothing remained that would assist in an identification. With the extent of the destruction, the clearing should have reeked for yards away, but whatever it was, it left neither a scent behind nor anything of Takeo beyond his skin and tissue."

Raguel stared at him.

"Have you nothing to say?" Reed asked tightly.

"Your brother and Ms. Hollis dropped off the radar this afternoon."

"She doesn't trust you." And Reed was beginning to feel similarly. He might have commented on the weather for all the concern Raguel was displaying.

"She needs to."

"Then give her reason to." Reed straightened. "I don't understand what you're doing—or more aptly, *not* doing. How is a novice supposed to?"

There was a long silence, then, "Is she safe?"

"So far."

"Are you going to her now?"

"If you don't mind."

"Tell Cain to report in. I want to know where in Upland they are."

Reed smiled. "You could send a team with me, you know. I wouldn't mind. I'm sure they wouldn't mind either."

"You worry about your job, Abel. I will worry about mine."

With a mocking bow, Reed skirted the archangel and his guards, and crossed through the busy bar. The location of their assignation didn't escape a deeper perusal. Raguel said he had a meeting there that he couldn't be late for. However, Reed suspected there was more to the choice. Perhaps it was a definitive statement of Raguel's disregard for the unfolding events of the day.

But if that was the case, why was the archangel so

certain of his safety? Had arrogance truly made him ignorant? Or did Raguel know more than he was willing to admit?

Eve woke to an icy deluge. Choking, she struggled to curl away from her torment and found herself strapped to a spindle-backed chair with her wrists bound in her lap.

Blinking, she glared at the young wolf who held a newly empty bucket in his hands. The air stunk of blood, urine, and shit.

"What is it with Infernals and water?" she snapped.

He simply stared at her, his face devoid of expression. He looked to be around sixteen years old. His hazel eyes were cold and barren, soulless. His hair was a mop of dark curls, his chin was weak, and his lips were full and pouty. The boy had the sullen look down to a science. His jeans were baggy and ripped in several places, and his Gehenna Masonry windbreaker was filthy.

"You shouldn't have taken her," admonished a voice from a speakerphone on the wall.

The tone was androgynous, or perhaps it only sounded that way because of the white noise in the background. Was the owner the other boy she'd seen in the convenience store?

Infernal or not, there was no way two teenage kids pulled off an endeavor as enormous as this one by themselves. An adult owned the masonry and secured the permits, vehicles, and contracts. And an adult certainly knew about this hellhole.

Eve shuddered as she studied her surroundings.

The space was decorated in horror movie chic. A lone naked lightbulb hung from the ceiling, casting a distinct foot-wide circle. The cement floor was stained with reddish-brown splatters she thought might be blood. There was a noticeable pattern to it, a distinct line where unmarred floor gave way to gory floor. On the very edge of the circle of light was a horizontal bar of silver metal—the edge of a gurney, like the ones she'd seen in the medical examiner's room on *CSI*. It had been pushed aside to make room for her.

Beyond the gurney, the shadows whimpered and writhed. Because of the intensity of the wattage above her, Eve's nictitating membranes weren't useful at all, leaving her blind but for the young wolf standing in front of her.

"I tried to draw them away, but they didn't follow," the boy said petulantly. "By the time I came back to see where they'd gone to, they were digging around the kiln room. What else was I supposed to do with her?"

He tossed the bucket aside. It crashed into something metallic and Eve jumped. A dog's frightened bark rent the air. A kennel, maybe? The resultant din of scratching and shifting suggested there were several creatures restrained in the darkness.

"How did they find us?" the voice asked.

"How the hell would I know?" the wolf muttered. "If not for Jaime, I wouldn't have even known we were being watched."

"What did Jaime do?"

"He didn't do anything, besides knock his girlfriend up. He had a delivery in Corona, which only took him an hour and a half, so he came back hoping to make another run. He noticed them sitting in a car on a side street before he left and again when he came back. He thought it might be Yesinia's dad looking to take a bat to him. He mentioned it to me, and I checked it out."

"Mortals do have their uses."

"Occasionally."

"Where's Cain?"

A maniacal light lit the boy's eyes. "Cain is dead."

Eve winced, her gut churning. An ache grew in her chest and spread. Laughter came from the speaker. Again, the sound held both masculine and feminine notes. Like a prepubescent boy whose voice had not yet fully changed.

"You think you killed Cain?" the person asked. "*You?* Better demons have tried and they have all failed."

"The tengu grabbed him."

There was a pause. "How many of them?"

"Twenty or more. However many there were in storage."

"Well, perhaps they've at least injured him. I'll check on him when I get there."

Eve realized then the poor sound quality was not entirely inherent to the speaker in the phone. It was the sound of traffic. Whoever was talking was on the way. Her heart dropped into her stomach.

"So what do you want me to do with her?" the boy asked, his feet shuffling on the gruesome floor.

"She might be more valuable to us alive than dead. If Cain survives—which he has proven is inevitable— he might forfeit a great deal for her return."

Fury started to burn its way through Eve's fear. She was sick of being mauled. No amount of chocolate could improve her mood enough to avoid the nuclear meltdown she felt was coming. And there was one basic undeniable truth—there was no way in hell she'd allow anyone to use her against Alec.

Her head turned slowly, her eyes narrowing in an attempt to see a way out. Where was she? The house on Falcon Circle? If not, she was screwed, because she would have no idea where she was, or which direction to run for help.

Eve glanced down at her watch. Through the water droplets on the face, she saw it was just after one in the morning. The kid couldn't have moved her too far from the masonry. Not enough time had passed.

If this was a real slasher movie, this room might be a basement of horrors. But this was California, where earthquakes made basements a rarity. She was either on the ground floor or above it. For some reason, that made her feel better. As long as she was above the ground, she might have a chance of escaping to the street outside or being seen from a window. If she screamed loud enough, she might be heard.

The door is to your left.

The sound of the female voice took Eve aback. She glanced around furtively. One of the animals was talking to her and she didn't sound good. Her voice was weary. Resigned.

It opens inward. If you make it to the hallway, run to the right and don't stop.

Eve had no idea how to reply without her voice, how to say she would come back for them if she lived through the night. She refused to leave them behind and let them suffer whatever fate awaited them on that gurney.

We're counting on it.

Mentally girding herself, Eve wiggled in her seat, trying to see if her legs were bound in any way. They weren't.

"You can bleed her until I get there," the person on the speakerphone said. "Just don't drain too much."

The wolf's slow smile sent Eve's anger into overdrive. A rough growl escaped her. She lunged forward, aiming her shoulder at the boy's stomach like she'd seen football players do when tackling. The maneuver worked. They both tumbled to the ground and crashed into a malodorous kennel. The animals began to bark, hiss, and screech.

Shouting came through the speakerphone. "What's going on? *Tim?* Answer me! What the fuck is happening?"

Struggling to her knees, Eve then lurched to her feet. One with the darkness now, her night vision kicked in, allowing her to see the proliferation of bloodstained tools hanging on racks suspended from the ceiling. There were also at least a dozen kennels holding animals so ravaged, Eve couldn't tell what species some of them were.

"Bitch!" the boy cried, swinging for her legs with both arms.

Eve stumbled, then turned and kicked at where he lay on the floor. "Asshole!"

Reaching the door, she fumbled for the knob. Grasping hands scratched her ankles and shins but couldn't get purchase. Yanking the portal open, Eve leaped around it and fled to the hallway.

Behind her, the wolf cursed and gave chase.

*   *   *

Alec bypassed the patio area of the masonry at a run, heading toward the main gate that led to the street. His footfalls combined with the Marks' behind him in a rhythmic pounding that built his anxiety. He was a yard away from the gate when a familiar figure appeared on the other side. The man grasped the wrought-iron bars, revealing the diamond-shaped detail on the back of his right hand—a detail that was identical to the one on the kid from the convenience store.

"Bad timing, Charles," Alec bit out.

"What are you doing here, Cain?"

The Alpha of the Northern California pack was in the wrong place at the wrong time. Alec wasn't in the mood to play. "Leaving. Get out of my way."

"I'm looking for someone; a young male from my pack." One hand dug into his pocket and withdrew a newspaper image of the Upland Sports Arena. In the periphery, the boy stood beside a Gehenna Masonry truck.

Alec smiled. "Good luck with that."

The Alpha's eyes glowed golden in the moonlight. He was tall and sinewy, handsome in a way that lured too many mortal women astray. He was dark and intense. Magnetic, some said. And wily enough to avoid Jehovah's wrath. At least so far. "It can't be a coincidence that you're here."

"You're the one outside of your territory."

Charles settled more firmly on his feet, showing his determination to block the exit as long as necessary. Since the padlock was on the exterior of the gate, Alec wouldn't be able to access it without reaching through the bars, a move that would put him at an unacceptable disadvantage.

"Point me in the right direction," Charles said, "and I'll step aside."

"There's no help for your rogue wolf. Go home."

"I can't let you kill him."

"That's not your decision to make."

"He's young, and he's my son." Charles's knuckles whitened. "His mother was a witch. Her parents believe I'm denying him his magical birthright. They've turned him against me."

"I don't give a shit."

"Because he's a half-breed," the Alpha continued, "he can't control his wolf, so he's rejected it and fled."

Alec's arms crossed. "You're breaking my heart."

"Let me handle this within the pack."

"It's too late for that." The evening breeze blew through the bars, ruffling through Alec's hair and filling his nostrils with the stench of Infernal. "Among other things, a Mark has been taken."

"Whatever Timothy has done, it's been at the will of his grandparents. Let me give them to you in return for my son."

"I want my Mark," Alec bit out, agonizingly conscious of how much time had passed since Eve had been taken.

"I understand. I want to help you."

"Then get out of the way."

The Alpha's grip loosened. "Do we have a deal?"

Alec inhaled sharply. "Sure."

Eve was right. The mark did burn with a lie.

CHAPTER 20

I t was a hallway, and at the end there was a faint, almost imperceptible glow.

Eve raced toward it, suddenly aware of just how much swinging arms helped a person to run. With her wrists bound in front of her, she felt off-balance and front-heavy.

The screeching cries of the animals ceased abruptly with the closing of the door Eve had fled through, telling her the horror room was soundproofed in some way. The thudding footfalls of her pursuer, however, were loud and clear. And gaining on her.

Flanking either side of the hallway were other doors, only a few, but they were all closed. There was no wayward moonlight to give her bearings. There was no artificial illumination and no windows to tell her where she was. Only the glow at the end of the tunnel that hinted at a window.

The hallway emptied into another. She turned the corner and found herself dodging sofas and end tables.

Moonlight flooded the space through picture windows. She was on the ground floor. If she'd been a religious person, she might have sent up a prayer of thanks. As it was, she thought it was about time she'd been given a freakin' break.

She saw the double-door exit that led to the outside. *Almost there . . .*

"Stupid slut!" the boy grunted, skidding into the wall as he rounded the corner behind her.

Eve sensed a tackle coming and leaped the last yard to the door. The mark burned with a rush of power, giving her the strength required to shatter the lock and leap out into the night.

Her foot hit the ground wrong and she stumbled . . .

. . . directly into the chest of an immovable masculine form.

Fishtailing around the corner of Falcon Circle, Alec stood on the brakes and squealed to a halt before the brown house at the end of the street. It was the only unlit home on the cul de sac; a dark hole in a suburban tapestry of welcoming lights. Behind him, a dark blue Suburban filled with Sara's guards and a black Porsche driven by Charles followed suit. Bringing up the rear was a van of wolves. The multitude of vehicles clogged the driveway and spilled out to the middle of the street.

Alec hit the pavement running, the driver's-side door of the Focus left hanging open.

This sort of melee was not the way things were done. Sting operations, raids, ambushes . . . Aside from being strongly discouraged because of their inevitable attention-grabbing value, they weren't in Alec's repertoire. He preferred the quiet, clean kill.

The soles of his boots skid around the corner of the garage. He charged toward the front double-doors.

One side burst open in a rush and a running figure tumbled out, crashing into Alec. If his heart could have stopped, it would have.

"What the fuck is going on?"

The voice wasn't Eve's.

Eve didn't need to look up to know that the man holding her was Reed. His scent was unmistakable and relief filled her.

But she was still pissed.

Leaning into him, she kicked back with one leg, nailing the pursuing kid directly in the chest. The force of the blow traveled through Eve and was absorbed by Reed. The young wolf caught air and was thrust backward at least a yard. He slammed into the stationary side of the door, colliding with an audible crack of his head against the thick glass. Knocked unconscious, he slid down and came to rest, sprawled and harmless.

"Nice," Reed said. He assessed her physical condition. "You're wet again."

"Was I ever dry?" She held out her bound wrists. Her hands were shaking terribly, but there was nothing she could do about that. "Take this off!"

"Where's Cain?" His fingers deftly unraveled the nylon rope that restrained her.

"Fending off tengu." At least she hoped he was still fending them off. The knot in her stomach tightened.

Reed freed her. "Let's go save his ass, then."

Eve kicked at the wolf's sneakered foot. "We need to keep an eye on him. He's your brother's target."

"I'll restrain him." He doubled up the rope in his hands and snapped it.

"There are also dogs in there . . . animals," she said, pointing at the showroom. "They're hurt bad. And someone else is coming. They're on the way here. I don't know how many. Only one guy was talking, but who knows if there were more with him. Or her. The voice was wierd."

"We'll need Cain," he said grimly. He was so calm, so self-possessed. And wearing a ridiculously expensive suit that smelled of a woman.

Eve pushed the thought aside. "Right. Tie up the boy. I'll get Cain."

A wry smile curved his lips. "By yourself?"

"There are only two of us. What else can we do?"

"I asked for reinforcements." He pulled out his cell phone. "Let me see where they are."

"Okay, then. We have a plan."

"We do?"

"Sure. I have a way with tengu. They'd rather pick on me than Cain and that should give him a break." She caught Reed by the lapels and shook him. At least, she tried to. He didn't budge. "Don't get hurt. You hear me?"

Reed winked. "I'll be sure to protect your favorite parts."

"Jeez," she muttered. "You're terrible."

"Hey." He caught her arm before she turned away. His voice was low and grave. "Be careful."

"Will do." Eve took off running toward the back of

the lot, skirting all the statuary and fountains that littered the patio area of the showroom.

They weren't nearly as frightening as before.

Alec stared down at the kid he had by the shirt. It was the other boy from the convenience store. Another wolf, although Alec wasn't certain which pack claimed him because his details were hidden beneath his clothing.

"Where's Evangeline?"

"Who?" the kid asked. "Dude, you're tripping. What the hell are you doing tearing down the street like the *Dukes of Hazzard*? You scared the crap out of me."

"Where's your friend Timothy? The kid you were with earlier?"

The young wolf scowled. "How the fuck should I know? He hasn't come back from work yet."

The Alpha's voice rumbled through the darkness. "Do you know who you're talking to, Sean?"

The boy's eyes widened with fear. Not because of Alec, but because of his Alpha. He began to struggle violently. "Let me go!"

Alec looked at Charles.

"He ran away with Timothy," the Alpha explained, his gaze never leaving the writhing teenager. "Where is he, Sean?"

There was an undertone to the Alpha's voice that drained all the fight out of the kid. He sagged in Alec's grip and said, "I think he's still at work. He called a little bit ago and asked for Malachai to meet him there."

"Malachai?" Alec asked.

"His grandfather," Charles explained.

Still at work. Alec released the kid and exhaled harshly. Was Eve still at the masonry? Had she been right under his nose?

All this time . . . wasted.

"Back up!" he yelled, skirting Charles and the other wolves to return to the Focus. "Back the cars up!"

A female Mark attempted to run by him. He caught her arm. "Get a hold of the team we left with Mariel," he said. "Tell them to search the premises."

"Yes, Cain." As she ran to the Suburban, she pulled out her cell phone.

Alec slid into the driver's seat and put the car in reverse. Once again he'd screwed things up. He should have killed the boy when he had the chance.

He wouldn't make the same mistake twice.

Eve wrenched open the door to the rear building. Heat assailed her, as well as an exceptionally noxious odor.

She ran in. The kiln was on, and there was a dark-clad man feeding bags into it. Eve briefly debated whether he was a friend or foe, but the barest whiff of sweetness revealed him to be a Mark. She wanted to know why he was there, but that could wait. A quick glance down the length of the room confirmed that the tengu were secured.

"Where is he?" she asked.

"Looking for you," the Mark said. He assessed her from head to toe. "Are you okay?"

"Not really, no." Eve tried to look collected, but the

sudden release of terror and tension left her limp like a deflated balloon.

"You didn't get yourself hurt, did you?"

Something about his tone bugged her. "It's not like I planned to get snatched, you know."

"Well, we all know you didn't plan to *not* get snatched either. You have no business being on a mission like this at your stage. Look how much trouble you've caused."

"Excuse me?" Her hands went to her hips. "Who said I wanted this gig?"

The Mark made some kind of grunting noise that she found offensive.

She shook her head. "I'm going back to check on the wolf-boy in the showroom. He had better social skills."

"Hang on," he muttered. "I'll go with you. Just let me wash this crap off my hands."

Eve opened her mouth to protest.

"Don't argue." He rolled his eyes. "You need someone to watch out for you before you get yourself killed."

"I've kept myself alive so far, haven't I?"

"By the will of God," the Mark argued. He moved over to a plastic utility tub sink in the corner.

As he busied himself there, Eve glanced around impatiently. The tengu were eerily quiet and she couldn't help but wonder what condition Alec had left them in.

Her foot tapped with frustration. She really wanted to say "to hell with you," but the fact was, this guy was trained and she wasn't. He was also sporting attire that suggested his position was an important one, or at least one that was distinguishable from the basic Mark in some way. Surliness aside, he could help her and she wasn't in a position to reject assistance of any kind.

His cell phone went off, playing a "Low Rider" ring tone.

"Can you hur—" she snapped, facing him. "Holy shit!"

Water poured from the tap like a twisting rope, wrapping around the Mark's body and face. He struggled, but any sounds he would have made were muffled. He was blue from his exertions and lack of oxygen.

"Hey!" she shouted. "Back off. It's me you want."

The Mark was dropped to the floor, unconscious. Maybe dead. She couldn't tell.

Leaving Eve alone with the Nix.

Reed straightened from a crouch with the bound teenage boy tossed over his shoulder. Opening the showroom door, he carried his burden inside. He tossed the kid on a waiting room sofa and took stock of his surroundings.

Gehenna Masonry had the sort of upscale style that Reed gravitated toward. They'd spared no expense in their presentation. The couches were leather, an espresso machine waited by the receptionist's desk, and samples of materials, colors, and tiles were mounted on mahogany displays.

A clever disguise, he thought. Not what he would have expected.

His gaze returned to the unconscious teenager. There was no greater proof of the masking Cain had suspected than the body in front of him. Reed had no idea what kind of Infernal it was. If not for the present circumstances, he wouldn't even know the boy *was* an

Infernal. That was almost as frightening as the look on Eve's face when she'd burst out of the showroom. He'd felt her fear as if it was tangible, but seeing it had been too much.

Yet she continued bravely, worrying over both Cain and himself. She'd only been marked a couple of weeks, but she was more concerned about the oldest members of the mark system than she was about her novice self.

Where the hell was Sara's team? After what he'd paid for them, they should be here.

Reed reached into his pocket, withdrew his cell phone, and turned it on. The phone played a little tune as it powered up, followed shortly by the beeping that said he had text messages and voicemails waiting. The subdued sounds were loud in the stillness. He glanced around warily, then moved toward the receptionist's station. It was time to shed some light on the situation.

He was reaching for the switch on the wall when the stench of rotting soul wafted by his nostrils. Reed shifted from behind the desk to the waiting area. He sniffed the air around the kid and frowned. Werewolf.

"It wears off," he murmured, a smile forming. If they destroyed all knowledge of the masking agent, things could go back to the way they'd been before.

Reed turned the lights on in the showroom, then took off down the hallway in search of the employee and purchasing records. Anyone or anything connected to the masonry would have to be secured. He dialed Mariel.

"Abel," she greeted. "Where are you?"

"At the masonry, where are you?"

"Cain found some suspicious materials and he wanted me to get them to the Gadara lab immediately."

"Cain is with you?" Reed spun around and headed back into the waiting area. Eve was on a goose chase. Or worse, walking into danger.

He paused at the end of the hallway. The couch was bare but for a gnawed length of rope.

The wolf was gone.

Reed was so horrified by the thought of Eve in danger that he failed to sense any hazard to himself until a sharp-ended metal rod pierced clean through his right shoulder from back to front.

Bellowing in pain, he dropped the phone. He gripped the protruding end of the pipe and yanked it free. It was four feet in length, hollow, and about an inch in diameter. Pivoting, Reed wielded it against his attacker. The blow struck the assailant in the face and he crumpled.

It was an elderly man, if the silver threading the dark hair at his temples was any indication. A mage. Sprawled at Reed's feet in his mortal guise—khaki slacks, loafers, and polo shirt. Harmless by all appearances.

Reed healed his wound and freed his wings. They unfurled through his garments to extend their full span. His features and voice contorted, taking on the face of his fury. The air stirred around him, swirling in response to the surge of his power.

The mage recoiled as he realized his mistake. A wand lay on the floor next to him, but he was too stunned to reach for it. He'd thought he wounded a fragile Mark, perhaps even Cain, not a *mal'akh* with full gifts.

Stupid. He should have smelled the difference.

"Vengeance is mine!" Reed roared, thrusting the pipe

through the mage's heart with such strength it cracked the floor beneath him.

Blood bubbled on the mage's lips, but he smiled. "And mine." He exploded in a burst of white hot embers, leaving only a body-shaped pile of ashes around the protruding spear.

Reed scowled. Then he smelled the smoke. His gaze lifted to the hallway. Shadows danced on the walls, betraying licks of flame.

"Eve."

Retracting his wings, he turned toward the front door. As he neared the exit, it wrenched open and Cain raced in.

"Where is she?" his brother demanded.

Three of Sara's guards came in after him. Followed by a group of wolves. One was clearly an Alpha—Charles Grimshaw, one of the more powerful pack leaders.

"Where are the tengu?" Reed queried. "Wherever they are, is where she is."

Alec gestured toward the blood on Reed's shirt and vest. "What happened to you?"

"*That* happened." Reed pointed to the ashes on the floor. "A mage."

Smoke began to pour from the back rooms, rolling down the hallway like a churning wave.

"Malachai," Grimshaw said. "Where is my son?"

"Down there." Reed pointed toward the rear of the building.

The wolves ran headlong into the fire.

Reed looked at Cain. There was a flash of comprehension in his brother's eyes.

Together, they raced after Eve.

* * *

Eve backed warily away from the Nix, who took on a human shape but remained clear as water. She'd seen something like it in a movie once. *The Abyss,* she thought it was. A bark of laughter escaped her. She was losing her mind. Here she was, about to die, and she was thinking about motion pictures.

"It's warmer in Las Vegas," the Nix purred.

She would have expected that his words would come out garbled because of the water, but he sounded normal. At least as normal as Germanic-accented English could sound.

"Why would I care about the weather in Vegas?" she retorted, reaching into her pocket.

"Have you seen the water show at the Bellagio? It's magnificent. You always come away with something new. Tonight, I found out where you were."

"Lucky you."

"Not so lucky for you."

Eve shook her head. "Why me?"

"I do what I'm told," he said, his lower half beginning to swirl like a vortex.

"What?"

The door opened. Eve gasped in relief and turned her head to find Reed.

What she found was the wolf.

Her heart went to her throat. *Reed. Are you okay?*

"Sorry to interrupt." The kid grinned. "I'll leave you two alone."

"You little shit!" She lunged toward him.

But he skipped out, slamming the door. A second

later a heavy thud against it suggested he'd blocked the exit in some way.

The Nix laughed and sidled closer. He was toying with her. She knew he could nab her in less than a heartbeat, but he wanted her to squirm. He wanted to frighten her half to death before he killed her.

Eve backtracked toward the kiln. Her plan was lame and probably doomed, but it was all she had. As she moved closer to the kiln it became warmer. The Nix advanced, smiling.

She pulled the small pouch from her pocket, praying the plasticized lining was intact. Otherwise, she was screwed.

"What is that?" he asked, his lower half spinning with such agitation that he looked like a genie.

"A present for you."

"Oh?"

Tearing the package open, she was relieved to find green powder inside. It hadn't gotten wet. "Do you like limes?"

"What?"

Eve leaped to the side of the kiln opening and the Nix surged toward her. She tossed the powder at him and the water took on a verdant cast. The eddy slowed and he tilted precariously. She quickly ripped open another and chucked that at him, too. The Nix tottered toward her.

"W-what have you d-done?" he gurgled.

Focusing on her super strength, Eve caught him as he tipped. She tossed him onto the rollers, then shoved his inert, semigelatinous form straight into the kiln.

He screamed and she stared, horrified. The floor

began to shudder, then the walls. Dust sifted down from the exposed metal rafters. The pallet truck bounced along the violently vibrating floor and the door to the tengu room dislodged.

Eve grabbed the downed Mark and dragged him to the exit. She tried to open it, but it wouldn't budge. Pounding against the door, she shouted for help, trying to be heard over the horrible whining that emanated from the kiln. The tengu raced toward her in a rambunctious aggregation.

"Help!" she yelled, beating at the door. "Help!"

Suddenly the door gave way and she fell . . .

. . . straight into Alec's arms. He squeezed the air from her.

"Time to go," he muttered, tugging her out. He reached back in for the Mark, tossing him over his shoulder in a fireman's carry.

Reed stepped out of the shadows. He held the young wolf by the scruff of his neck. He tossed him into the kiln room and shut the door. Then he picked up a length of wood and propped it against the portal, trapping him inside.

The sound of sirens turned Eve's head and she saw the showroom engulfed in flames.

"The animals!" she cried, setting off at a run.

Hard arms caught her about the waist and held her back. She fought against Reed's hold, but he was too strong.

"Eve," he said, his voice to her ear. "It's the Lord's will."

But it was too senseless for her to accept. If God had loved them, he would never have allowed them to suffer as they had. He would have allowed them some tiny bit of comfort before death. Instead he'd used her to give them hope, then cruelly shattered it.

"We've got to go," Alec said, running toward a group of people dressed like the guy he had slung over his back.

"Where are the wolves?" he asked when they reached them.

"Still inside," a female Mark replied. She stuck two fingers in her mouth and whistled.

Another Mark came running from a shedlike building. As he drew to a halt before them, he reported, "It would take days to sort through all the materials in there."

A tremendous whining noise came from the kiln building, the sound of metal stretching and tearing. Alec shook his head. "We don't even have minutes." He looked at Eve. "What did you do to it?"

"I put the Nix in there."

"Dear God," the female Mark breathed.

"Shit," Alec muttered. "That thing is going to blow. Run!"

Eve sprinted behind him to the car in a daze. They managed to drive a block's distance before the kiln exploded.

The fireball was seen from miles away.

CHAPTER 21

Gadara paced behind his desk in the penthouse office of Gadara Tower. Dressed in jeans and a white denim button-down shirt, he looked both handsome and leisurely. However, he definitely *wasn't* the latter.

"You are a menace, Ms. Hollis," he said grimly. "There is no other word for you."

From her seat in front of the archangel's desk, Eve glanced first at Alec, who sat on her left, and then Reed, who sat on her right. Two days had passed since the incident in Upland. Yesterday had been recovery time to make up for the twenty-four hours without sleep the day before. Today was the day of reckoning.

"You told us to take care of the tengu," she reminded. "We did."

"By destroying a brand-new air-conditioning unit and crushing a custom Lexus," the archangel retorted. "You failed to mention that when you related the events a few days ago."

"Think how much the tengu would have cost you over the long haul," Alec suggested. "We saved you money."

"And what is the benefit of the disaster in Upland?" Gadara queried crossly.

"You told me to get my hands dirty," Eve said.

He paused, glaring. "You blew up an entire city block!"

"I didn't, the Nix did."

"How did you manage that, by the way?" Reed asked in a conversational tone. As usual, he was dressed to the nines and looked very divine.

"Jell-O."

"Really? Clever."

"Totally an accident. I didn't think it would work."

Alec reached over and picked up her hand. The complete opposite of his brother, he was wearing leather pants and a T-shirt. "But it did. It was brilliant."

He didn't say it wasn't a coincidence that she had picked up instant gelatin in the convenience store, but she knew he was thinking it.

"Excuse me." Gadara's palms hit the desk and he leaned forward. "Are we done patting ourselves on the back?"

"Ya know," Eve drawled. "If I didn't know better, I would think you *wanted* us to fail."

"Ridiculous," he scoffed. "I benefit only when you succeed, but at this rate, you will drive the firm into bankruptcy."

"I have a plan," she said. "I'll just stay home quietly until it's time to start training."

It took a moment for his glower to fade into a reluctant smile. "You start training next week."

"Oh?" Reed straightened from his lounging position. "Whose rotation is it?"

"Mine"

Eve didn't miss the sudden tension in the men on either side of her.

"Better me than Sara, yes?" Gadara asked, staring at Reed.

Reed made a choked noise. Alec shook his head.

"Rotation?" Eve asked.

"The archangels share training duties in a rotation," Alec explained.

"Oh." She looked at Gadara.

"I am the best," he said modestly.

She laughed. "Of course you are."

"Anything from Hank regarding the stuff Mariel brought back from the masonry?" Alec asked.

"Like Ms. Hollis's gelatin idea," the archangel said, sinking into his seat, "Hank says it is very clever. But there is something missing, and considering the creators are mages, Hank is certain there was an incantation of some sort involved."

"I wonder how many people knew the recipe," Reed said.

"Not many, would be my guess."

"Mine, too," Alec agreed. "The rarer it is, the more value it had to Malachai and his wife."

"Hank believes it would have been a couple's spell," Gadara continued, "something a man and woman would cast together in order to affect the largest number. By your accounts, several types of Infernals were successfully able to use it."

"Unless there were several kinds of masks," Eve offered.

All three men looked at her.

She shrugged. "Just sayin'."

"I killed Malachai," Reed said. "The rest of the materials were destroyed in the explosion."

"The house on Falcon Circle was raided," Gadara finished, "and anything of interest was removed. I have a team investigating the various leads we found there."

"The Alpha might be able to help us find the woman," Reed suggested.

"I doubt it." Alec's face was grim. "We killed his son. He's not going to be feeling too charitable."

"If the grandparents hadn't led the boy astray, he probably wouldn't have attracted notice. The fault lies with them."

"Try telling that to a grief-stricken parent," Eve said. "They don't always have their head on straight."

"Right." Alec squeezed her hand.

"Anything else?" she asked Gadara.

He reached into the wooden cigar box on his desk and withdrew one. She wondered what he did with them, since he didn't smoke. Just gnaw on them until they got soggy? The thought grossed her out, so she pushed it aside.

The archangel studied her. "In a hurry to go?"

"Yes, actually."

"Stay on the radar," he admonished. "It is there to protect you."

"No worries. I have a date with my couch and the first season of *Dexter* on DVD."

"Odd viewing choice."

Eve stood and all three men pushed to their feet. "Considering my life? Are you kidding? It's like watching *Leave It to Beaver*."

She moved toward the elevator. Alec followed after her.

"Abel." Gadara's voice arrested everyone. "I'd like you to stay and go over your report regarding the death of your Mark."

Reed nodded and hung back.

Turning inside the car to face him, Eve's gaze met his just before the doors closed.

His wink good-bye followed her all the way home.

Yellow police tape and a crime scene sticker sealed Mrs. Basso's door. Eve couldn't help but stare at it as they passed. Alec tossed an arm around her shoulders and tugged her closer, offering support.

"This is terrible in so many ways," she said.

"I'm sorry, angel."

"I loved her." She struggled to push her key into the lock of her door. It was hard to see through tears.

Alec took her keys from her and worked his way through the dead bolts. He pushed open the door and gestured her in.

"I liked her," Eve continued, setting her Coach bag atop the console table where she kept her gun. The screen door to the patio was open and a crisp sea breeze wafted through her sheer curtains, billowing through them like a ship's sails. "Really liked her. Some people you only like a little, some you only like on certain occasions, and some you only like when you're drunk. But I liked her all ways and all the time."

He pulled her into a tight embrace.

Her hands fisted in his shirt. "I'm going to miss her. And I'll probably hate whoever moves in next door."

"Don't say that," he murmured. "Give them a chance."

She rubbed her face into the cotton of his T-shirt, drying her tears. "What am I going to do with you?"

"Can I offer a suggestion?"

Leaning back, Eve met his gaze. "I mean about our living arrangements."

His mouth curved in a smile that curled her toes. "Of course I'll move in with you, angel. I was just waiting for you to ask."

"My dad would kill me."

"This coming from the gal who survived a tengu, a Nix, and a wolf in a week?"

"They have nothing on my dad's silent treatment, let me tell you." She pulled away. "I mean he's silent most of the time, but when he is peeved about something, he becomes *really* silent. Oppressively silent. I hate it. Makes me squirm."

"Guess I better go with plan B, then."

She frowned. "What's plan B?"

"Moving in next door when the police are done with it."

"What?"

"It's perfect."

"It's creepy."

"She was a sweet old lady, angel. She's with God now; she's not hanging around worrying about us."

The doorbell rang.

They both stilled. Alec arched a brow in silent query. She shook her head. Knocking came next, an annoying impatient rapping.

"Ms. Hollis?"

Eve groaned in recognition of the voice.

"*It's Detectives Ingram and Jones from the Anaheim Police Department. We'd like to speak with you.*"

Blowing out her breath, she went to the door and opened it. "Hello, Detectives."

"Can we come in?"

"Certainly." She stepped out of the way, her heels rapping on the hardwood floor. She'd dressed for business to see Gardara—skirt, blouse, and chignon. Now, she was doubly glad to be formidably attired.

The two policemen entered and she was once again struck by what an odd pairing they were. One short and thin, the other tall and portly. But there was a synergy between them that told her they had been working together a long time.

"Would either of you like some coffee?" she asked.

"Sure," Jones said, unsmiling.

Eve led the group into the kitchen and began preparing the coffeemaker. "So what brings you to my door?"

"We found a local florist who remembers selling water lilies on two separate occasions to this man," Ingram said.

She looked over her shoulder. The detective held up a sketch artist's rendering. Mostly she found the ones she saw on television to be useless for identification purposes, but this one was good. It looked eerily like the Nix. She took the carafe over to the sink.

"Have you seen this man, Ms. Hollis?" Jones asked.

"No." The mark burned.

"What about you, Mr. Cain? Have you seen him?"

"I haven't, no." Alec, moved to the cupboard that held the mugs.

"I don't believe you," Ingram said bluntly.

Eve sighed and filled up the water reservoir of the coffeemaker. "I'm sorry about that."

"So are we." Jones propped one foot on the rail that ran along the bottom of the island. "You see, either both you and Mrs. Basso received flowers—which is what we think happened—or another woman in Huntington Beach has been targeted. The rest of the lilies were purchased at various locations in Anaheim. We don't want to waste our time on you, if there's another victim out there."

Holding her tongue was killing Eve. She could hear the frustration in the detectives' voices and it broke her heart. She hated to send them on a wild goose chase, but what else could she do? Telling the truth wasn't an option.

Alec pulled the bag of coffee beans out of the freezer. "Did you look at the security tapes?"

As Eve took the bag from him and poured the beans into the grinder, her hands were steady but she was shaking inside.

"We did," Jones admitted. "This man visited Mrs. Basso."

"But not Ms. Hollis," Alec finished.

Eve realized he'd planned ahead and doctored the video. She was both grateful and admiring.

The din of the grinder blocked out all conversation for a few moments, then she filled the filter and turned on the coffeemaker. She wiped her hands on a dishtowel and faced the two detectives.

"I really wish I could help you," she said softly.

Ingram smiled grimly and toyed with his handlebar mustache. "We think you can, Ms. Hollis. You'll be seeing us around until we're sure either way."

"I'll have to stock up on coffee, then."

Alec moved the mugs from the counter to the island. "Now that the pleasantries are out of the way . . . Cream and sugar, anyone?"

Eve was curled up on her living room sofa watching *Wildest Police Videos* when the knock came to her front door.

She debated ignoring it. Today was the first day in three weeks of training where she didn't feel like she had been hit by a truck. She didn't want any unwanted visitors ruining it. Even with her ability to heal rapidly, Mark combat training was hard work and it was six days a week. She'd come to seriously appreciate the classroom-only days. And Sunday. Now known affectionately as "vegetation day."

The knocking came again, louder.

With a small grunt, Eve pushed to her feet. Out of habit, she paused at the console table by the door and withdrew her gun. Then she peered through the peephole. Alec stood there, smiling.

"Angel," he called out in that rumbling purr that caressed like warm velvet. "It's just your friendly neighbor."

Pulling the door open, she waved at him with her gun hand. He was wearing shades, a tank top, knee-length Dickies shorts, and pure sex appeal. No one wore it better.

He pushed his sunglasses up and smiled. "Pretty soon you'll be more deadly than that weapon."

"I still like the way it feels." She hefted it reverently. "Weighty, solid."

With one hand on the jamb, Alec leaned in. She watched, riveted. He stopped with his lips a hairsbreadth away from hers.

"I've got something weighty and solid," he murmured, his breath gusting across her lips. "Wanna take it for a ride?"

"That's so crude," she whispered back. "I think it turned me on."

He kissed her. "I was talking about my bike."

Her mouth made a moue.

"I want to take you out," he said. "Let's have some fun and relax a little."

"We can have fun here."

"And we will." His dark eyes burned with promise. "Later."

"What's wrong with now?"

Alec laughed. "Much as I love having sex with you—and you know I do—we've never been on a date."

Eve frowned. "A date?"

"You. Me. Outside. In the sun. Doing things together in public that won't get us arrested."

"What things?"

He shouldered his way in and plucked the gun from her hand. "I was thinking we could take a ride down the coast to San Diego. It's a beautiful day."

She watched him return her weapon to its padded case and zip it up. Then he tucked it back into the drawer.

A date. Something warm and fuzzy expanded in her chest. "Let me change."

"Don't. You look hot."

Eve looked down at her outfit of shorts and tank top.

Totally, ridiculously unsafe for motorcycle riding. But then again, there were some perks to being marked. Alec had hyper reflexes and she was built like a tank. Kinda. Sorta.

"If you turn off the television," she said, "I'll go get my boots."

Alec caught her arm. "Wear those." He pointed to the flirty flip-flops tucked beneath the console.

"Not very practical on a bike," she pointed out.

"Let's be impractical. It's Sunday. You're supposed to take the day off."

She opened her mouth to protest.

"Have I ever told you," he purred, "how sexy those little flowers you have painted on your big toes are?"

Eve slipped on the shoes. "What's in San Diego?"

"Seahawks versus Chargers."

"That's such a guy date," Eve teased, smiling.

He grabbed her keys and shades. Then he pulled her out to the hallway and locked the door. "We'll take care of the girl parts later."

AUTHOR'S NOTE

There are some projects in an author's career that are inspired. The Marked series is definitely that for me. Eve came to me like Athena of Greek mythology, springing from my head fully armed and prepared for battle. Her story was then expanded upon by random synchronicities. I won't attempt an explanation for how often random events offered prompts and clues at the exact moment I needed them, but I'm grateful.

Residents of Huntington Beach and Anaheim will note that I took creative license with locations. The fictional Henry's Ice Cream shop is located where Lorenzo's Pizza used to be on the corner of Cerritos and Euclid. Both the Circle K and Lorenzo's are gone now, leaving a hole in my life that only Lorenzo's pastrami sandwiches could fill.

St. Mary's Church as described in the Marked series is nothing like the actual St. Mary's by the Sea, which is located in a different part of the city and is much smaller and older. My St. Mary's more closely resembles Saint Vincent de Paul in some aspects of appearance and location, but it's fictional in every way.

I've taken other liberties with my beloved hometown area. Locals will spot them; non-locals won't care. I hope you enjoyed the story in either case!

APPENDIX

THE SEVEN ARCHANGELS

1. These are the names of the angels who watch.
2. Uriel, one of the holy angels, who presides over clamor and terror.
3. Raphael, one of the holy angels, who presides over the spirits of men.
4. Raguel, one of the holy angels, who takes vengeance on the world of the luminaries.
5. Michael, one of the holy angels, to wit, he that is set over the best part of mankind and over chaos.
6. Sarakiel, one of the holy angels, who is set over the spirits, who sin in the spirit.
7. Gabriel, one of the holy angels, who is over Paradise and the serpents and the Cherubim.
8. Remiel, one of the holy angels, whom God set over those who rise.

—The Book of Enoch 20:1–8

THE CHRISTIAN HIERARCHY OF ANGELS

First Sphere—Angels who function as guardians of God's throne
- Seraphim
- Cherubim

- Ophanim/Thrones/Wheels *(Erelim)*

Second Sphere—Angels who function as governors
- Dominions/Leaders *(Hashmallim)*
- Virtues
- Powers/Authorities

Third Sphere—Angels who function as messengers and soldiers
- Principalities/Rules
- Archangels
- Angels *(Malakhim)*

ABBREVIATED PLAYLIST *(in no particular order)*

"Killing in the Name of"—Rage Against the Machine
"Blasphemous Rumors"—Depeche Mode
"California Love"—Tupac
"Carry on Wayward Son"—Kansas
"Dead or Alive"—Bon Jovi

More extras at www.sjday.net

Turn the page for an excerpt from

EVE *of* DESTRUCTION

Sylvia Day writing as S. J. Day

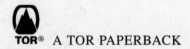

TOR® A TOR PAPERBACK

CHAPTER 1

Evangeline Hollis woke to the scents of Hell—fire and brimstone, smoke and ashes.

Her nostrils flared in protest. She lay on her back, unmoving, willing her brain to catch up with her circumstances. Licking her lips, she tasted death, the bitterness coating both her tongue and her mouth in a thick, immovable wash. Her muscles shifted in an attempt to stretch and a groan escaped her.

What the hell? The last thing she remembered was . . .

. . . being burned to a crisp by a dragon.

Panic assailed her with the memory, quickly followed by her mind lurching into full awareness. Eve jackknifed up from her sprawled position, sucking in air with such force it was audible. She blinked, but only inky darkness filled her vision. Her hand reached up to her arm and her fingertips found the raised brand there. The Mark of Cain—a triquetra surrounded by a circlet of three serpents, each one eating the tail of the snake before it. The eye of God filled the center.

The mark burned whenever she took the Lord's name in vain—which was often—and whenever she lied, which was a little less often but useful on occasion. When dealing with Satan's minions, playing dirty leveled the playing field.

Where the fuck am I? In her upright position, the smoky stench in the air was magnified. Her nose wrinkled.

Maybe I'm in Hell? As a longtime agnostic, she still struggled with facing the reality of God. Heaven, Hell, souls . . . They were concepts that couldn't be explained with reason.

Besides, if there was a merciful God and a Heaven, she'd be there. She had only been cursed with the Mark of Cain for six weeks, and she hadn't yet been properly trained in how to kill Infernals, but during that short time she had eradicated a tengu infestation, killed a Nix, and managed to vanquish a dragon. She'd also helped to put a lid on a major new threat to the good guys—a concoction of some sort that allowed Infernals to temporarily hide in the guise of mere mortals. *And* she'd managed to get Cain and Abel to work together for the first time since they were kids.

If all that wasn't enough to save her soul, she would take her chances with the Devil. Maybe he'd have a better sense of fair play.

As Eve's mind struggled to catch up with her present circumstances, the sound of singing penetrated the fog of her thoughts. She couldn't understand a word, but it was familiar all the same. The language was Japanese; the voice, her mother's.

The idea of sharing Hell with her mother was oddly both comforting and chilling.

Sylvia Day is the #1 *New York Times* and #1 international bestselling author of more than a dozen award-winning novels translated into over three dozen languages. She has been nominated for the Goodreads Choice Award for Best Author and her work has been honored as Amazon's Best of the Year in Romance. She has won the *RT Book Reviews* Reviewers' Choice Award and been nominated for Romance Writers of America's prestigious RITA award twice. Visit the author at www.sylviaday.com, facebook.com/ authorsylviaday, and twitter.com/sylday.